Praise for the novels of
New York Times bestselling author Sharon Sala

"Drama *literally* invades the life of an A-list Hollywood star, and the race is on to catch a killer."
—*RT Book Reviews* on *Life of Lies*

"A wonderful romance, thriller, and delightful book. [I] recommend this book as highly as I can.... Exciting... and will keep you glued to the pages until you reach the end."
—*USATODAY.com*'s *Happy Ever After* blog on *Life of Lies*

"In Sala's latest page-turner, staying alive is the biggest challenge of all. There are appealing characters to root for, and one slimy villain who needs to be stopped."
—*RT Book Reviews* on *Race Against Time*

"[An] emotional thriller, packed with action, love, regrets, and criminal activity that will make your blood boil.... A phenomenal story."
FreshFiction.com on *Race Against Time*

"[T]he Youngblood family is a force to be reckoned with.... [W]atching this family gather around and protect its own is an uplifting tribute to familial love."
—*RT Book Reviews* on *Family Sins*

"[A] soul-wrenching story of love, heartache, and murder that is practically impossible to put down.... If you love emotional tales of love, family, and justice, then look no further.... Sharon Sala has yet another winner on her hands."
—*FreshFiction.com* on *Family Sins*

Look for Sharon Sala's next novel
DARK WATER RISING
available soon from MIRA Books.

SHARON SALA

IN SHADOWS

mira

mira

Recycling programs
for this product may
not exist in your area.

ISBN-13: 978-0-7783-6926-4

In Shadows

Copyright © 2018 by Sharon Sala

For questions and comments about the quality of this book, please contact us at
CustomerService@Harlequin.com.

www.Harlequin.com

Printed in U.S.A.

I dedicate this book to the faceless, nameless, quiet heroes who remain in shadows to keep us and our country safe, and to their families, who sacrifice so much to help them do it.

I will never know your names, but I pray for you every night to complete your missions.

And one day, when it's time for you to come out of hiding, I pray for the rest of your life to be full of happiness and sunshine.

You have earned it.

IN
SHADOWS

One

The showerhead was still dripping when Shelly Mc-Cann walked out of the master bath into the bedroom. Her steps were slow and measured as she dropped the dirty clothes in the hamper and glanced at the clock. It was almost midnight. She was going to hate herself in the morning when the alarm went off at 6:00 a.m., but it was hard to sleep alone.

She turned down the bed and was just getting ready to crawl between cool sheets when she heard a *beep, beep, beep, beep* and knew someone had just turned off her security alarm.

She spun toward the doorway, her heart hammering so hard she could barely breathe as she heard the solid thud of footsteps moving toward her. Someone was running down the hall!

All of a sudden the dark silhouette of a tall man with long hair filled the doorway of her bedroom. Her legs went weak.

"Oh my God, oh my God."

Seconds later she was in her husband's arms, returning kiss for kiss, pulling off his jacket as he removed his shoulder holster, unbuckling his belt so he could push the jeans down his legs. At the same time, he ripped the snaps open on his shirt, then reached for her night-gown and pulled it over her head.

Shelly was trembling. It had been so long since she'd seen Jack. At least a month. And when he sat down on the bed, she pulled off his boots so he could take off his jeans.

There was no foreplay and no need. He wrapped his arm around her and fell backward onto the bed, tak-ing her with him.

Shelly was hot and wet and crying, "Hurry, Jack, hurry," when he slid between her legs and began a steady, rhythmic thrust.

"Love you, baby, love you, love you. Ah God, you feel so good," Jack whispered, and then tunneled his fingers through her long curly hair and kissed her.

It was always like this. The first time in hunger and desperation with no way to control what was happen-ing. Sex lit the fuse, and the fuse was short.

Shelly was riding that glorious heat when the cli-max exploded within her. She screamed, which broke what was left of Jack's control. He tensed, shuddering from the power of the climax rolling through him. Their ragged breathing filled the space around them, and for a few minutes more they held on to the afterglow, lying motionless in each other's arms.

Then Jack finally raised up on both elbows and smiled at the well-loved look on her face.

"Hey, baby."

She sighed. "Hey, yourself," she said, and put her hands behind his neck and pulled him close.

"I missed you so much," Jack said, as he leaned down

and kissed the hollow at the base of her throat. "Are you okay at work? Nothing happening that's causing you trouble?"

"It's all good. Being a CPA is smooth sailing. Numbers don't argue and they don't lie. Only people."

He was running his hands along her body, and it was making him hard again. He knew she could feel it, because she shivered.

"Again?" he asked.

She wrapped her legs around his waist and pulled him deep inside her. And so the dance began again, only this time slower. By the time they hit detonation again, she was out of her mind.

Two hours later, Jack was getting dressed while Shelly watched from the bed.

"How much longer is this assignment going to last? It scares me," she said.

He sat down beside her, aware of the fear in her eyes, and thought she became more beautiful to him with each passing year. He'd loved her since he first saw her in ninth grade—a tall, skinny blonde with wild, flyaway curls and braces on her teeth. By the next year they were inseparable, and nothing had changed after all these years except the ring on her finger and his job.

"I'm sorry, Shelly. I promised you this assignment will be my last undercover job and I meant it. I can't give you a time line, but I can keep that promise. Can you give me that much?"

Shelly crawled into his lap and put her arms around his neck.

"I would wait for you forever," she whispered, and

leaned into his kiss, shivering from the touch of his hands on her bare body.

It was Jack who finally called the inevitable halt as he grasped her by the shoulders.

"I love you so much, but I have to leave. I've already been gone too long. I don't know when I'll get to see you again," he said, then made himself get up and finish dressing.

Shelly was trying to distract herself from dissolving into tears. "You do know all that long dark hair is kinda sexy."

He grinned as he stomped his feet down into his boots and then pocketed his car keys.

"Not nearly as sexy as you sitting naked in that bed."

She laughed.

He blew her a kiss and was gone.

She heard the security alarm being reset and then nothing, which meant he had parked somewhere else and came to their house on foot. One of Jack's first concerns with every undercover job he'd been on was to make sure the perps never found out Shelly existed.

She glanced at the clock. *Three hours of sleep. Oh my God. But he was worth it.*

She lay back down, pulled the covers up over her bare body and cried herself to sleep.

Five blocks over, Jack was standing in the shadows only yards from his car, searching the area to see if he'd been made. He stood motionless for a good ten minutes until he was satisfied there was no one awake in his vicinity, then walked out of the shadows, got in his car and drove away.

The city streets of Houston were never devoid of traffic, but it was sparse compared to what it would be after the sun came up. He drove straight toward the Port of Houston, to a warehouse on Morgan's Point owned by his current boss, a man named Adam Ito, who ran an import/export business.

Ito had been on the Feds' watch list for at least three years, a suspect dealing in black market weapons to whatever country was willing to pay his price. So far, they'd never been able to pin anything on him, which was Jack's latest assignment. Find the evidence to take him down. But four months undercover was getting old.

By the time he got back to the warehouse it was nearing 4:00 a.m. He parked up near the building, pocketing his keys as he reached the entrance, then knocked. The door swung inward, bringing Jack face-to-face with Mahalo Jones, the man who ran Ito's work crew.

Mahalo frowned. "Where da fuck you been?"

"Chasing tail. Get out of the doorway," Jack growled.

Mahalo's frown deepened, but he stepped aside, then yelled at him as he was walking away.

"It's a good thing you didn't turn up late for the shipment comin' in. Boss man would have had your ass."

Jack turned on one heel and in seconds was in Mahalo's face, jamming a finger into his chest.

"I chased ass because it's *my* damn life, and I'm here because a shipment isn't due for hours, which means I am not late, and I don't take crap from anyone, so save your damn opinions for someone who cares. Got it?"

Mahalo looked like he wanted to punch Jack in the face just to watch him bleed, but he didn't. Judd Wayne—Jack's alias—was known as the kind of guy who would fight until one of them was unconscious... or dead.

When Mahalo didn't say anything, Jack nodded. "That's what I thought," he said, and headed for the crew's lounge area.

All he wanted was one of the cots to grab a couple hours of sleep, but the hair was standing up on the back of Jack's neck as he walked away. He could feel Mahalo's hate, but that went both ways. When he got to the lounge area, he eyed the cots scattered about the room.

There were seven other men sleeping in this room, and two empty bunks. One empty bunk was at the back of the room, and one at the front. He chose the one closest to the door, giving him a quick exit should the need arise. He pulled the nine-millimeter Glock from his shoulder holster and laid it beside the pillow.

The airless room reeked from the varied odors of unwashed bodies and the remnants of week-old pizza slices, but discomfort was all part of the job. He hung his jacket over a ladder-back chair against the wall beside the bed, took off his boots and then rolled over onto his side facing the door. With the Glock held loosely in his hand, he thought of Shelly and closed his eyes.

Adam Ito was buck naked, facedown on a massage table, slick with essential oils and groaning from the footsteps of the tiny Asian woman named Ling, who was walking down the length of his back. Every time he felt something pop in his spine, he moaned. When she dropped off the side of the table in a single, catlike motion and told him to turn over, his pulse reacted.

He knew what was coming next and held his breath as she climbed back up, straddled his legs and slowly lowered herself down onto his very slick, very hard erection. She was tight and hot and he came inside her before she was all the way down.

After a leisurely shower together, and a blow job that sent him to his knees, he sent Ling on her way and got dressed, before leaving his playhouse to head home.

It was nearing 1:00 a.m., and Tommy, his limo driver, was waiting in the driveway when Adam exited the small, unassuming house on the outskirts of Pasadena. The night sky was clear, but the lights of a city as vast as Houston made stargazing difficult.

Adam took a deep breath, imagining he could almost taste the salt air of the seaport city, and then went down the steps to go home. Tommy opened the door to the limousine without speaking. As soon as Adam was seated, the driver shut the door and quickly left the area.

Adam Ito felt good all the way to his bones. He was pleased with his very perfect, very orderly life.

The next morning, Tommy was again waiting beside the limo for his boss, but this time it was at Adam's estate in the Memorial area of Houston. When he saw him coming toward the limo, he jumped out to open the door.

Despite the heat, Adam was wearing a white suit and shirt along with snakeskin shoes in a silver-gray leather. The only bit of color about his person was a Gucci necktie in robin's egg blue. He led with his chin as he approached, indicative of how Adam also lived his life.

"Good morning, sir," Tommy said, and bowed as he opened the car door.

Adam acknowledged the deference with a nod. "Good morning, Tommy. Straight to the office today."

"Yes, sir," Tommy said. "Ginger tea with lemon in the bar," he added, and quietly closed the door as his boss settled into his seat and poured himself a cup of hot tea to enjoy on the ride downtown.

Within twenty minutes, they were caught in a traffic snarl on the 610 Loop and waiting for it to clear when Adam's cell signaled a call. He glanced down at caller ID and immediately closed the window between him and the driver before he answered.

"Yes?"

"There is a very hot shipment of long-range missiles available. They are prototypes. Are you interested?" the caller asked.

"Prototypes? Do they work in existing launchers and how long range are we talking about?" Adam asked.

"Yes, to the launchers, and five hundred kilometer range. They came straight off an assembly line. The lot needs to move, ASAP."

Adam frowned. "How many?"

"A thousand…in twenty crates," his contact said.

Now it was time to get down to business. "What's the price?" Adam asked.

"Twenty million."

Adam snorted softly. "Granted that's a good price, but for untested missiles?"

"That's the going rate and they are not untested, just yet to be used in warfare. Think of the surprise effect of being three hundred miles away from an attack target. Launch at night…and unless they have high-tech radar on the ground, you're golden."

"What's the accuracy?" Adam asked.

"Testing shows a seventy-five percent success rate right now. You know you'll be making ten times over the buyout when you sell."

Adam didn't hesitate. "Delivery date?"

"Today is Wednesday. You will receive delivery at 3:00 a.m. Friday morning. They'll produce the products, if both parties are satisfied, you will make the money transfer into his chosen account, then they will unload at your warehouse. It'll be up to you to get the crates inside a shipping container. Once you're good to go, one of those ship-to-shore cranes will do the rest."

"And your cut?" Adam asked.

"The usual one percent of your cost."

"I want you on-site for this one," Adam said.

The caller's voice sharpened. "You know that's not going to happen. Ever. If this business model bothers you, it will be simple to offer the goods to other buyers."

Adam frowned. He didn't like to feel controlled in any way, but he chose not to push the issue. "Fine," he said, as the line went dead in his ear.

He dropped the phone into his jacket pocket and glanced up. They were moving again.

Still wearing the afterglow of Jack's unexpected visit, Shelly walked into work in baby blue slacks and a white short-sleeve blouse. She'd pulled the long curls away from the sides of her face today, clipping them at the nape of her neck with her favorite silver clip, but it was the big smile on her face that drew her coworker's attention.

"Morning, Shelly. Who took you to bed last night?"

Shelly's comeback was tinged with surprise that Mitzi would ask that, and worry that she'd let part of her private life slip into where she worked.

"What kind of a question is that, Mitzi Shaw? Do I ask you how many times you and Joe do the dirty?

And just for the record, I took myself to bed and the smile was because I felt like smiling, and now I don't."

Mitzi frowned. "Dang. I was only making polite conversation."

"In no way is that question part of polite conversation. Lord... I may as well work in a bar," Shelly muttered, and went to her own cubicle to begin her day.

She kept books for five different businesses at Bates and Davis, the accounting firm where she worked, and she was good at her job. Most of the time working with numbers was calming to her. There were no variables in accounting. Numbers told the story, and if they didn't balance out, then the search would be on. Shelly liked sure things.

Like how she'd felt the first time she'd seen Jack walking into a classroom her freshman year of high school. She'd been absolutely positive that he would love her and that they'd live happily ever after.

That was her first sure thing she marked as memorable. And it still held true today. She couldn't wait for the case he was working on to be over.

When noontime came, Mitzi ambled over to Shelly's cubicle and then peered over the divider.

"Want to go to lunch with me, or are you still too pissed?"

Shelly hit Save on the program she was in, then looked up.

"Yes, I'll go to lunch with you. We'll talk about your love life instead."

Mitzi blushed. "Zinger...and a good one. I promise no more 'inquiring minds want to know' shit, okay?"

Shelly smiled. "Yes."

"How does Chinese sound?" Mitzi asked, as Shelly grabbed her purse.

"Like a good idea. It's right across the street, which leaves us a little more time to enjoy the meal, instead of rushing back."

Outside was slap-in-the-face hot, which left no time to dawdle as they walked down to the crosswalk. Traffic was thick and it was loud. Pissed-off cabdrivers were honking at each other, trying to maneuver their cabs three lanes wide on a two-lane street.

"Lord, remind me why I thought Houston would be a swell place to live," Mitzi muttered, as sweat beaded on her upper lip and on the back of her neck.

Shelly pointed at the crosswalk light and then they started walking within the moving crowd. Her purse was crossways over her shoulder with the bag pulled around in front of her chest, and held firmly within her grasp. As a law officer's wife, safety first had been drilled into her from the beginning of their married life.

About halfway across, she felt the strap give on her shoulder and then a hard yank. She tightened her hold as she pivoted and saw the man behind her. He was holding the cut purse strap with one hand, and the knife he'd used to cut it in the other. Without thinking, she reacted just as Jack had taught her, kicking out as she spun, using the momentum of the turn to land a bone-breaking kick straight on the kneecap.

She heard it pop over the loud blare of the traffic and followed up the kick with the heel of her hand, ramming it into his nose.

Blood splattered as the thief dropped the purse strap. His knee went out from under him as his eyes rolled back in his head. He dropped in the middle of the cross-walk, flat on his back, unconscious.

Mitzi was screaming. Traffic had come to a complete stop all four ways, and as the crowd parted around them, a city cop cruising past witnessed the last half of what was happening.

He hit lights and siren as he radioed in the assault, and then he pulled his vehicle up to a curb and got out, already directing traffic before the man got run over.

"Get him out of the street!" he yelled, and three young men came running to move him to the sidewalk.

Shelly was rattled and she was angry. He'd ruined her Coach purse, which had been a Christmas gift from Jack.

"Ma'am, are you hurt?" the policeman asked, as Shelly and Mitzi followed the crowd out off the street.

"No, just shaken," she said, and held up the strap on her purse. "I felt him cut it."

Mitzi wasn't screaming anymore, but she was trembling.

"How did you know to do that?" she asked.

Shelly shrugged. "My husband taught me."

The cop handcuffed the thief, who was already regaining consciousness, sat him up so he wouldn't choke on his own blood and then called for an ambulance.

"I'll need your information," the cop said.

"We're on our lunch hour," Mitzi said, and then realized that had nothing to do with what had just happened, and shut up.

Shelly was too rattled to cope with both Mitzi and the cop. "Mitzi, go eat. There's no need for both of us standing here missing lunch."

Mitzi hesitated. It didn't seem right abandoning her friend.

"Seriously, Mitzi. I have to do this, you don't."

Mitzi finally nodded. "Okay. I'll bring you takeout," she said, and looked over her shoulder twice as she walked away.

Shelly's hand was beginning to hurt a bit, but she could move everything just fine, which meant nothing was broken. She pulled out her ID and began giving her statement while the sun continued its high noon phase, making the top of her head feel like it was on fire. At first she was just uncomfortable, but in a few short minutes she began feeling sick.

She could hear approaching sirens and started watching the traffic, praying for their arrival. But after a couple of minutes when they still hadn't come, she interrupted the officer's inquiries.

"Officer, either I get out of the sun, or you're going to need another ambulance."

He looked at her. She was pale and shaking like she was cold, which was impossible in Houston heat.

"It's not going to take much longer," he said.

"No, you don't understand," Shelly said. "I feel nauseous and dizzy."

And just like that, the sirens were suddenly screaming in her head as cop cars and an ambulance pulled up simultaneously from different directions. But it was too late. Just as she had cautioned, her legs went out from under her and she was on the sidewalk.

Someone was trying to help her up, and people were talking to her, but she couldn't focus.

"Get me inside somewhere cool. I need water," she kept saying.

Someone handed her a bottle of water, and other people were lifting her to her feet and walking her inside the nearest business, which happened to be a florist shop. The immediate swath of cool air that washed over her body felt wonderful, but she was still weak and shaking.

One of the owners came running with a folding chair from the workroom, and another came with a handful of wet paper towels. Shelly drank water and held the wet towels on the back of her neck until she began feeling better. Finally she felt good enough to give Mitzi a call, glossed over what had happened and asked her to come to the florist when she was through to walk her back to the office.

The cop who'd kept putting her off finally had his perp on the way to ER and was free to come check on her.

"I'm really sorry, ma'am. I didn't fully realize the seriousness of how you were feeling. Do you want me to call an ambulance for you?"

"No, I'm already feeling better. I'll be okay, and my friend is going to walk back to the office with me."

"You're sure?" he asked.

"Yes, I'm positive. And thank you for the rescue."

He grinned. "You rescued yourself. I didn't do anything but pick him up off the street. And by the way, kudos to your guy. He was a good teacher," the cop said, and left.

The shop owner came up front to check on her again between customers, then gave her fresh cold towels and another bottle of water.

Shelly took it all gladly. "You've been so kind. Thank

you for helping me out like this. As soon as my friend shows up, I'll be out of your way."

The man patted her shoulder. "You aren't in anybody's way and I'm glad we could help. Take care now, and call out if you need anything more."

Shelly was blinking back tears as he walked away. Everyone was being so kind, but the only person she wanted was Jack, and that was impossible.

A few minutes later, Shelly saw Mitzi coming up the street at a lope. Her purse was on one arm and Shelly's to-go lunch in a sack on the other. Then she was inside the store, crying.

"I shouldn't have left you. I'm so sorry, sweetie. I'm so sorry. Are you feeling better? I can call a cab for you and send you home. I'll tell Willard what happened when I get back to the office."

Shelly shook her head. "I think I'll be—"

"No, I insist. You were attacked by a mugger! You're white as a sheet and have no business going back to work. I'm going out to hail a cab. You watch through the window and come out when you see it stop."

Going home was suddenly the most important thing she needed to do.

"Yes, yes, okay, I think I will," Shelly said. "And thank you."

Mitzi handed her the sack she was carrying. "Here's your lunch. It's on me. You get home, get comfy and eat, then spend the day resting. You had the best smile on your face when you came to work this morning and now this. Horrid people. Lazy, horrid thief."

She leaned down and gave Shelly a quick kiss on her forehead and out the door she went.

Shelly stood up, mostly testing her equilibrium before trying to walk again, and sighed with relief. She was certainly steady enough to be mobile. She watched from the window until she saw the cab stopping, then left the shop.

Hit with the heat and humidity again, Shelly was suddenly glad she'd opted to go home.

"Thank you again," she said, as Mitzi helped her inside the cab.

"You're welcome. Now mind what I said. Rest."

"Yes, yes, I will," Shelly said.

Mitzi shut the door.

Shelly gave the driver her address and then leaned back in the seat and closed her eyes.

Two

Adam Ito was in his warehouse watching his men unloading crates of decorative urns and tea sets from a shipping container that had just come in from China.

His crew boss had the manifest, carefully checking numbers against the pallets being unloaded. Mahalo's size and girth were massive, and the amount of sweat on his bald head and dark skin gave his large body an ebony sheen. To Adam, who was a fan of sumo in his native Japan, Mahalo was so massive he was almost beautiful.

But then his gaze shifted to the man operating the forklift, and *beauty* was not a word he could associate with him. Judd Wayne had a rolled-up black-and-white bandanna tied around his head. The old T-shirt he was wearing had the sleeves cut out. He was sweat-soaked, plastering everything he was wearing to his body like a second skin, and he exuded sexy—something Adam envied.

Even though Judd did his job, he was an unknown, which always made Adam uneasy. And, from the complaint Mahalo made against him this morning, it appeared Judd wasn't averse to pushing boundaries. Adam understood the male need for sex, but how long did it take to find a hooker, these days?

Adam stayed for another half hour to reassure himself they had the job well in hand, then returned to his limo to enjoy the cool air. He'd already given Mahalo the news about the special shipment coming in Friday morning and told him to ensure the crew would be available and on the dock by 1:00 a.m.

He poured himself a glass of sparkling water, added a few cubes of ice from the ice bucket and took a quick sip, appreciating the effervescence. After one last glance at the crew in action, he pressed the intercom.

"Tommy, take me home."

"Yes, sir," the driver said, then put the limo in gear and left the dock.

Mahalo breathed a sigh of relief as he watched the boss's exit—he didn't like it when Ito stayed to watch—then returned to the task at hand. One glance at the manifest indicated two more pallets in the container and then they'd be through. Before they scattered for lunch, he needed to let the guys know about the new orders, so he left the warehouse to round them up. They arrived at their own speed and then had to wait for the last one to come out of the bathroom. As soon as he arrived, Mahalo began.

"Listen up. Mr. Ito has a special shipment coming in at 3:00 a.m. Friday morning and he needs all of us here."

The men shifted from one foot to the other. One showed his displeasure by spitting tobacco juice from the wad in his jaw only feet from where Mahalo was standing.

A half dozen of them let fly with complaints. But the undercurrent of grumbling ceased instantly when they saw the look on the crew boss's face.

"Shut the fuck up," Mahalo snapped. "I want every one of you here at the warehouse before midnight Thursday night. I know the boss said 1:00 a.m., but if you don't show, it's on my head. I want to know you're here before he is, and no excuses, or don't come back at all and pray you never see me again." He stared straight at Judd Wayne when he said it. "A shipment will be unloaded here and we have to transfer it into the container ASAP. You know the drill."

Judd wasn't one of them complaining. He had a feeling this was going to be the shipment he'd been waiting for.

"Are we through for now?" Judd asked.

Mahalo glared. "Why? Want to chase some more tail?"

"No. I'm hungry and there's a food truck just down the pier. Want anything?"

Mahalo blinked, absently rubbing his big belly. "Uh…sure, why not? Whatever they have, I want two."

When he reached for his wallet, Judd held up his hand. He'd stood up to Mahalo earlier, and now it was time to smooth things over. "It's okay, boss. This one's on me, but I'm driving. Too damn far and hot to walk it. Back ASAP."

"Hey, Judd, got room for me to hitch a ride?"

Judd glanced behind him. It was Munoz.

"Yeah, sure, why not?" he said.

A couple more of the men followed behind him, one on a motorcycle, a couple of them in a beat-up Jeep.

They stood in line for shrimp tacos, and when they

finally reached the counter, they placed their orders and paid, then stepped aside to wait for delivery.

Jack was eyeing a pelican perched on a nearby pier when he heard the men start to laugh. He turned around to see what was funny and realized they were all looking at a little television inside a truck.

"Whoa…look at her! You wouldn't want to make that one mad."

Jack moved closer.

"What's going on?" he asked.

"Look…they're showing it again," Munoz said. "Just watch."

At first all Jack saw were the backs of people crossing a street, but when he recognized the florist shop in the clip, his heart skipped a beat. The building Shelly worked in was on the opposite side of the street from that florist.

"Look! Here's where you see some dude trying to snatch this woman's purse. See! There's the knife in his hand. He's already cut the strap off her shoulder and is trying to pull it out of her grasp. Now watch this!"

Jack kept thinking, why did that person film what was happening instead of calling out a warning? Then he saw that long curly hair and knew before the woman turned around it was Shelly. He felt sick but hid his shock. He watched her look over her shoulder, saw the fear on her face, but then all of a sudden she kicked sideways, hyperextending the mugger's knee. He couldn't hear the man's shriek but could see his face contorting in pain.

"Now here comes the hammer," Munoz said.

And that was exactly what it looked like. Jack gritted his teeth as he witnessed her finish the rotation with her arm extended, her fingers curled, aiming with the heel of her hand. And just as he'd taught her, she used the momentum of her body to increase the impact of the blow. Blood spurted from the mugger's nose as his head snapped back, and then he was down. People were crowding around her again as the clip ended.

"Man, she is one fine bitch," Munoz said. "I wouldn't mind tapping that."

Jack resisted the urge to punch him and closed his eyes, remembering clearly the self-defense lessons he'd given Shelly for weeks on end.

Then the woman in the food truck called out a name.

"Judd, your food is ready."

He made himself focus and stepped up to the window. "Thanks," he said, and then headed for his car.

He started it up to get cool as he waited for Munoz, and picked up one of the tacos from his order and began to eat. The food settled his hunger but not his anxiety. He needed to hear Shelly's voice to make sure she was okay.

A short while later he and Munoz drove back to the warehouse. Mahalo was waiting in the doorway when they arrived.

"Two orders of shrimp tacos and they're damn good," Jack said.

Mahalo took the bag. "Thanks," he said, and ambled off into the shore side of the warehouse to catch some of the sea breeze while he ate. Jack grabbed a bottle of water out of the old refrigerator from their lounge area and followed, not for the conversation, but the cooler air.

Houston was an amazing city, but for a man who'd been raised in Colorado, it was too damn hot. He leaned back against a bench right in front of a broken window overlooking Galveston Bay and took a drink, savoring the cold liquid sliding down his throat.

Mahalo knew he was there, but he was clearly not in the mood for talking, and that was fine with Jack. They'd gotten into it earlier when he'd been out late, but the last thing he needed was any extra heat on him because Mahalo was pissed. It was better to stay quiet and amicable. The big man ate, and Jack finished off his water, then tossed it into a nearby trash barrel.

The bay was full of ships, some anchored offshore waiting their turn to off-load. One was already sailing out of the harbor as Jack looked up. He wondered which ship was designated to carry Ito's illegal cargo. God, he wanted this job over with, and he wanted to hear Shelly's voice.

"Hey, boss!"

Mahalo looked up.

"Are we done for the day?"

"Yeah," Mahalo said.

"Then I think I'm gonna head out. I'm going back to my place. I want a shower and to catch some z's before we report back here tomorrow."

Mahalo swallowed what he was chewing. Even though he wasn't in charge of their time off, he gave Jack a hard look. "Ten p.m. tomorrow night and don't you fuck up on me. You drive the forklift."

Jack slid off the bench. "I'll be here."

Munoz walked over as Jack passed him. "You leavin'?"

Jack nodded and kept on going.

"Hey, you wanna hang out tonight…maybe play some pool down at Smokey Joe's?"

"I'm going home and sleeping until I wake up to-morrow," Jack said.

Munoz shrugged. "Yeah, okay. Next time."

Jack just kept walking. He noticed Munoz glance at the boss, then leave before Mahalo gave him something to do.

The moment Jack got in his car, he grabbed a burner phone from the glove box and made a call to Shelly as he was driving away. The phone rang and rang, and he was bordering on panic when he finally heard her voice and realized she'd been asleep, which also meant she was home. Shit. She never left work unless something was wrong.

"Baby, it's me."

He heard her breath catch, and then she was crying.

"I am so glad to hear your voice," she said.

"I saw what happened to you on the news. Are you okay?"

"Yes, I am now. The mugger didn't hurt me, but I had to stand out in the heat too long and I fainted."

Jack groaned. "Are you alright now?"

"Yes, yes, I swear. Mitzi was the one who sent me home, and I'm glad she did."

Jack was bothered and it showed in the tone of his voice. The guilt he felt at leaving her alone for such long periods of time never eased.

"I'm never there for you when you need me and I know it, but something is going down within the next thirty-six hours that may put an end to this assignment. Bear with me, baby. I can't wait to come home."

Shelly wiped away tears with the tail of her T-shirt. "I'll be here, whenever you do. Just stay safe. That's all I want."

"Okay. Gotta go. I'm about to get into the middle of noon-hour traffic. Love you so much."

"Love you more," Shelly said, and disconnected.

Jack felt the disconnect all the way to his bones, then dropped the burner phone into the console and took the on-ramp onto a freeway, accelerating into flight mode, which was the designated speed for Houston.

It took him forty-five minutes to get back to his apartment building. After he parked, he ran all the way up the outer steps to the third floor, then down the open hallway to room 355.

He checked the lock to make sure it hadn't been tampered with, then slipped inside, locking the door behind him. All the shades and curtains had been pulled so the rooms were dark but still easily navigated by light coming in between the slats in the shades. He paused in the hall to adjust the temperature down five degrees because he liked to sleep in the cold, then went to the bedroom and stripped.

He turned on the bathroom light as he entered, eyed the day-old beard and his wild hair and turned on the water in the shower. As soon as the steam was rising, he got in and soaped his entire body twice before he felt clean, then did the same thing to his hair. Before he left the shower, he grabbed the shaving cream and his razor and started to finish the job, then hesitated and laid the razor back on the rack. Clean was one thing. Looking well-groomed was not the look he was going for. He towel-dried his hair and then dried himself.

He was looking for the blow-dryer when he caught a glimpse of something in the fogged-up mirrors and jumped. Just for a second he thought someone else had snuck in, until he realized it was him.

"Dammit," he muttered, and swiped a towel across the mirror to clear away the condensation. He was always on edge, on the alert. In this line of work, he had to be. But now his own reflection was startling him. He was ready to be done with it all.

He swiped his hand across the condensation and cleared a patch of the mirror. He had what he considered an ordinary face with a jawline leaning toward square, which was now covered in black whiskers. Even though Shelly called him "her hunk," he saw only regular features and a nose that had been broken twice. He had his father's eyes—almost as black as his hair.

Thinking of his father came with the usual pang of sadness. His parents were long since dead.

He'd been undercover so long this time around that it was becoming harder to remember normal. Maybe after what he'd learned today his luck would change.

He went from the bathroom back into his bedroom, pulled down the sheets on his bed, then sat down and picked up his phone and made a call to Charlie Morris, his contact at the FBI.

Charlie answered promptly.

"Special Agent Morris."

"It's me. I have something for you."

"What's up?" Charlie asked.

"Some kind of a special shipment is coming in at the warehouse this Friday morning at 3:00 a.m. As soon as it arrives, we load it into a shipping container. Don't know where it's bound, but whatever it is, I know it's contraband or we'd be doing all this in broad daylight like all the other shipments coming in and going out."

"Good job," Charlie said. "I'll let them know, and

remember that you're going to be arrested with all the others."

"Yeah, no problem. I'm sick of this gig," Jack said.

"I can only imagine," Charlie said. "Stay safe."

"Thanks," Jack said. He disconnected and then rolled over onto his side, pulled up the covers and was asleep less than a minute after his head hit the pillow.

But Charlie Morris didn't roll over and go to sleep. He was already notifying their boss, Deputy Director Wainwright, who would start the ball rolling on organizing the bust.

Charlie's partner, Nolan Warren, overheard enough of the conversation to know something was finally breaking. As soon as Charlie delivered the message, Nolan asked, "Is this all about the Ito case?"

Charlie nodded. "It appears so. I sure hope so for Jack's sake. He's ready to come in."

"I wouldn't be any good at undercover work," Nolan said.

"It wouldn't be my choice of assignments, either," Charlie said, and then logged out. "I'm going to have lunch with Alicia. See you later."

"Give her my best," Nolan said.

"Will do," Charlie said, then grabbed his suit coat and gun and paused on his way out to let their clerk, Fred Ray, know where he was going.

Fred was a skinny redhead who wanted to be a field agent in the worst way but kept failing one portion of the test that really mattered. He could fire a gun, but he never hit anything. So he rode desk duty and envied the field agents from afar. When he saw Agent Morris coming, he paused what he was doing.

"Going to lunch?" Fred asked.

"Yes, having a late lunch with Alicia."

Fred grinned. "Noted. How is your wife these days? She should be due soon, right?"

The very mention of the baby was all it took to put a huge smile on Charlie's face.

"She is eight months and three weeks pregnant, so 'any day now' is how her obstetrician puts it."

"Frieda and I have three, so I know how you feel. Enjoy your lunch and my best to your wife."

"Thanks, man," Charlie said, and walked out of the office with a bounce in his step.

Thursday night had finally arrived, and none too soon for Jack. He was antsy to get to the warehouse and to bring this case to a close. It was starting to rain as he arrived on the dock and it was habit to check out his surroundings. As far as he could tell, there was nothing out of place. He took note of the fact that he was thirty minutes early and kept driving until he reached the warehouse.

As he got out of his car, he saw the lights were on in the building and the main door was ajar. At least Mahalo was thinking ahead and not making them all wait in the rain for him to open up.

A couple of men were already inside playing cards on top of a crate when Jack walked in. Mahalo was on the phone—with the boss, Jack assumed. Adam Ito was always present, whether a shipment was coming in or going out. He couldn't imagine him missing an important job like this.

Mahalo saw him come in, nodded once to approve

his arrival and then lumbered away, making sure he was too far away to be overheard.

Jack sat down, glanced at his watch and then leaned back. He pulled out a pocketknife and began cleaning his fingernails, then picked up a chunk of wood that had broken off from one of the pallets and began whittling it down for lack of anything else to do.

Munoz arrived a couple of minutes later, and then another man, and then another until all of them were on the scene. Mahalo came back to the front of the warehouse and motioned at Jack.

"Go make sure that forklift is fueled up and in working order, then bring it up."

"Yeah, okay," Jack said, and headed back to where the forklift was parked.

He checked everything including oil pressure, filled up the gas tank, raised the lift up and down a couple of times to reassure himself that it was also working, then drove it up front and parked.

"Good to go," he told Mahalo, then went into the bathroom to wash the grease and oil from his hands.

By the time he was finished, someone had claimed the chair he'd been sitting in, so he climbed up on a stack of wooden crates and sat, his long legs dangling off the side.

Now they waited.

It was just before 2:00 a.m. when Mahalo got a call. He answered, listened, then dropped the phone back in his pocket and activated the switch that raised the massive warehouse doors. As the doors went up, Jack began hearing the approach of an incoming helicopter, but instead of passing overhead, it sounded as if it was landing.

Before he could figure out what was happening, he saw Ito set a briefcase down at the top of the stairs, then noted Ito's guards coming down from the second floor and looked away. Son of a bitch. Ito came by chopper, not the limo. Jack didn't have a way to give the Bureau a heads-up but had to believe they were already on-site somewhere and had seen that for themselves.

He also noted the two special bodyguards who came down ahead of him were armed to the teeth. As soon as they reached the last step, they stood to one side, waiting as Ito descended. After a few remarks to the guards, Ito began making the rounds, checking out his men.

Jack knew it was only a matter of time before he got to him, and he braced himself. Nothing was ever good enough for the man.

Then he overheard Ito telling Mahalo that the delivery was coming in a bit early, which made Jack nervous. *Dammit!* Another slight change of plans. But when Adam Ito finally got to him, he barely noted his presence. Jack breathed a little easier as he readjusted his shoulder holster and sat quietly, waiting for everything to unfold.

Before Ito's arrival, time moved slowly, but after his appearance, it flew. It was ten minutes to three in the morning when they heard a truck approaching.

The rain had stopped a short while before, so when Mahalo heard it, he walked out to make sure it was their delivery, then gave the truck driver a thumbs-up and motioned him inside.

The delivery was a little early, but not enough to matter. Jack started to get down from where he was sitting, but then Mahalo motioned them all to wait. The buyer and the seller had a little business to attend to before the unloading began.

Ito's bodyguards matched his stride as he moved to the open doorway of the warehouse. Then all of a sudden another man appeared out of the night, also with guards. Jack couldn't see his face clearly, but he heard Ito call him Dumas. He couldn't hear what was being said from his location, but when Mahalo ran back upstairs to retrieve the briefcase, he guessed it might be the laptop he'd need to transfer the money.

At the same time Ito was getting set up, Dumas had his men unload two crates from the truck so that Ito could preview the goods. From his perch, Jack got a glimpse of the lettering on the side of the crate. ATacMS, then MGM and then a series of numbers, but it was the words below it that shocked him. *Prototypes*. That meant new stuff. Weapons that could quickly turn the tide of a firefight. The hair crawled on the back of his neck. These weapons could not leave this dock.

Then he began looking at the men with Dumas, and when he zeroed in on one of them, his heart stopped. There was a man looking straight at him, and the moment their gazes connected, the man grinned. It was one of Jack's snitches who went by the name of Ritter, and he was already pointing and shouting.

Oh hell.

Jack had but a few seconds to react. The only door out of the warehouse was barred by armed men, and running up to the roof would get him nowhere. Ritter's ID had just declared him dead meat. He leaped to his feet and ran across the stacks of crates, moving toward the broken window at the back of the warehouse.

"Stop him! Stop him! He's a Fed. You have a fucking Fed in on this? We're all going down!" Ritter kept screaming.

Adam Ito spun around, and when he saw Judd Wayne leaping from one stack of crates to another trying to get away, he started shouting.

"Kill him! Kill him! Don't let him get away!"

Ito's men were shooting now, and so were the others. Jack pulled his gun as he ran and fired into the crowd without looking back.

His heart was pounding, bullets flying all around him. He heard one whiz by his head. The broken window was only a few yards away when he heard the chopper warming up above him. Dammit. Ito was going to get away.

The sound of gunfire echoed all around him as he leaped over the chasm between the last two stacks of crates. Without slowing down, he lowered his head, put his arms up to protect his face and went headfirst through the broken window.

He'd made it but was falling down, down toward the water! Then seconds before impact, it felt like his entire right shoulder had been ripped from his body. He hadn't made it after all.

He went into the water on his back, knocking the air from his lungs. While he was struggling to catch a breath, the water closed over his face and then he was sinking.

"I got him! I got him!" Munoz said. "Fuckin' Fed. Damn pig. He's fish bait now!"

But his glee was cut short as the warehouse was suddenly swarming with federal agents.

Dumas had been trying to get his goods back on their truck and off the pier, but it was too late. More shots were fired, but this time it was the Feds doing the shooting. Four men dropped, and then the rest were so greatly outnumbered that they responded to the agents' orders and began dropping their weapons and surrendering.

Agent Charlie Morris had been waiting for this night for months. Jack McCann was his friend, and he was finally going to bring him in. But as he searched the line of men down on their knees, he realized Jack was missing.

One of Ito's men laughed.

"You looking for your snitch? He went out that window with a bullet in his back, and I hope the son of a bitch is dead."

Charlie hid his shock as he immediately turned, grabbed a couple of other agents, and they took off running. By the time they reached the edge of the dock and looked out into the dark expanse of Galveston Bay, he saw nothing. His gut knotted.

He radioed in for boats and search teams, while he and his men began a land search, dividing up and running along the pier in both directions in hopes they'd spot him close by.

Within thirty minutes, there was a boat on scene with searchlights on the water, slowly circling the area, looking for a survivor, or a body.

Jack might have passed out from the pain, except for the shock of the cold water. In desperate need of oxygen and with his shoulder on fire, he was swimming upward with his one good arm as fast as he could go. Just when he thought his lungs were going to burst, he surfaced.

The first breath of air was a game changer. Treading water, he looked back. Feds were all over the place now, and above, the receding lights of a chopper in the sky.

Adam Ito!

The son of a bitch did it. He was getting away, which meant as long as Jack was alive, Ito would be chasing him until one of them was dead, and that would put Shelly in constant danger. The agents would figure out what happened to him and begin looking for his body. He couldn't let himself be found, and he was beginning to weaken. He had to find a way to get ashore.

He began to kick his legs again, but his boots were full of water and pulling him down, so he rolled over onto his back to float, kicking his legs to propel himself as far away from that loading dock as he could get.

Away from the lights of the city, the night sky above him was beautiful, peppered with light from stars that had long since burned away. He could hear voices now and then coming from the anchored cargo ships, but he couldn't make out what they were saying. He kept kicking and floating, although he was getting weaker and the stars were dimming. It took a few moments for him to notice he was caught in the outgoing tide. It was pulling him out farther from shore, and farther into the bay.

Dammit. After everything, this was not the ending he had envisioned.

His legs felt like lead. He felt himself sinking.

Oh no. My Shelly. So sorry. Love you forever.

And then the stars went out.

"Paul! Grab him, dammit! He's sinking!"

Paul Faber glared at his fishing buddy. "I see that, Lou. Get me closer."

Lou accelerated the outboard engine, maneuvering their skiff right beside the drowning man, and a heart-beat later, Paul leaned over, grabbed him by a leg and pulled him into their boat.

"Good job," Lou said. "Is he alive?"

Paul was on his knees as he moved their lantern a little closer to the body and began checking for a heart-beat.

"Barely," he said, and started doing CPR as Lou hit the gas on the outboard motor and aimed the skiff through the bay back toward their landing on the op-posite shore.

It wasn't until Paul saw blood mixing with the water beneath him that he realized the man was hurt. He has-tened his chest compressions and was soon rewarded when the man choked, then started coughing up water. Paul turned him over onto his side so the water could run out, and that was when he saw the bullet hole in his shirt.

"This guy's been shot."

"Oh man! Think we should call the cops? No, wait! What if they ticket us for fishing out here after dark?"

Paul frowned. "You gonna measure a man's life against some measly fine?"

And then the man between them suddenly groaned and spoke only two words in a deep, raspy voice.

"No cops."

Jack didn't remember anything but the sight of the stars above him as he'd begun to sink, so coming to in a rowboat with strangers was something of a shock.

"What's your name? Are you a criminal?" Paul asked.

Jack coughed, then shook his head once. "No name.

No perp. Smugglers… They shot… Help… Hide…"
Then he rolled over onto his back as a wave of blinding pain pulled him under.

Paul eyed the man closely and made a knee-jerk decision. "Fine, we'll call him Dude, and I'm betting five bucks he's some kind of cop. *Perp* is cop talk." Then Paul got up on his knees and pulled off his shirt.

"What are you doing?" Lou asked.

"Gonna pack this wound and hope it slows down the bleeding until we can get him help."

Lou frowned. "He said no cops. Doctors have to report gunshot wounds on patients."

"I know that. I'm not taking him to a hospital. I know a guy," Paul said.

"We both found him. We'll both take him," Lou said.

Paul folded his T-shirt into a thick cloth pad, then yanked off the man's T-shirt and used his skinning knife to cut it straight up the front. He began pulling on the thin knit fabric to elongate it, then started rolling it up, turning it into a long, thin rope.

Sweat was dripping out of his hair and into his eyes as he shoved the pad he'd made against the open wound, and tied it down as tight as he could with the makeshift rope.

"What made you think to do something like that?" Lou asked.

"Two tours in Afghanistan," Paul said, and then looked toward shore. "We're almost there. As hot and muggy as this night is, he shouldn't feel this cold. Hurry. I think Dude is going into shock."

Three

The moment Lou reached the landing, Paul jumped out and ran to the Jeep. He backed the trailer down into the water, then helped Lou winch it up and fasten it down. As soon as they were on solid ground, they lifted Dude out of the boat and into the back seat of the Jeep. Paul jumped into the driver's seat, leaving Lou to keep an eye on the victim, and took off as fast as he dared drive.

"Where are we going?" Lou asked.

"To see a medic I served with. His place is just off Tri-City Beach Road. I'm calling him now. What's Dude's status?"

Lou reached over the seat to check his pulse. "Heart still beating."

Paul nodded, listening as his call began to ring. Once, twice, three times it rang, and then Paul heard a familiar voice, cursing and coughing between breaths.

"Faber, you sorry bastard—" *cough, cough* "—do you know what time it is?"

"Not exactly. I need your help. Bringing you a man we fished out of the bay."

"I don't resurrect drowning victims. Either you re-suscitated him, or you didn't."

"I resuscitated him, but he's been shot. If you can stop the bleeding, I won't ask more."

"Dammit all to hell, you sorry bastard. I don't want to be mixed up in anything shady."

"Please, Muncy. I have a feeling about him. I think he's one of the good guys. Just save him. I'll get him off your property as soon as you say I can move him," Paul said, and then waited. There was a long moment of silence, and then he heard a resigned sigh.

"You're gonna owe me. How soon will you be here?"

"Fifteen minutes, more or less."

Muncy grunted. "I'll be waiting."

Paul disconnected. "He's gonna do it!"

Lou glanced over his shoulder. Dude was gonna owe them big-time—if he lived.

Special Agent Charlie Morris was still on the dock in front of Adam Ito's warehouse, watching the search-ers out in the bay. This should not have happened. He was sick at heart, trying to come to terms with his part in letting Jack McCann down.

They'd searched the waters all around the docks, around the ships still anchored offshore and all around Morgan's Point. They'd done all they could do until day-light, which actually wasn't far away. The sky in the east was already getting lighter. He rubbed the back of his neck as he stared at the vast expanse before him.

"Come on, Jack…where are you, buddy? I'm not gonna give up on you until they show me the body, and don't make me face that, because then I would have to tell Shelly we failed you."

His phone rang as he was waiting for sunrise.

"Special Agent Morris," he said.

"Agent Morris, this is Fred. I'm sending you the info you requested via email. Check your phone. It's a large attachment. Let me know if there's anything wrong."

"Thanks, Fred. Will do."

He hung up, then pulled up his email, then began searching for the file. It had to do with who owned the warehouse where the bust went down. He was guessing Ito owned it, but he needed confirmation. To his surprise, Adam Ito co-owned it with his father, Ken Ito, who was a resident of Tokyo, Japan, which meant Ito senior was far beyond their jurisdiction.

The gleam from the headlights was bouncing off the corner posts of the driveway as Paul turned off the beach road and sped toward Muncy's house. It had been a while since his last visit here, but he distinctly remembered getting stone-faced drunk at a wake for a vet friend who had committed suicide. It had taken him two days to sober up enough to drive home.

"Porch light is on!" Lou said, as the house came into view.

"And that's Muncy on the porch," Paul added, pointing to a bare-chested man wearing a pair of gym shorts and cowboy boots.

"I see you two share the same tailor," Lou said, eyeing Paul's bare beer belly.

Paul didn't answer. He was too busy trying not to run over the baying mastiff that came out to greet them.

"What the hell is that animal?" Lou muttered. "It's huge."

"That's Dwayne, named after the actor Dwayne Johnson."

"The Rock. I get it. Both of them oversize," Lou said. "Now please tell me he's friendly, or I'm not getting out of the Jeep."

"He's fine," Paul said, then braked and killed the engine.

Muncy was already calling down the dog as Paul jumped out. Lou followed reluctantly, still uncertain whether he was going to survive the trip from the Jeep to the house.

"I'm gonna pull him out. You catch his legs," Paul said.

Lou nodded, and together, they got the unconscious man past the dog and into the house in one piece.

"Muncy, this is my fishing buddy, Lou Parsons. Lou, this is my old friend Muncy Peters."

Muncy nodded, but he was more focused on the man they were carrying. "Bring him this way, and put him belly down on the island," he said, leading the way through the living room to the kitchen.

"Good lord," Lou said, eyeing the white sheet hanging off the kitchen island like a tablecloth, and the assortment of medical supplies on the counter behind them.

He grunted as they lifted Dude up, then carefully rolled him over onto his belly, turning his head to the right.

"Hell of a bandage," Muncy said, eyeing the wet, bloody pad they'd tied onto his shoulder.

Paul shrugged. "It's all we had."

Muncy checked for a pulse. "Barely there. He needs a transfusion, but it's not gonna happen here. You two, stand on either side of him in case he wakes up. After all the crap it appears he's been through, it would be a damn shame if he broke his neck falling off the operating table. Paul, move that hot soapy water where you can reach it and clean him up."

Lou's eyes widened, but he held on to their patient as the other two began working.

Muncy began by scrubbing his hands and arms, then putting on a pair of surgical gloves, while Paul began cleaning the man's entire back with hot water and soap.

"That's good enough," Muncy said. "Now pour this grain alcohol into the wound, and then some of it into the pan with my instruments, then stand aside."

Again, Paul did as he was told, then moved aside as Muncy picked up a surgical clamp. It wasn't the tool he needed, but it was all he had.

"Help me, Jesus," Muncy said, as he eased the probe into the wound, then kept moving it around until he felt the bullet. Muncy stopped and took a couple of slow, deep breaths to calm his nerves.

"Did you feel it?" Paul asked.

Muncy nodded. "Going to try to get a hold on it," he said. "Hey, Lou, stand on the other side of me. You're in my light," Muncy muttered.

"Yeah, sorry," Lou said.

Silence ensued as Muncy worked, until finally he latched on to the bullet and pulled it out. "Got it!" he crowed, and dropped it into a small dish. "I'll clean out the wound now and sew it up. That's all I can do for him. I think he'll live. Are you satisfied with that prognosis?"

Both men nodded, somewhat in shock at what they were witnessing.

Paul kept an eye on Dude. He had not moved once through the entire process until Muncy began pulling the edges of the wound together with neat, tiny stitches. At that point, every time Muncy took a stitch, Dude moaned.

"Just like Granny's quilting stitches," Muncy muttered, as he knotted off the last stitch.

He checked the man's pulse again, gave him an injection of antibiotic, and another one of painkiller, and then applied a clean bandage. "I'm finished and he's still alive, which says more for the dude's fortitude than my skill."

"Now what?" Paul asked.

"Get him out of those wet clothes and off my kitchen island and I'll make breakfast," Muncy said. He began gathering up his equipment, dropping each tool into a deep pan of water simmering on the back burner of his range, and threw the rest of the bloody bandages away.

"Where do you want us to put him?" Paul asked.

"Down the hall in the spare bedroom."

"Will do," Paul said. "Lou! Grab his feet."

"Lord have mercy," Lou muttered, trying not to think of eating off the makeshift operating table as he helped Paul strip the guy and carry him down the hall.

Muncy ran ahead to turn down the covers, then helped ease him down on his side. They propped pillows behind his back to keep him from rolling over onto the wound and pulled up the covers, then paused in the hall to adjust the thermostat on the central air before going back to the kitchen.

Paul paused, then leaned over and quietly spoke into the unconscious man's ear. "Hey, Dude! Don't die. Okay? Just don't die."

Adam Ito flew out of United States airspace in the dark and was in Mexico before daylight. He took a plane from Mexico City back home to Tokyo in the bright light of day without being challenged, but he did not breathe easy until the plane was in the air. His entire syndicate—the one he'd spent years building—was gone, and all because he'd taken a traitor into his midst.

It was certain that all of his men had been arrested, so he had no immediate people to call to find the details about what happened. His last order had been to kill Judd Wayne, and if he wasn't already dead, Adam would find out his real identity and finish the job himself.

Oblivious to anything but the subconscious need to keep breathing in and breathing out, Jack's body was struggling to hang on to life as the sun rose on another day in Houston.

He had no conscious thoughts, just intermittent flashes of random memories that disappeared as quickly as they came.

Sitting beneath a Christmas tree when he was little, calmly unwrapping everything under it.

Chasing his dog, Trip, through the woods back home in Colorado Springs.

Shelly walking toward him as she came down the aisle.

And then back into a deeper state of unconsciousness.

The alarm went off in Shelly's bedroom, signaling the beginning of another day on the job. Grumbling beneath her breath, she rolled over and shut it off as she threw back the covers, getting up before she was tempted to go back to sleep.

Going back to work yesterday had been a little rough, especially since she'd had to take a cab back downtown because she'd left her car in covered parking the day before. But as the day progressed, she'd felt better and better. By noon, she was almost her normal self, but not enough to brave the Houston heat.

She had asked Mitzi to bring her a sandwich when she came back from lunch, then kept working. Tomorrow was payroll day for all of her accounts, so the accounting had to be done and the paychecks sent to direct deposits at respective banks. By the time she drove herself home that evening, she was satisfied she'd come to no lingering harm and was completely caught up at work.

Shelly flipped on the TV to listen for a weather report as she headed to the bathroom, and was in the shower when they aired the report of the FBI bust of stolen army weaponry at one of the shipping docks, and the arrest of the people involved.

She turned the set off as she went into the kitchen to grab a little breakfast before she headed downtown, and was happily oblivious to the fact that the FBI had divers in Galveston Bay, looking for the body of her husband, who was being viewed as missing and presumed dead.

As soon as the sun came up, Paul took Lou home, then dropped the boat off at his place and was back at Muncy's house by midmorning with a sack of burgers and fries and a giant chew bone for Dwayne. The mastiff sniffed the sack but happily settled for the rawhide chew and plopped down with it on the porch. Paul walked in with the food, partly as a balm to Muncy for putting up with his uninvited guests, and partly because Muncy loved burgers and fries.

"Whatcha got there?" Muncy asked, as Paul headed toward the kitchen.

"Burgers," Paul said. "Want one or four?"

Muncy grinned. "I'll start with two. Don't mind if I do," he said, digging his hand into the sack and coming up with two paper-wrapped burgers and one of the to-go boxes of fries. "Coffee's fresh if you want some."

"I do," Paul said. "I'm gonna take some food and the coffee back to the bedroom."

"What are you going to do back there? I just checked on your patient. His blood pressure is good and his heart rate is steady."

"Because he's *my* dude. I fished him out of the water. Biggest fish I ever caught and I don't intend to lose him," Paul said. "Besides, it's not like I got anyone waiting for me at home. If you want me, you know where I'll be."

Muncy watched his friend walk out with the food, then finished off one of the burgers before he went outside to finish watering his vegetable garden.

Paul softened his steps as he walked into the bedroom, put the food and coffee down on a small table near Dude, and eased himself down in the easy chair beside it. The man's color was still pale, but he was breathing slow and easy.

"You just hang in there," Paul whispered, then peeled the paper away from a burger, and as he began to eat, he couldn't help but think what a turn his life had just taken.

Being retired had been sucking big-time, but for the moment, he had purpose. And after watching the breaking news reports about the FBI bust in Galveston Bay this morning, he fully believed Dude had been telling them the truth. Now all he needed was for him to pull through and tell him the rest of the story.

Agent Charlie Morris was still on the scene, waiting for word from the divers who'd been in the water since daybreak. He could see the boats of all three diver crews who were searching the bay in grids. So far, they had nothing to report, and Charlie couldn't bring himself to go home.

He'd called Alicia twice this morning to check on her and give her updates. She knew Jack and Shelly, too, and was heartsick for what seemed to be a horrible end to a dear friend.

Charlie heard the tears in her voice and felt the same sadness. This still didn't seem real, and he wasn't going to believe it unless he saw a body.

When his radio squawked, he grabbed it.

"Agent Morris. Go ahead."

"Sir, this is Search Team One. We've cleared grid three and we're moving on to grid four."

"Thanks for the update," he said, and sighed as he looked out across the bay. "Come on, Jack. You know I'm not gonna leave till we bring you home, one way or another."

Jack surfaced so fast he gasped, thinking he was still under water, only to realize he was naked and dry, and in bed in someone's house. He stared at the sleeping stranger asleep in the chair near him, then gazed around the room in disbelief.

Who is that, and where the hell am I?

He started to move, then moaned. Damn but his shoulder hurt. So, he had been rescued, but by who?

"Hey," Jack said.

Paul sat up with a jerk, then smiled as he headed toward the bed. He laid a hand on Jack's forehead to feel for fever. It was warm, but not drastically so.

"Dude! Welcome back. Can I get you anything? Water? Something for pain?"

"I need to use the bathroom," Jack said.

"Right!" Paul said. "Hold that thought. I'm gonna get help." He left the room yelling for Muncy.

Muncy came running, thinking there was a dire emergency and wondering what else he could possibly do to keep the man alive without getting him to a hospital.

"What's wrong?"

"He woke up and needs to pee. I need help getting him upright."

"Well, that's a good sign," Muncy said, and followed Paul back into the bedroom.

"I'm Muncy Peters. This is my house. Think you're strong enough to stand up?"

"We're gonna find out," Jack said.

"I could bring you something to pee in," Muncy offered.

"Just help me up," Jack said.

They got him to the bathroom, and by the time they had him back in bed, his face was beaded with sweat.

"You look like shit," Muncy said. "I'm gonna go heat up some beef broth. You need the homemade kind, but I'm not Martha Stewart."

Paul propped him up into a semi-sitting position and then pulled up the covers so the cool air coming through the vents wouldn't chill him.

"My name's Paul Faber. Me and my fishing buddy,

Lou Parsons, fished you out of the bay around 3:00 a.m. this morning. Muncy Peters is an old friend. He was a medic in Afghanistan during the early days of the war."

Jack was listening intently. "Did I say anything to you?"

"You said you were shot. You said no cops and you wouldn't say your name. I've been calling you Dude," Paul said.

"So no one knows I'm here but you guys and your friend Lou?"

Paul nodded. "And Lou won't talk and neither will we."

"Good. The less you know about me, the safer all of you are."

"You're one of the good guys," Paul said. "That's all I need to know."

Jack tried to say thank you, but he was already slipping away again.

Paul removed one of the pillows from behind his head and then eased him back down and straightened the covers.

"I think I missed my calling," he muttered, as he eyed Dude one more time before going back to the kitchen. He needed coffee to stay awake.

Shelly finished up and logged out for the day, ready to be home, but not all that ready to face the drive in rush hour traffic.

Her boss, Willard Bates, stopped by her desk as she was locking it up.

"Good job getting the direct deposits for payroll done on your accounts, Shelly. Considering you did it despite missing half of the day on Wednesday, you pulled off quite the feat."

"Thank you, sir. I know I'd want my paycheck to show up when it's supposed to."

Willard nodded. "That's the kind of work ethic we appreciate here. Ron Davis and I have talked, and we both agree that you are due for a step raise. There will be a twenty percent increase to the salary you're already drawing, so congratulations. You've proved your loyalty and drive to the firm time and time again. You deserve this."

Shelly beamed. "Thank you, sir! That's very much appreciated."

He nodded. "Of course. Have a good evening, and we'll see you Monday."

"Yes, sir, bright and early," Shelly said, and left the office with a bounce in her step.

Forty-five minutes later, she pulled up into the drive, hit the remote and pulled in as the garage door went up, but she didn't get out of her car until the door was all the way down. It was yet another safeguard Jack had taught her a few years back after a rash of assaults happened as women were driving into their garages.

She hurried into the house and disengaged the alarm as she kicked off her heels, relishing the feel of the cool hardwood beneath her bare feet as she went down the hall to change.

After changing into shorts and a loose T-shirt, she retrieved the mail and took it with her into the kitchen. To celebrate her raise, she got a piece of dark chocolate from the candy dish on the kitchen table, popping it in her mouth before going to make herself a glass of sweet tea.

As usual, she picked up the remote and turned on the flat screen hanging over the sideboard before getting the tea from the refrigerator. It was time for the six o'clock newscast, and she was curious as to what was happening in the world while she'd been at work.

The moment the sound came on, she heard the word *FBI*, then *dive crews searching Galveston Bay*. Her heart stopped as she turned around. But the on-the-scene reporter wasn't giving details other than referring to what was already old news…that the Feds had recovered stolen military weapons and that men had been arrested.

"Then what are they still searching for?" Shelly muttered, staring intently at the screen.

Then she thought of Jack's last call, about something big going down, which, if it worked, would end his undercover work for good. The news anchor was still talking as the camera zoomed in on a man standing on the dock looking out into the bay. It was Charlie Morris, and the look on his face was not happy.

All of a sudden the hair stood up on the back of her neck. If this had already gone down, then why wasn't Jack home? At the least, why hadn't he called?

The camera shot pulled back to an overhead view of all of the dive crews scattered across the bay, and she started to shake. What if something had gone wrong? What if it was Jack they were looking for? The thought of losing him was impossible to fathom.

She staggered backward, grabbing on to a kitchen chair to keep from falling as wave after wave of fear washed over her.

"Not Jack. Please, God, not Jack."

Four

Adam Ito had all kinds of technology available to him in his Tokyo home, but the Japanese media didn't report on day-to-day business going on in one of the many US cities unless it affected them directly. He wanted to know details of what was going on, but all of his contacts he might have called were in jail, where he would have been, too, if he hadn't arrived in his chopper.

He finally got through to an associate who lived in West Texas, a neo-Nazi named Newton Rhone who had bought arms through Adam more than once to outfit his own army. Newton was a skinhead with big dreams and an ego to match, and the only person Adam could think of who wouldn't rat him out.

When someone finally answered the number Adam had called, he recognized Rhone's raspy voice.

"This is Rhone."

"Hello, Mr. Rhone, this is Adam Ito."

Rhone grunted audibly. "I almost didn't answer this unfamiliar number. And I am surprised to hear your voice. Thought you were behind bars with your men."

"I'm not that easy to catch," Adam said.

"Good for you, but what the hell do you want?" Rhone snapped.

Adam frowned. How quickly attitudes change when weakness is revealed. He shifted into his own version of "don't fuck with me" and posed his question.

"I want nothing from you but information. If you are unwilling to give me an update on what's happening, then I'll file that away for future reference and leave you alone," Adam said.

Ito made certain Rhone heard the displeasure in his voice, and he'd know what Ito was capable of when he was unhappy. He'd made sure to leave a man with notched ears and missing the end of his nose the last time he'd been displeased.

"No need to be pissed off at me," Rhone said. "Ask your question."

"I know you aren't in Houston, but I assume you listen to the news."

"Yeah, so what about it?" Rhone asked.

Adam ignored the sarcasm. "I want to know what kind of story the Feds are releasing about a recent bust they made in Houston. Have they, in any way, acknowledged the man they had undercover?"

"All I can tell you about the Feds is that they're searching Galveston Bay, presumably for a body, because they have multiple dive crews on it. But they don't say who they're looking for, or which side he was on."

Adam pinched the bridge of his nose and then stared up at the ceiling, willing himself to stay calm.

"Thank you. I could make it worth your while to stay informed on this search if you so wished, so that the next time I called to check in, you would have updates for me."

Rhone didn't want to be connected with the man in any way, but he also didn't want him as an enemy. "Yeah sure, whatever," he said.

"Thank you. I will be in touch," Adam said, and disconnected, but his worst fears had been realized. His men were all in custody, and likely Dumas and his crew, as well.

This information certainly put to rest the idea of finding a way to set a new operation up in a different location out of the United States. No one would want to do business with a man who'd been duped by the Feds. His growing rage toward Judd Wayne was impossible to express.

The next time Jack woke up, Paul was still there, and with hot beef broth waiting. Paul was adamant Jack needed to drink as much as he could stomach. He'd bled a lot and was certainly low on blood, which would mean he was low on iron. The iron-rich beef broth was the best solution Muncy could offer for a man who needed a transfusion but with no way to get it.

Considering the fact that Dude was still nude, Paul couldn't help but notice his well-toned physique as he sat up on the side of the bed with a blanket draped across his lap and legs.

"How you doing?" Paul asked, as he watched him sipping the broth. "Hurting much?"

Jack shook his head as he blew on the broth to cool it.

"You aren't much of a talker, are you?" Paul asked.

Jack paused and looked up, then managed a slight smile.

"I have been known to recite the Gettysburg address with a few beers under my belt."

Paul laughed. "That's a good one, Dude."

Jack took another sip. "This is good."

"I'll give your compliment to the chef," Paul said.

Jack paused. "Your friend Muncy. Do you trust him?"

The smile slid off Paul's face. "Yes. You're safe here."

"What about the other man? There were two of you… before I mean. Right?"

"Lou? Yeah, he helped me save you. Look, I know you don't know us…and I don't want to know what you're about, but Lou isn't the kind to talk about his business and Muncy and I spent two tours apiece in Afghanistan and Iraq fighting bad guys, so we know that type, and you're not one of them. We got your back for as long as you need it."

"As soon as I'm a little stronger, I'll be gone and you can forget you ever saw me."

Paul pointed at the broth. "I reckon you should drink some more of that."

Jack picked up the mug and downed the broth.

"Want anything else?" Paul asked.

"News. What's happening?" Jack asked.

"Oh, that stolen weapons bust is newsworthy. Feds recovered missiles stolen from the US Army and arrested a bunch of people." Paul hesitated, then added, "They have all kinds of divers out on the bay looking for a body."

Jack stared down at the floor without speaking, then finally nodded. "Good enough," he said.

Paul glanced out the window. It was moving toward nighttime.

"How would you feel about taking a car ride? I told

Muncy we'd be out of here as soon as you could be moved."

"Do I have clothes?" Jack asked.

"Everything but a shirt. Muncy will provide that."

"Then yes, I think I can do that," Jack said.

"Good. As soon as it gets dark, we'll leave. It's about thirty minutes to my house. You'll be safe there and comfortable enough."

"I appreciate all this," Jack said.

Paul nodded. "No big deal. Sit tight. I'm going to get your clothes."

Jack wanted to call Shelly so bad he ached. But he couldn't take a chance on anyone thinking he was still alive. They would go after her to get to him, so she would be safer if he stayed hidden and kept her in the dark as long as possible. Right now, he had to see if he was strong enough to walk. He reached for the bedpost and, using it to steady himself, he pulled himself upright.

The room was spinning, but the longer he stood there, the steadier he became. As soon as the vertigo passed, he made his way out of the room and across the hall to the bathroom. By the time he got back, Paul was there with his clothes.

Shelly was still in the kitchen, staring at the television long after the news was over. Sunset had come and gone. Streetlights were on, but she sat in shadows, hiding from a burgeoning truth she didn't want to face. Jack was the most important person in her life. No. Jack *was* her life. She could barely remember a time when he wasn't in it. This couldn't be happening… She had to be wrong. She was succumbing to all of this panic because it was her worst fear coming to life—the one where he never came home.

Finally, she made herself move.

"You're not a damn bat. Get up and turn on some lights," she muttered, as she got up and flipped the light switch.

The kitchen was immediately illuminated. She saw her empty glass still by the refrigerator and made herself that glass of iced tea. The cold, sweet brew was the perfect color of amber as she poured it over the ice. She took a sip, savoring the sweet taste of her favorite black tea, then dug around in the pantry until she found a box of sesame seed crackers. She took it and her tea into the living room, turning on more lights as she went, and then, as was her nightly habit, turned on the porch light. It was her version of a candle in the window. Wherever Jack was, he counted on her to stay strong.

The shades were pulled, the curtains drawn. As she settled into her favorite recliner, the familiarity of the room eased her even more. A picture in her line of vision was of her and Jack standing at the rail of their cruise ship with the wide blue sky above them, and the vastness of the Pacific Ocean behind them. It was one of her favorites from the last vacation they'd taken. The fact that the cruise was almost five years ago spoke to the huge change their lives had taken since Jack began working undercover.

She popped a cracker into her mouth and turned on the television again, but it was a different show and a different room, and she managed to deny a lingering level of fear. She began getting sleepy around midnight and turned off the television.

She went through the house locking up and set the

security alarm by the front door, then headed for the shower. She caught a glimpse of herself in the mirror as she entered the bathroom—the fear was still there, banked like embers, and she quickly looked away.

When she finally did go to sleep, she dreamed.

"Shelly...baby...do you want multicolored lights on the Christmas tree or what?"

Shelly looked up from the box of ornaments she was sorting, gauging the size of the tree with the number of multicolored strings that they had to work with.

"I love the multicolors, don't you? They make it seem more like the way trees were decorated when we were kids."

Jack grinned.

"I remember one year when I was a kid, Mom wanted one of those silver metallic trees. She called it retro because it was what Grandma McCann had when Mom was a kid. She found one at a flea market and was so excited to put it up, but by the time she had it decorated, the silver leaves were shedding like crazy. Dad laughed. Mom cried, and then he was sorry he laughed, but it was too late. She was already disappointed by the tree failure and Dad's teasing topped it off."

Shelly was completely caught up in the story. "So what happened?"

"They sent me to bed. It took me a few more years before I figured out that Dad's method of apologizing was sex. I'm pretty sure they made love under that damn tree because he was still picking pieces of those aluminum leaves out of her hair the next morning."

Shelly laughed. "That's awesome."

Jack let her laughter wash through him, filling the well of his love for her all over again, then laid down the strands of lights and crawled across the floor on his hands and knees to where she was sitting.

"What are you doing?" Shelly asked, as he raised up on his knees beside her.

"Going to make love to you under our tree," he said, then wrapped his arms around her shoulders and pulled her down onto the carpet.

Shelly moaned in her sleep. The sensation of him sliding inside her was so real that she came within seconds, then woke to the realization that everything but the climax had been a dream. Afraid to give rise to the fear she'd banked earlier, she rolled over onto her side and pulled the covers up to her chin.

Paul glanced over at the man in the seat beside him. He was pretty damn stoic for a guy who'd more or less drowned just a short time ago, never mind being shot in the back. Tough as a boot heel, he was. He couldn't help but admire the trait.

Paul had already tried making conversation, but he gave it up when he didn't get any responses. The pain on Dude's face was highlighted by the dashboard lights, but it was less than it had been. Probably because Muncy had put his arm in a sling and given him the last of the Novocain in a shot before they left.

"Not long now," Paul said.

"Good," Jack replied, and then leaned back against the headrest and closed his eyes.

Paul could almost believe Dude was actually resting, except for the white-knuckle grip he had on his seat belt. About five minutes later, he took an off-ramp, pulled up to the first stop sign and then turned right. Dude didn't bother to look up.

"I'm so damn sorry," Paul muttered.

"No way, man. I'm alive because of you guys. I can take all kinds of pain to stay that way."

Paul just kept driving, making no apologies for the occasional rough spot on the streets, or the number of turns he had to take to get home, but when they finally pulled up into his driveway, Paul exhaled softly.

"We're here," he said. "Sit tight. I'll come help you out," he said.

Jack waited.

A couple of minutes later, they were inside the house. Paul locked the door behind him before turning on lights, then put his arm around Dude's waist. "Walk with me," he said. "My spare bedroom with its own bathroom is at the end of this hall."

Jack couldn't see how far the hall went because he was too busy focusing on putting one foot in front of the other.

Paul turned on lights as they went, and when they reached the last door at the end of the short hall, he swung it inward and turned on the lights.

"Take a seat in the easy chair while I turn down the bed. The sheets are clean because I don't have company, so there's that."

Jack eased himself down and then leaned forward and put his head between his knees to keep from passing out.

Paul yanked back the covers, then rushed over to where he'd left Dude and quickly pulled off his boots and then the borrowed Kick Some Ass T-shirt from Muncy.

"I'll get your pants off as soon as you get to the side

of the bed," Paul said. "Now, put your arm around my neck and I'll help you stand."

Jack was moving on autopilot but managed to do as he was told. When he got to the side of the bed, Paul unsnapped the jeans and then pushed them down to his knees.

"Sit down and lean back," Paul said, and as soon as Jack's butt hit the mattress, Paul swung Jack's legs onto the mattress and then pulled the jeans the rest of the way off. "Okay, Dude, is there anything you need before I leave you to rest?"

"Water," Jack said.

"On the way," Paul said, and ran out of the room. Dude had already stretched out on the bed when he got back, but Paul helped Dude sit up enough so that he could drink, then set the glass on the bedside table and eased him back down onto the pillows.

"My room is up one door and across the hall. I'm leaving my door open, so if you need anything in the night, just yell out. I'm a really light sleeper."

"Thanks, man," Jack whispered.

"No problem," Paul said, and then turned on the small lamp on the table beside an old, white rocking chair and turned out the overhead lights as he left.

Jack's head was spinning. Every time he closed his eyes, it felt like he was falling, but he paced his breathing and managed to slow down the rapid pace of his heart until he finally fell asleep.

But sleep wasn't restful. The Novocain hyped his dream state to the point that it became nightmares. He kept dreaming of Shelly calling out to him, but he didn't know where she was, and he couldn't move.

When she started crying, he woke and reached out to comfort her. Then he remembered where he was.

He also knew what he was doing by staying hidden. He was breaking her heart.

Charlie went home at sundown when the dive crews quit for the day. He already had the word from headquarters via a message from Fred that they'd finish out the grid search tomorrow, and if nothing popped, it would be called off. His guilt was at an all-time high. Never in his career had he felt more responsible for what had happened. Jack had depended on them—on him—and they'd all failed him. He was already facing the fact that most everyone believed Jack's body had drifted out to sea with the outgoing tide.

His steps were dragging when he walked in the door, but seeing Alicia coming toward him with her arms outstretched, and feeling the baby bump between them, was the healing he needed.

"I'm so sorry, darling," Alicia said. "Does Shelly know anything?"

"No, but all of the news coverage and the fact that Jack isn't calling probably has her scared to death. I don't know how I'm going to tell her. I can't believe this is even happening. I feel so damn responsible."

"No, Charlie, no. How many times have you talked about the dangers attached to your job—and you aren't even doing undercover work! Jack accepted the risks that came with his position and it was his choice. He chose that. No one forced him into the life."

Charlie hugged her. "Thank you, baby. I needed to hear that."

Alicia slipped out of his arms, then put his hand on

her belly. "Feel that? Your son hears your voice. He's glad Daddy is home."

Charlie broke into a big smile. "I can't wait to meet this little guy."

"Me, either. We're going to be great parents. Now come with me into the kitchen. Dinner is almost ready and I decanted your favorite wine."

Charlie thought about the list of bills in his office that he needed to pay, but he couldn't resist her offer. "You're singing my song," he said, and followed her and the enticing aromas.

Jack eventually woke to the scent of brewing coffee drifting into his room. He remembered enough to know not to roll over on his shoulder and managed to sit up and then swing his legs off the side of the bed. Almost immediately, the vertigo hit again, but he stayed where he was until it passed, then got up and made his way to the bathroom. When he came out, there was a pair of gym shorts on the bed.

He eyed the sling Muncy had put on him, but since he didn't have any broken bones and it was limiting to his mobility, he opted to leave it off as he sat down to dress. He broke out in a shaky sweat as he bent over to put on the shorts and had to rest before he got them as far up as his knees. Now he was going to have to stand to finish the job.

He was still dizzy as he tried to get up, so he leaned the back of his legs against the bed to steady himself until he could get the shorts up where they belonged.

"Damn good thing I wasn't trying to get those jeans on by myself," he muttered, and then reached for Muncy's ass-kicking shirt. The fact that it was oversize was lucky, or he would never have been able to get it on by himself.

His hair was a work in progress. He'd either have to accept the wild man look or ask for help to get it tied into a ponytail. He wanted a cup of coffee in the worst way, so he slowly made his way out of the room. He'd barely made it a few steps down the hall before wondering how far he could get without passing out.

Fortunately for him, Paul showed up.

"Well, damn, Dude. Looking good here. Need a shoulder to lean on?"

Jack nodded.

Paul was considerably shorter, but it was to Jack's advantage and he used his shoulders for a crutch and made it to the kitchen, where he finally sat.

"Okay?" Paul asked.

Jack nodded again, too winded and in enough pain he didn't want to talk about it.

"Coffee coming up. How do you take it?" Paul asked.

"Black, and if I haven't already said it, thank you for all of this."

"It's all good, Dude. Here's your coffee. I'm not much of a cook, but I do breakfasts pretty good. Want eggs fried or scrambled?"

"I'll eat them however you make them," Jack said, and tested the coffee with a tentative sip. It was too hot, but otherwise good, and it would cool. Then he glanced at the clock over the stove. It was almost 10:00 a.m. "What's the news on the dive crews this morning?"

"They were still at it last time I checked," Paul said. "Remote is on that cabinet behind you and so is the TV."

Jack eased himself around, reached for the remote and turned the TV on, then searched until he found a local station. Within minutes a news crew was breaking into regular programming with an update on the latest regarding the FBI bust at Morgan's Point. When Jack saw his friend Charlie Morris standing behind the bank of microphones, he froze. The look on Charlie's face was grim. And then he began speak.

"As of nine thirty this morning, we have called off the search teams and will be clearing the area shortly."

"Who or what were you searching for?" a reporter called out.

"At this time, that's still classified information. We are aware there have been some assumptions made that we were searching for military-issue missiles or weaponry, but that is not the case. We appreciate your interest and concern, but the public is not in danger in any way and never was."

Another reporter spoke out. "Then can we assume you were looking for a body?"

"As I said, it's still classified information. Thank you," Charlie said, and walked away.

Jack didn't realize he'd been holding his breath until Charlie left the podium. He combed his hair back away from his face and then aimed the remote and turned the TV off.

"Eggs are done, Dude," Paul said, and set down a plate of fluffy scrambled eggs at each of their places, followed by a stack of buttered toast.

Jack turned around, looked at the food in front of him and nodded.

"Looks good." He started to pick up his fork with his right hand, then paused and switched hands. "Being ambidextrous comes in handy now and then," he said, and forked up a bite, chewed and swallowed while Paul watched. "Tastes good, too," he said.

Paul grinned with satisfaction, reached for some toast and then dug into his meal.

Jack was quiet, speaking only to ask Paul to pass the saltshaker.

Paul shoved both salt and pepper shakers toward him, then got up to refill their coffee.

"I guess that was weird," Paul finally said.

"What was weird?" Jack asked.

"Well, they think you're dead and you know you're not."

Jack looked up then and surprised himself by grinning.

"Yeah, that was weird as hell."

"It'll be hard on any family you have."

The grin on Jack's face slipped, but he never acknowledged the fact that he had any family to notify. Paul seemed like a good guy, but he wasn't giving Shelly's existence away to anyone.

Shelly was cleaning house—something she did every Saturday, but this time it was to keep from losing her mind. She'd seen the news report. She'd heard Charlie say they were calling off the search. And she knew enough about the FBI to know that if someone from the Bureau died, nothing would be said until family was notified. But here it was almost noon, and she hadn't received any phone calls or unexpected visitors. So she went from one job to another in panic mode, praying like she'd never prayed before that it wasn't going to be her.

It was a little after 1:00 p.m. when she finally put

away the mop and vacuum cleaner, hung the feather duster on a hook inside the cabinet in the utility room and went into the kitchen to wash up. Even though the air conditioner was running, she was hot. The thought of something cool to drink sent her to the refrigerator.

She had just opened the door to get a bottle of water when the doorbell rang. Breath caught in the back of her throat, and her heart started to pound, but she couldn't move. The crazy thought went through her mind that as long as she didn't answer the door, Jack would still be safe.

But the doorbell rang again, and then someone knocked on it as well, and Shelly made herself move. She was all the way into the living room when she saw the dark government-issue sedan parked at the curb. It was at that point that time began slowing down. It felt as if she was walking through a dream sequence and any moment the alarm would go off and she would wake up. She unlocked the dead bolt and then opened the door, and when she saw Charlie Morris and another agent with him, she thought she was going to throw up.

Charlie was heartsick. He'd brought his partner, Nolan Warren, with him because he didn't have the guts to come alone. He could tell by the look on her face that she already knew, yet it was his job to say the words.

"Shelly, may we come in?"

The anger she felt was unexpected. "No. Just get it said."

He reached for her arm, but she took a step backward, not wanting to be touched. Charlie understood.

"As you wish. Shelly, I'm so sorry, but from what we can gather, it seems that Jack didn't survive the bust. We don't know how, but his cover was blown. He jumped out a window over the bay when the shooting started, and was shot in the back on the way down. We have not been able to recover the body."

Shelly reeled as if he'd just slapped her. "So, you not only got him killed, but you lost him, too?"

"We tried to—"

Shelly stepped back and shut the door in their faces and turned the lock. She was shaking so hard she couldn't breathe, and there was a pain spreading in her chest that was surely going to kill her. But when it didn't, she threw back her head and screamed, and then screamed again and again until she fell to the floor, curling up like a baby in the womb, refusing to be birthed again into an ugly, ugly world.

Outside, the two men were still standing, unable to decide what to do. Charlie already knew neither one of them had any living relatives, and he had no way of knowing if she had close friends or anyone she could call.

It was Nolan Warren's instinct to help people who were in need, and yet in this instance they'd made it worse.

"Dammit, Charlie, what do we do here?"

Charlie laid a hand in the middle of the door and then shook his head and turned away.

"We can't do anything. They'll send a chaplain. They'll offer grief counseling. But Shelly's going to tell them all to go to hell, and I don't blame her. We lost our inside man and we're going to have to live with that."

Their steps were slow as they walked back to their car and then drove away.

Five

Shelly had cried until her eyes were swollen, her throat was raw and she was so weak it was an effort to breathe. Now she lay motionless on the floor, staring at the underside of the sofa and trying to come to terms with what had happened, but nothing felt real. It was a nightmare of epic proportions and she kept waiting to wake up. From where she was lying, she could smell the lemon oil she'd rubbed onto her dining room table and chairs, and the clean, just-mopped flooring beneath her.

Eventually, she drifted off to sleep and then woke abruptly, trying to remember why she was on the floor, and when she did, her heart broke all over again. She was on the floor, and Jack was in the water, and she'd never see him again. She didn't even have a body to bury. The indignity of what was likely happening to his body was horrific. She couldn't get the images of it out of her head.

Then she heard footsteps outside on her porch, and then to her horror, there was a knock at the door.

She didn't plan to answer, but if the mailman was knocking, he had something needing a signature before he could deliver. Either she got up now and dealt with it, or she'd have to drive all the way down to the post office and take care of it later, and that wasn't happening. She knew she looked horrible, but she didn't care.

She dragged herself to her feet and opened the door. The smile on the mailman's face froze, his voice mirroring his sudden concern.

"Mrs. McCann! Are you alright?"

"No, I'm not, Billy. I just received some bad news."

"Oh no! I'm so sorry to bother you, but this package needs a signature before I can deliver it. Do you mind?"

He held out what looked like an oversize cell phone and a small stylus, and she signed where he pointed. Then he handed her a box wrapped in plain brown butcher paper.

"My sympathies," he said, and ducked his head as he turned and walked away.

Shelly closed and locked the door, then picked the mail up from the floor, dumping it all on the kitchen table before going to wash her face. She caught a glimpse of herself in the mirror as she walked in and shuddered. Her skin was red and blotchy, her eyes were horribly swollen and her bottom lip was bleeding. She had no idea how that had happened.

She began splashing her face over and over with cool water until her eyes were no longer burning, dried herself off and then looked in the mirror again. Not much had changed. Her eyes still mirrored shock and they were so swollen it hurt to blink. So now she knew. Washing away grief was not a thing that could happen.

She went back to the kitchen and picked up the box. There was no return address on the outside, so she tore into the wrapping, then opened it. There was a note inside and yet another, smaller jeweler's box inside. And then she recognized the handwriting.

"This isn't happening," she moaned.

Happy Absentee Anniversary, Baby. I'll make it up to you when I get home.
Love you forever,
Jack

The note fluttered to the table as she pressed her hands over her heart. The jeweler's box loomed like an elephant in the room, and the tension was only going to get worse until she looked at his gift.

"God help me," she whispered.

Her hands were trembling as she reached for the box, and as she lifted the lid, the stunning sapphire ring within caught a ray of sunshine and winked at her. Blue was her favorite color, and the sapphire was her birthstone. She took it out of the box and slipped it on the ring finger of her right hand, then shook her head as fresh tears finally rolled.

"You are my forever love, too, Jack McCann, and it fits, just like you fit me. How am I ever going to live without you?"

Then she took off the ring and put it back in the box, gathered up the note and took all of it to her room. The king-size bed with the tufted turquoise spread was nothing but a reminder that she would never make love with Jack again. So many things would never be done again. She set the note and the jewelry box on top of the dresser, then walked away. There would be ugly reminders of his absence all over the place, and there was nothing she could do to hide them. He had been the only family she had left in the world, and now there was no one.

Her steps were slow, her feet dragging as she finally made the glass of iced tea and took it with her to the kitchen table.

She sipped it as she went through the mail like it was just another day, and only now and then did the tears well, but when they did, she covered her face and sobbed. In a way, part of her was already putting grief into its own compartment so she could function. She was seriously considering not telling anyone at work and just showing up on Monday as if nothing had happened. She never talked about Jack, so it was not as if they'd know the difference. And she had a feeling that sitting here alone in their home with nothing to do but remember and imagine would be worse. She'd give it more thought tomorrow, but today was for her. She didn't want to see or talk to anyone. She didn't want to hear people say how sorry they were, or hear the platitudes that would come later. She didn't want anyone to see her so beset with grief that she couldn't function. Jack was hers, and today she didn't want to share him.

But what she wanted and what she got were two different things. She was still going through mail when her doorbell rang.

"No," she moaned, and didn't move.

It rang again, and then like before, whoever it was began knocking.

"Go away," she whispered. "Go far, far away."

Finally, the knocking stopped, and her phone rang.

"Hello."

"May I speak to Shelly McCann?"

"You already are," she said.

"Ma'am, this is Harold's Florist. We are at your house and we have a delivery for you."

"Leave it on the porch," she said, and hung up.

She heard someone moving about outside the door and then heard a car starting up. She waited until they left before she got up and went to the door and looked out. There was a huge vase of flowers and a card poked out among the blooms.

She picked it up and carried it inside, pausing long enough to turn the dead bolt, then took the vase as far as the dining table before she removed the card.

It was a sympathy card from Charlie and Alicia. She left the card lying on the table beside the flowers. The longer she looked, the more resigned she became. This was really happening. She could hide from the world, but evidently not for long.

Jack was sitting in a lounge chair on Paul's back deck, shaded from the heat by the large roofed porch with an icy glass of sweet tea in the cup holder on the arm of the chair, and eating what was left of his ham sandwich. Paul was out in his garden picking tomatoes and stopping every few minutes to curse the heat before he bent back over to continue. Jack finally swallowed the last bite and washed it down with a big drink, then leaned back and closed his eyes.

Immediately, he thought of Shelly. Today was their anniversary, and if the gift he'd gotten her two weeks ago had been delivered, he was guessing the timing of its arrival had come on a bad day. He didn't have to ask to know if she'd already been notified of his demise. He knew how the Bureau worked.

His gut knotted, knowing what her reaction would

be. He'd broken a promise to her. In her mind, he didn't come back like he said he would, and he could only imagine what she was going through. He needed some kind of update about Adam Ito before he could move forward, but he didn't know who he could call. This whole situation sucked.

For Shelly, the day passed in a blur of visitors. People from the Bureau came knocking. A chaplain showed up to pray with her. She told him no, thank you, and shut the door.

A couple of hours later Charlie called. She saw caller ID and let it go to voice mail. Then Alicia called. Shelly knew she was due to deliver almost any day, and rather than give her something else to worry about, she answered.

"Hello."

"Oh, honey… We're so sorry. Charlie and I want you to know how much we love you."

"Thank you," Shelly said.

"Is there anything we can do? Do you need help planning services?" Alicia asked.

"Services? Why would I have any kind of service? I have no one to bury and no family to grieve with. Neither one of us did. Thank you for calling," she said, and hung up.

There were other callers within a couple of hours—all from the Bureau. She let them go to voice mail, then got in the car and headed for Beach City on Galveston Bay. It was as close as she could get to Morgan's Point. It was where the divers had been searching, so she had to assume it was where Jack had died. She needed to see it for herself and face the fact that God saw fit to leave him there, because right now she was having all kinds of trouble accepting that decision.

Her rage stayed with her all the way to Beach City, and then once there, she became sidetracked trying to find a place to park. Once she did, she put on sunglasses and walked down to the shore. By the time she got there, she was carrying her sandals, and despite the warm sand through which she was walking, she was shivering.

There were people swimming, and even more talking and laughing, and children were everywhere, running through the crowded beach like runaway puppies, but she'd never felt more alone. The wind was brisk, and as she started down toward the water, it caught and tugged at the loose curls in her hair until she gave up and let it down to blow freely.

Everyone down here was in swimwear, while she had on white denim shorts and a pale pink T-shirt. She walked all the way into the shallows, then stood with her feet apart, bracing herself against the ebb and flow of the ocean.

The water was cold. She imagined Jack falling into the depths and hoped to God he'd been unconscious when it happened. She stared out across the glittering, wind-driven water decorated in foam-curled ruffles along the edges of the waves and wondered how anything this beautiful could be so deadly. The ocean gave up her shells, her fish, even driftwood and sea glass. Why wouldn't she give up Jack? He didn't belong to her.

"He belongs to me," Shelly said, then took a few steps farther into the water. Now it was halfway between her ankles and her knees and for the first time she could feel the power and the danger. "He belonged to me," she shouted, unaware she'd said that in past tense. "Damn you! Damn you! He belonged to me."

A man came up behind her. "Ma'am, are you okay?"

Shelly jumped at the sound of his voice, then looked up at him through a film of tears.

"No, no, I'm not okay," she said, and ran out of the water, and all the way back to her car.

She was out of breath and sobbing when she finally got inside. She tossed her shoes on the passenger seat and started up the car to let it cool off.

"God! I would hate You for what You've done, but it wouldn't bring him back," she cried, and then grabbed a handful of tissues and swiped at her face in short, jerky movements.

By the time she pulled herself together enough to drive home, it was almost 6:00 p.m. It would be after seven, maybe later, before she got home. Going out to dinner on Saturday night was a ritual for many Houstonians, which meant more traffic than normal—if that was even possible. But there was no way to get home without going through it, so she put the car in gear and drove away.

It was almost eight o'clock by the time she drove the car into the garage and hit the remote to close the door. She sat until the door was down, then got up and went into the house, still barefoot and carrying her shoes.

She disarmed the alarm and then checked her phone and was shocked by the number of missed calls, then thought, so what? She was in no mood to see who they were from. She was windblown, sand between her toes, and slightly sunburned.

She headed for the shower and shampooed her hair first, then clipped it up on top of her head so she could finish her shower. It took every bit of energy she had left to blow dry her hair before putting on clean clothes.

As always, the cool hardwood was grounding as she went into the kitchen. She stood in the doorway, looking at the stainless steel appliances and the black gas cookstove, trying to imagine life without Jack. Her shoulders slumped. And yet in the middle of despair, her stomach growled, demanding to be fed.

Her eyes were bright with fresh tears as she put a piece of bread in the toaster and then began to scramble a couple of eggs. Within a couple of minutes she was standing at the stove eating eggs from the skillet, chasing bites with buttered toast and cold milk.

Her phone signaled an incoming call, which she chose to ignore, and as soon as she finished eating, she rinsed the dishes she'd used and put them in the dishwasher. The food settled her nausea. Now to check the calls.

She spent the next hour returning calls, leaving messages, deleting some without feeling the need to respond, and ignoring another call from Alicia. They'd said all that needed to be said to each other.

When she finished with the last call, she put her phone in the pocket of her shorts and then locked up the house, set the alarm and headed to her bedroom, turning out lights as she went.

Tomorrow was Sunday. She had a decision to make about work and was already leaning toward going back. She couldn't tell them her husband had died without lying about all the rest. No one at her work knew he worked for the FBI. She'd only ever told them he worked at the state level in a government position. They'd never met him. And if she told them he was gone, then they'd want to know about the funeral, and she would have to lie again, or tell them he was the body they'd been looking for and didn't find in the bay, and that would give away his ties to the Feds. It seemed simpler to keep quiet, but she still wasn't certain.

Adam was on his way to his father's estate in an exclusive part of Tokyo. He'd been summoned, which made him a bit nervous. Despite Adam being in his midforties, his father, Ken Ito, was still the head of their family and had an equal share in the import/export business Adam ran. His brother, Yuki, who worked in the Tokyo office, had not only known but had helped Adam hide the fact that they were pocketing a bigger cut of the money from the smuggled items than their father knew. However, the FBI bust had ended more than the arms dealing. It had also brought the import/export business to a halt, which would obviously impact more than just their family business. There was the cartel to deal with, as well.

He arrived at the family home on time but was startled to see so many cars there. Adam had been expecting his father would want to see him alone, that he would be furious and ready to tear into him about what he'd let happen, yet all of these vehicles signified some sort of gathering. He parked and got out, glad he'd chosen a black silk shirt to wear under his white suit and tie, reflecting dignity, as opposed to casual comfort.

He strode to the door with his chin up in a quiet gesture of defiance and knocked. One of their servants let him in and directed him to the dining area. He entered confidently but stopped midstride when he realized who his father had invited to their home. He looked at the stern faces of the men sitting at the long table, and it was suddenly very clear to him the danger he was in. He didn't know what to say or how to react. His brother, Yuki, was standing at the end of the table but wouldn't look up at him. When Adam tried to make eye contact with his father, Ken held up a hand.

"Do not look at me!" his father barked. "Move to the end of the table beside your brother."

Adam felt their judgment. "But there is no chair there," he said.

His father's face was emotionless, but the rage in his voice was evident. "That is because neither of you are guests. Stand and accept your punishment!"

Adam moved to stand beside his brother, and when he did, he saw the frantic beat of Yuki's pulse in a vein down the side of his neck. He took a deep breath, then looked into the faces of the men sitting around to judge him. They were crime bosses from all parts of the world, he knew, and some of the most dangerous men on Earth. He felt sick to his stomach wondering if he and his brother were going to leave this house alive.

"We have already voted," Ken Ito said. "It is due to my compatriots' consideration for me that neither of you will be executed."

Yuki swayed on his feet, obviously from relief.

Adam bowed his head. "Thank—"

"Do not speak!" Ken said.

The power and rage in his father's voice was something he had never heard. It took everything Adam had to stand his ground.

"My sons have destroyed everything I worked years to grow. You have destroyed the links that we here at this table used through that business, and all because of

greed and stupidity. You had a traitor in your organiza-
tion and didn't even know it! And during an audit of our
now defunct business in Houston, Texas, you and Yuki
were also traitors to the cartel…and to me! You have
been stealing money from me, from all of us. Now you
have nothing, and all of your employees, and your last
client and his employees, will soon be in prison, likely
for the rest of their lives. We also know that the man
who betrayed you is still an unknown. His body has
not been found. You do not know if he's alive or dead.
This list of mistakes is long and unforgivable. And so
we have decided your punishment."

Adam took a deep breath, waiting…staring straight
into his father's gaze.

"You are both banned forever from Japan. If you
come back here again, I will kill you myself."

Yuki moaned. He was shaking to the point of being
unable to stand.

As for Adam, the vow was a gut punch he hadn't
seen coming, but his father was not finished.

"But I am not a heartless man. Adam, you also ran
out on your men and left a job unfinished, so you will
return to the States and make sure the man who betrayed you is dead. If he is not, you'll do whatever
it takes to draw him out—if that means finding and
threatening his family, so be it. But if you don't, I will
come to Houston and I will kill you myself. Now get out
and take your brother with you. I no longer have sons."

Then every man at the table, including his father,
stood up and turned their backs on him.

Adam walked out of the room, too stunned to let
emotions color his reactions, while Yuki stumbled along
behind him. Their mother was standing in the hallway,

sobbing. When Yuki would have run to her, she dropped the suitcase she was holding and ran away.

Yuki picked up the suitcase and followed his brother. He put the bag in the back seat, then got into the passenger seat and put his hands over his face.

As for Adam, reality finally hit as he was driving away. He would never see his father or mother again, or the snow-capped mountains of his mother country. Would his longtime friends even know what happened to him? Would they forget he'd ever existed? What had he done? What the hell had he done? He'd talked Yuki into doing this, and now neither of them would ever be able to return home again. Right now he could honestly say it had not been worth it. Getting back into the United States without being arrested would be almost impossible after the mess of the bust, but they'd given him no choice.

By the time he got back into the city, he'd gone from sorrow to regret, from rage to determination. And since he would never set foot in Japan again, he and his brother went straight to their bank and had everything transferred to respective numbered accounts in Switzerland.

Finally, Yuki began to talk as Adam drove back to his Tokyo residence.

"What are we going to do?" Yuki asked.

Adam glanced at his younger brother, then shook his head. Where Adam was slender and handsome, his brother was stocky and his features coarser, less refined. Yuki looked like their mother's family. Adam looked like their father. And the intelligence level was the same. One a follower. One a leader.

"We are going to avenge the family name to stay

alive, and then we…you and me…are going to become men to be reckoned with. We will take down those old men, one dynasty at a time. The first to go will be our father. What's his will be ours."

Yuki's eyes widened in utter fear at the thought of taking out the heads of the cartel, but he had nothing different to offer, and so he rode in silence, wondering how long he would survive in the harshness of the underworld.

When they reached Adam's home, he dismissed his brother with a wave of the hand.

"Occupy yourself for a while," Adam said, and began packing important papers and clothes before he got on the phone and chartered a jet with a flight plan to Mexico. Afterward, he called all of the household staff together, told them that he was closing up the house and wouldn't be back. He gave each of them what amounted to six months of their respective salaries and thanked them for their service.

Their shock was evident, but manners were everything, and so they bowed, thanking him for his consideration. He should have returned the bow. It was tradition, but he'd been exiled, and his growing rage superseded cultural niceties.

Within the hour, a limousine arrived. The driver loaded up the brothers' luggage, then seated them before heading to the airport. Yuki was crying without sound. It both hurt and aggravated Adam. His brother was behaving like a child, but there was nothing he could say that would make it better.

As for Adam, he couldn't help but look at the city through which they were passing to remind himself to be grateful he was still breathing.

Six

Once they arrived on the tarmac, Adam and Yuki were welcomed onboard the chartered jet by a male flight attendant. His Slavic features were offset by the whitest blond hair Adam had ever seen.

"Good afternoon, sirs. I am Roland. Welcome to Indigo Charters. If you will both follow me, I'll show you to your seats."

Adam glanced out one of the windows as they moved toward the center of the plane and saw men loading their luggage onto the plane. He nodded in satisfaction.

"May I take your suit coats?" Roland asked.

Yuki took his off and handed it over, while Adam turned his back and held out his arms, waiting for the attendant to remove it.

Roland hung them up, then showed the men to their seats.

"Would either of you care for a drink before take-off?"

Normally, Adam's only drink of choice was sake, but after being rejected by Japan, he chose an American drink.

"Bourbon."

"Yes, sir," Roland said, then turned to Yuki. "And what about you, sir?"

"Sake," Yuki said, and cleared his throat.

The brothers were buckling up as Roland returned with their drinks and a small plate of appetizers. "Lunch will be served after we have reached our altitude."

Adam took the whiskey and downed it in one gulp. "Once more," he said, as he set the shot glass back down on the tray.

Roland hastened to fill the order because the pilot was readying for takeoff.

Adam took the second drink and then held it between his palms as the pilot began to taxi toward the runway, while Yuki was pouring himself a second drink from the decanter of sake. Within a few minutes they were given the go-ahead for takeoff. As the jet began to move faster and faster, Adam leaned his head against the headrest and, for the first time, met his brother's gaze and allowed himself to feel the pain. There was a moment of shared sorrow before he swallowed past the knot in his throat and looked away.

At this moment, he hated his father almost as much as he hated Judd Wayne.

Shelly knew by noon Sunday that she was going back to work. The job would be her saving grace. She didn't have any idea how widows' benefits worked in the Bureau and right now didn't trust them to take any better care of her than they had Jack. She'd just received that step raise at work, which would make some difference in her take-home pay, and thanks to Jack's foresight, the insurance policy they had on their home mortgage would pay off the house. She would figure out the rest of it as she went.

Having made that decision, she sat down at the kitchen table with a bowl of soup and the box of crackers. The soup was canned. The crackers were stale. It didn't matter. She couldn't taste it and ate only for sustenance.

Her phone rang again in the middle of her meal.

"Hello."

"Hello, Mrs. McCann. This is Reverend Wilson, and I was wondering if I might stop by this afternoon to pay my respects."

"No, you may not," Shelly said. "I don't know you, sir. I am not having a failure in my faith…only in the FBI. I am not discussing my life or my future with you. I do not need to be prayed over. I've spent the last four months alone waiting for my husband to finish this undercover job. It was going to be his last. Did you know that?"

"No, ma'am, I did not, but—"

"There are no buts. I made myself clear enough already. Please stop bothering me. Regardless of your title, you are a stranger. Do not call me again. Understood?"

She heard a sigh, then the man cleared his throat.

"Yes, ma'am, I understand. My sympathies to—"

Shelly hung up in his ear. "Still wanted to have the last word," she muttered. "Probably runs over time with his sermons, as well."

She looked down at the cooling soup but couldn't manage another mouthful. She got up and poured it down the garbage disposal, tossed the stale crackers into the trash and refilled her sweet tea, then took it outside to the back patio.

The pool in the backyard sparkled in the sunlight. She looked away as she chose a seat in the shade, then set her glass of tea on the table, leaned back in the chaise lounge chair and glanced down at the sapphire ring she was wearing today.

The ache in her chest was a part of her now. She had accepted the grief as she might have accepted a broken leg. It had happened, now she had to figure out how to live with it until time wore away the sharp edges.

The privacy fence between her and her neighbors was eight feet tall, but she still heard voices and laughter, as well as the cry of a child who hadn't gotten her way.

Someone else was playing music from her favorite station. She and Jack often made love to that music. Then she put a hand over her heart as new tears began to roll.

"Okay, God, I did not see this coming, and I'm not sure how I'm going to survive it without losing my mind. I need help, so anything positive that You can send my way will be appreciated."

Jack was slowly gaining strength, drinking Paul's beef broth without argument, understanding the need to rebuild the iron in his body. Every time he felt fatigue, which was often, he went right back to bed and slept his way through it. By the time Monday morning rolled around, he was extremely sore, but slowly gaining strength.

He ate what Paul put in front of him, thought of Shelly with every waking moment and dreamed of Adam Ito as he slept. This wasn't over. It would never be over until Ito was either behind bars or dead.

* * *

Charlie was at work Monday when Fred came up to his desk with a manila envelope.

"This was dropped off for you," he said.

"Thanks," Charlie said. "Just lay it on the desk. I need to finish my thought on this report."

"Will do," Fred said, and headed back to his desk.

A couple of paragraphs later, Charlie ended the report and had just hit Save when he got a call from Alicia.

"Hey, babe, what's up?" Charlie asked.

"Honey…you need to come home. My water broke. It's time to go to the hospital."

Charlie was between panic and joy.

"Now? Oh my God. It'll take me thirty minutes to get there and another twenty to get you to the hospital. Are you going to be okay for that long?"

"I don't know!" Alicia said. "Mom and Dad are on their way here to bring us some produce from their garden. They should be here anytime."

"Then have them take you to the hospital and I'll meet you there, okay?"

"Yes, okay. I'm so excited, but I'm scared, too."

"I know, baby, but it's going to be alright. I will be there waiting when you get there. I won't let you down."

"I know. Oh—Mom and Dad just pulled up into the driveway."

"Great!" Charlie said. "I'll see you soon. I love you so much. We're finally going to meet our little guy."

Alicia laughed nervously. "Gotta go let them in the house. See you soon," she said.

"Tell your dad I said to drive carefully. He's carrying precious cargo."

"I will. I love you," Alicia said.

Charlie's heart was pounding as he hung up, but he was smiling. He called the deputy director, told him what was happening and where he was going, and gave Fred a thumbs-up as he left the office.

"It's go time," he said. "Alicia is on the way to the hospital."

"Fantastic," Fred said. "Drive safe."

Charlie laughed. "That's the same message I sent to my father-in-law."

It rained in the night.

Shelly woke to the sound of it blowing against the bedroom windows and got up to watch the storm. It was coming down hard enough that the streetlights were merely smudges of yellow on a charcoal canvas. She hoped Jack wasn't working out in this weather—and then she remembered. Wherever he was, the weather wasn't going to affect him.

She crawled back into bed, but the ache in her chest was too big to contain. She rolled over onto her side and cried herself to sleep. The next time she woke up, the alarm was going off and her cell phone was ringing. When she saw it was her office calling, she quickly answered.

"Hello?"

"Shelly, it's Willard Bates. I'm so sorry to be calling you this early, but we're calling all of the employees to catch them before coming in to work today."

Shelly sat up. "What's wrong?"

"Not exactly sure how it happened, but the sprinkler system went off in the office last night and everything is saturated."

"Oh no! Are the computers ruined, too?"

"We don't yet know the extent of damage," he said. "But we have the assurance of knowing our backups are all safely stored in the home office's security system."

"Oh, that's right! Thank goodness."

"At any rate, just consider the first part of this week as days off with pay. I'll be sending out group texts to keep everyone updated as it goes, and you'll receive notice when it's safe to come back to work the same way."

"Alright. Thank you for letting me know before I got out into the middle of traffic. I'm so sorry this happened."

"Of course, and so are we. I'll be in touch."

The call ended.

Shelly put down the phone and then got up to go to the bathroom. Normally, having extra days off with pay would be welcome, but not this time. She didn't know what to do with herself or how to spend this day. Then she heard her phone signal a text and glanced at it. It was from Charlie. She pulled up the text and then sighed.

We have our boy. Eight pounds, two ounces and twenty one inches long. We named him Charles Jonathon and will call him Johnny. Mother and baby are doing fine.

She sent a simple Congratulations, then went to get dressed. That's how the universe works, she thought. One life ends as another begins. While some people are so deep into grief they can't function, others are celebrating wonderful milestones. It felt like a slap in the face to know how happy they were, while she was dying inside. Her voice was shaking, her words bitter on her tongue.

"Yes, Lord, thank You for the reminder that the world does not revolve around me."

* * *

Jack had slept through the rain, but the evidence of it was still there when he woke to sunshine Monday morning. Water was dripping from everything into glistening puddles.

When he got to the kitchen, he found a note from Paul telling him to help himself to cereal and coffee, and that he was going to the supermarket and wouldn't be long.

Jack ate a bowl of cereal standing up at the sink, then took his coffee outside. The day was already steamy, but the sun felt good on his face. He was grateful to be alive.

He took a sip of his coffee and made a face. It was too strong and too bitter for his taste, which made him think of the coffee Shelly made. It was always good. He longed to hear the sound of her voice. He wanted to call her and let her know he wasn't dead. But good sense told him now was not the time and to let it go.

Instead, he focused on a flock of monk parakeets taking flight from the queen palms around the pool at the house next door. From a distance, their flashy green feathers made them look a bit like green leaves caught within a gust of wind. When he looked up and saw the silhouettes of seagulls as they flew against the bright blue sky, he wondered how anyone could doubt the presence of a higher being. None of this was accidental evolution…it was God-sent.

And after what had gone down during this last bust, there wasn't enough money in the FBI budget that could keep him in undercover work. He wanted out. And he would have questions when he finally got to come in from the job, not the least of which had to do with the suspicious coincidence of having one of his personal snitches show up on Dumas's crew.

Jack closed his eyes, reliving the moment when he recognized Ritter. But as he did, he suddenly realized something he had forgotten in the ensuing chaos.

When Jack first saw Ritter standing beside Dumas, he was looking straight at him, but not in surprise.

"As if he knew I would be there," Jack muttered.

It was the first time he'd thought about someone on the outside possibly giving away his presence on Adam Ito's team, but to his knowledge, no one outside of the Bureau had known. He filed the thought away for another day and finished his coffee. He was dozing out in the sunshine when he heard a car coming up the drive. He went back inside the house to make sure it was Paul, and it was. Jack unlocked the front door and started to go out to help.

Paul had both arms full and was heading to the house when he saw Dude come out.

"No, no! Stay inside. I've got this," he said.

Jack didn't argue, but he did hold the door open, and then again when Paul went back to bring in the rest of the groceries.

"Lock us in," Paul said, as he walked in with the last load.

Jack did as he was asked, then followed Paul to the kitchen.

"Been up long?" Paul asked, as Jack sat down.

Jack nodded. "Awhile."

Paul put a package of cookies on the table.

"Oreos, Dude. Knock yourself out."

Jack grinned. Paul was still a kid about some things, and Oreo cookies were at the top of the list.

"I'm good for now," Jack said.

Paul shook his head. "Man, you don't know what you're missing," he said, then opened the package and popped one in his mouth as he finished putting up the purchases.

Jack started to refill his coffee, then winced at the weight of the full carafe.

Paul heard him grunt and turned to look at what was happening, then frowned. "Are you hurting?"

Jack nodded. "Some."

"Let me see," Paul said, then pulled up the back of Jack's shirt and lifted a corner of the bandage to take a look at the bullet wound on Jack's shoulder. "Well, hell. Looks as if you have an infection. I guess we shouldn't be surprised. That open wound was in the bay, for God's sake. I'm calling Muncy."

Jack frowned. That explained why he felt the way he did, but this was a delay in his healing he didn't want.

Paul saw the frown. "You need antibiotics, Dude. If Muncy doesn't have anything, you are gonna have to think about going to a doctor."

Jack didn't comment. He knew who he could call, but that would mean the Bureau knowing he was alive, and once they knew that he'd risen from the dead, so to speak, so would Adam Ito. And if Ito knew Jack was alive, it didn't matter how well Jack might hide. Ito wouldn't mess around looking for Jack. He'd go straight for the people Jack loved and make Jack come to him.

Paul was on the phone now, talking to Muncy, and while Jack was getting only one side of the conversation, he guessed Muncy was coming over.

"He's on the way," Paul said, hanging up.

Jack nodded. "Sorry about this."

Paul frowned. "Don't talk stupid, Dude. I'm starting to like you."

Jack reached across the table, got an Oreo out of the open package and toasted Paul with it before putting the whole thing in his mouth.

Paul grinned. "That's what I'm talkin' about."

About twenty minutes later, Muncy Peters arrived. Jack was already back in bed with a growing headache and a fever to match. He heard the men talking as they came down the hall toward his room, and then they were inside.

Muncy stopped beside the bed, then frowned as he touched Jack's forehead and chest.

"He's running a fever, for sure." Then he met Jack's gaze. "Feelin' pretty rough?"

"I wasn't, but as the day progresses, I'd say yes," Jack said.

"Well, let's see what's happening beneath your bandage," Muncy said. "Turn over on your side."

Jack gritted his teeth as he rolled over, then moments later felt Muncy removing the bandage.

"Oh hell no," Muncy muttered.

"That good, is it?" Jack asked.

"It's not unusual, but because you aren't on IV antibiotics, it's gotten a pretty good jump on us. Don't worry, we'll get you fixed up," Muncy said.

"How is it you have all this stuff on hand?" Jack asked.

Muncy snorted softly. "Son, you can buy anything if you know where to look for it. They sell pretty good first aid kits online, too. The kind that hunting and fishing guides might carry with them when they're up in the wilds. Now hang on to somethin', cause this is gonna hurt like a son of a bitch."

Jack barely had time to react before a sharp, stabbing pain shot through his shoulder and all the way up through the top of his head. He groaned and then gave up to the shadows pulling him under.

"He passed out!" Paul said, looking worried.

"Good," Muncy replied. "I don't know what he's been doing, but he's pulled a couple of stitches loose, too." He proceeded to clean up the wound, which started it to bleeding. Before he put another bandage on it, he poured some white powder down into the wound, then gave him another shot of antibiotic.

"What's the powder stuff?" Paul asked.

"Technically, it's sulfanilamide, aluminum sulfate and titanium dioxide, a clotting agent with antibiotics in it. I'm also leaving these capsules. Tell him to take two pills, twice a day. There's a ten-day supply in the bottle. If he's still sick after that, he better get his ass to a hospital."

"Yes, I'll tell him," Paul said. "Why isn't he waking up?"

Muncy frowned. "Because he's weak, and now he's sick, too. His body needs the rest. Just make sure he gets plenty of fluids and as much sleep as he can manage."

Paul nodded. "Yeah, yeah, I sure will, and I'll happily pay you to replace what you used on Dude."

Muncy shook his head. "Naw… I've got just as much invested in him getting well as you do now. It's a matter of pride. I don't like to lose a patient."

When Muncy began looking around for a trash bag, Paul stopped him. "I'll clean all that up," he said.

"Then I'll see myself out. Take good care of the dude and don't hesitate to call if this doesn't work."

Paul gave him a thumbs-up.

For the next twelve hours, Jack was awake only long enough to take medicine or go to the bathroom before he'd fall back into bed, either shaking from a chill or burning up from another fever. Part of the time he didn't know where he was, and when he was out, he was talking in his sleep.

Paul sat in a chair pulled up beside the bed. He knew now that Dude loved a girl named Shelly, and he had pretty much figured out that Dude was a Fed. It was the last part that worried him most. If Dude was a Fed, then there was only one reason why he didn't want anyone to know he was alive. Someone had ratted him out while he was undercover, and he didn't know who he could trust.

Seven

Shelly got a text on Thursday to come to work the next day. It was a relief. She'd spent most of the week so depressed that it had been all she could do to get out of bed to bathe and eat.

Now she was being forced back into the land of the living. She made herself stay up all day so that she'd sleep that night, and when the alarm went off Friday morning at the usual time, she didn't mind.

She had decided as she was driving into work that keeping Jack's death a secret was going to be too difficult for her to pull off. She needed to be able to concentrate to do her job, and that would be nearly impossible if she started out trying to live a lie. So as soon as she got to work, she went to Mitzi's cubicle.

Mitzi looked up and smiled.

"Hi! This was a bad way to have a few days off, right?"

Shelly leaned over the short wall and whispered, "I need you to come with me to Willard's office."

Mitzi was startled and it showed. "What's wrong?"

Shelly just shook her head and kept walking to their boss's office and knocked, with Mitzi right beside her.

"Come in," he said.

Shelly started talking as she was walking inside. "Sorry for barging in like this, but I need to talk to you and Mitzi privately, and I don't want to have to say this but once."

"Of course. Please both of you have a seat. Do you want a cup of coffee?"

Shelly shook her head. "No, thank you."

"I'm good," Mitzi said, and sat down in a chair beside Shelly.

Willard put his elbows on his desk and leaned forward.

"So, what's going on?"

Shelly's hands were curled into fists, and it was going to take everything she had to get this said.

"Something happened last weekend and I need for the both of you to know."

Mitzi started to worry, and Willard was no longer smiling.

Shelly's voice shook with every word. "My husband is dead. He was shot in the line of duty, and that's all I can really say about it."

The pain of saying that aloud was worse than she'd imagined, and there was no way for her to stop the tears that began rolling down her face.

"Oh my God, Shelly! I'm so sorry," Mitzi said.

Willard gasped. "I can't believe it. You never mention him, so...I didn't even know he was a cop."

"He was an FBI agent," Shelly whispered.

Willard's eyes widened. "FBI... Oh, wait! Oh my God, was he part of that bust they made on the stolen arms shipment?"

Shelly pulled a tissue from her purse.

"I really can't talk about any of that. I want to reassure you that coming to work is good for me. It helps me refocus on something besides losing him. I would so appreciate it if you did not spread this around. Being the wife of a federal agent has always been tricky. The fewer people who know the details of my life, the better off I'll be."

"Then this stays in here with us," Mitzi said. "If you choose to tell anyone else, that will be your call. Can I do anything for you? Take up some of your accounts until—"

Shelly stopped her. "No, and please ignore me if you happen to see tears. They come and go without reason."

Willard's voice was shaking. "I disagree. You have all the reason in the world to weep. Have you already had his service?"

"Not having one," Shelly said, wiping her eyes.

"Really?" Mitzi said.

Shelly sighed. "It's not what you think. They just never found his body."

Willard stood abruptly. "That big search the FBI had going on in Galveston Bay over the weekend...they were searching for him, weren't they?"

Shelly's stomach rolled. She couldn't think about that. "I'd like to get back to work now. Is there anything we need to know about water damage?"

Willard sensed her need to focus on work, and so he

began to explain what had happened and what they'd need to do to catch up.

"Yes, sir," Shelly said when he'd finished. She was trying to be all business, but her hands were shaking.

Willard felt so sorry for her that he could hardly think.

"My deepest sympathies," he said softly.

"Thank you," Shelly said. "I'd better get to work."

"I'm right behind you," Mitzi said.

They stopped at Shelly's cubicle. Mitzi turned around and hugged her.

"I just can't believe this has happened," she whispered.

"Neither can I," Shelly said, "but I need you to promise me something."

"Anything," Mitzi said.

"Don't talk about this. Not to anyone. His work was dangerous, and I don't know how it might affect me if everyone knows my business, understand?"

Mitzi nodded. "Completely. I won't even talk about it with my husband. But know if you need to talk, I'm here."

"I appreciate that. I think we need to get busy. We have quite a backlog to get through."

"Yell if you need anything," Mitzi said, and walked back to her cubicle. But just thinking about losing her husband and not being able to ever find his body was like something out of a horror movie. She sat down and went back to work before she burst into tears.

Shelly turned on her computer and began setting her workstation back up—getting everything she normally used out of the drawers and back up on her desk. Her heart ached and she was blinking away tears when she pulled up her first account. It was a struggle to focus, but after a while, routine kicked in and she lost herself in the job and the numbers.

Adam and his brother landed in Guadalajara, Mexico, without incident. He registered at one of the smaller hotels, under his own name, but that wouldn't be for long. Adam was still growing the mustache he had begun when he was in Mexico the first time, and he went from combing his hair straight back to parting it on one side. He was wearing glasses he didn't need, and he had also started smoking, two things Adam Ito would have not done.

Yuki was beginning to realize the life they would be living and was regaining some of his attitude. Even though he hadn't been the fireball Adam had always been, he'd had his own brand of power.

Money went a long way in Mexico, and anything could be had here for the proper price. Even new identities, which came with a stolen car from across the border. After a new paint job and a switched license plate, the gray Jeep Cherokee now belonged to Adam, aka Lee Tanaka, who would be traveling with his friend Soshi Yamada. In two days, Adam would be in Texas again with his brother at his side.

Charlie Morris went in to work on Friday with a box of cigars and a picture of his son taped to the lid. He passed them out to everyone in the office, gathering congratulations like he used to get merit badges in Boy Scouts. He was proud of their new family and bragging about Alicia's ten-hour delivery to anyone who would stand still long enough to listen. But when the clamor died down, he was all too aware that his best friend wasn't here to share his joy.

He took a cigar and headed outside, his steps much slower than when he came in. As soon as he reached one of their break areas, he headed for a bench in the shade. His intent was obvious as he methodically unwrapped the cigar, but then his cell phone rang. He glanced at caller ID, frowned and then let it go to voice mail. He dealt with personal business at home, and the business of being a federal agent when he was on the job. He snipped off the tips of the cigar before reaching for his lighter. As he leaned back, he glanced up through the limbs and leaves to the bits and pieces of blue sky.

"For you, buddy. This wasn't supposed to happen," he said softly, then put the cigar in his mouth and lit up.

It took a couple of draws before the hand-rolled cigar caught fire, and then, in memory of Jack McCann, he blew a smoke ring.

"It's not exactly a halo, but it's the best I can do," Charlie said, and then sat back with tears in his eyes, thinking of all the shit that had gone wrong, and smoked the cigar down to a stub.

The weekend was rough, but by the following Tuesday, Jack's infection was gone and his strength was better than it had been since he'd been shot. He still had some antibiotics to finish off, and after that, there was nothing more these men could do for him. He was itching to get back on the streets and find out what he could about Ito, and to check on Shelly without her knowing it.

The car he'd been driving either was still on the dock or had been towed off by the FBI, so he had to adjust his plans for transportation. The first thing to do was get to his apartment, get his motorcycle and gear out of the storage unit that came with it, and pack up the clothes he had there. No one on Ito's crew or the Bureau had known where he lived, not even Charlie. His rent was still paid up to the end of the month, so his things should still be there. He also needed to get into his home when Shelly was at work.

Whether he was a hundred percent or not, it was time to get down to business.

Paul was taking burgers off the grill for their supper, but he'd had an eye on Dude all afternoon. Something was changing. He was feeling better, which probably meant he was getting antsy.

"Okay, they're done. Let's get back inside before these dang flies carry us off," Paul said.

Jack opened the door for his host and followed him in.

"Why don't you get whatever you want to drink," Paul suggested. "I'm still working on my Coors."

"Since I'm still taking meds, I'll settle for sweet tea," Jack said, and poured some in a glass of ice and carried it to the table.

They put their own burgers together, adding condiments and extras to suit themselves. Paul dropped a handful of potato chips onto his plate and then shoved the bag in Jack's direction and took a big bite.

"Damn, this is good, if I do say so myself," he said.

Jack grinned.

Paul chewed and swallowed, and was still eyeing Dude as he reached for his beer.

"You're itching to leave, aren't you?" Paul asked.

Jack looked up, a little surprised he'd been that obvious.

"I have a big mess to clean up, and it's not going to happen until I can get back on the streets."

Paul took another bite, nodding as he chewed. "I get that. All you gotta do is tell me when you're ready to go. I'll take you wherever you want and drop you off, and we'll forget we ever met."

Jack leaned back in his chair, amazed by Paul's understanding of his situation.

"How do you feel about tonight?" Jack asked, and then took a big bite of his burger.

Paul was shocked.

"In the dark?"

Jack nodded. "In this life, I live in shadows. I can get around easier in the dark without being noticed."

"Then eat up, Dude," Paul said. "Looks like you've got a big night ahead of you."

"Listen, you guys saved my life. I don't forget things like that. When this is all over, there's someone I want you to meet."

Paul grinned. "That's a meeting I don't want to miss," he said.

The meal was over, the kitchen cleaned up, and except for Muncy's Kick Some Ass shirt, Jack was wearing his own clothes again.

He felt for his keys and wallet. The keys had been clipped to a belt loop on his jeans, which was why he didn't lose them in the bay, and the money he'd had in his wallet had dried without too much damage. His phone was somewhere at the bottom of Galveston Bay. But he had close to three hundred dollars on him.

Enough to gas up his motorcycle and get around the city, and the rest of what he needed was in the safe at home.

"Are you ready?" Paul asked.

Jack looked up, eyeing the slight paunch and the gray in Paul's receding hairline, but saw only the hero who'd had his back.

"I'm ready," Jack said. "We need to chart a course toward Pasadena. I'll direct you from there."

Paul nodded. "Then let's get on the road."

"At least this will be the last trip you have to make for me, and you'll have your life and your house back," Jack said.

Paul didn't comment as he turned on the porch light before they walked out into the night.

Streetlights lit up the neighborhood. Even as they were walking to the car, they could hear people outside up and down the block. Some were grilling, because they could smell the smoke, and from the reverberating sound of the diving board and the shrieks of laughter at the splashes, it was apparent Paul's next-door neighbors were outside in their pool. Such wonderfully ordinary lives. Jack wanted that back.

They were mostly silent all the way across Houston, and when Paul finally took the exit off the 610 Loop that would take them into Pasadena, Jack was sitting on the edge of his seat, watchful for the old neighborhood.

Less than two blocks from Jack's final destination, he told Paul to pull over at the service station on the next corner.

Paul pulled up at the pumps and killed the engine.

"I might as well fill up while I'm here," he said, and was reaching for the door handle when Jack stopped him and then held out his hand.

Paul grasped it, feeling the strength in Dude's grip. "Thank you," Jack said. "You are a righteous man, and we will see each other again."

They shared one quick handshake. Jack got out of one door and Paul got out of the other. Paul stood beneath the fluorescent lights watching Dude slip into the shadows of the alley between two buildings and then he was gone.

Paul turned back to the pumps, scanned his credit card and filled the tank. By the time he was back on the freeway and heading home, Jack was already at the apartment complex, climbing the three flights of stairs.

It felt weird, but at the same time normal, to be walking back into this apartment. It had been a little haven of sanity from the double life he'd been living. Now he wasn't so sure it was safe anymore.

Before, it was where he could call Shelly and talk without fear of being overheard—where it felt safe enough to close his eyes. But he'd been here over four months and had no way of knowing if anyone he knew had accidentally seen him going in or out, or if the Bureau had ever tailed him here. Since his body had not been recovered, he had no way of knowing if the place was staked out with people waiting to see if he came back, and he wasn't going to be here long enough to find out.

He hurried into the bedroom and began packing his clothing into a duffel bag, then his toiletries. He was moving around from room to room when he heard a fight break out in the apartment next door. At least one thing hadn't changed. That couple needed to part ways before one of them killed the other.

After a final check of all the rooms to make sure

he had everything, he slipped out of the apartment. He paused in the breezeway to make sure there was no one around, then hurried downstairs, crossed the parking area to the storage sheds that came with each apartment and opened shed 355. It had been a couple of weeks since he'd been on his motorcycle, but he kept it fueled and ready to ride, and now he was glad he had it.

He retrieved the key from where he'd hidden it, fastened the duffel bag behind the seat and rolled it out. The security lights reflected against the black metal on the Indian Springfield. He'd had this one a little over two years now and was glad he'd had the foresight to incorporate this into Judd Wayne's world.

He rolled his shoulder, testing the mobility. It was sore, but it wouldn't kill him. He went back to get his helmet, relocked the storage shed and climbed on. The bike fired upon demand. The deep rumble only hinted at the engine's power, but it was music to Jack's ears. He accelerated, wasting no time getting out of the complex. All he needed now was a motel for the night and time to figure out what his next move would be.

Shelly hadn't been at work more than an hour when Willard stopped by her cubicle to deliver a message.

"Excuse me, Shelly. Hate to interrupt such intent labor."

She paused, then swiveled her chair to face him.

"No problem. What's up?"

"We just got a call from the manager at Graze. That's your account, right?"

"Yes, sir. The newest one. We've had it about six months. Is anything wrong?"

"Yes, I'm afraid so. The owner, Colin Wright, was

found dead in the office of Graze this morning. It's assumed he never went home, because he'd been dead at least eight hours."

Shelly was in shock. "Oh my God… He was so excited to finally own his own restaurant. What happened? Do they know?"

"They didn't say, but we've been ordered to give them a final accounting. His wife is moving home to Michigan."

"Yes, sir, I'll get right on it," Shelly said, but her eyes were already welling. Desperate for a reason to escape, she reached for her coffee cup. "Excuse me. I need a refill," she said, and all but ran toward the break room.

Willard saw the tears at the same moment he realized how the news would strike her. He walked away, shaking his head at his own stupidity. It was her account, so she had to know, but he could have delivered that news with a little more finesse.

Shelly hit the break room and sank down onto the sofa, set her cup onto the coffee table and buried her face in her hands. It was the mention of the grieving wife that had been the trigger this time, but these days she was primed to lose it on a daily basis.

She cried until she heard footsteps, then jumped up and ran into the bathroom and shut the door.

"Shelly, it's me. Are you okay?"

Shelly sighed. Mitzi didn't miss a thing.

"I'll be out in a few. I'm alright, but thanks for checking."

"Let me know if you need anything," Mitzi said.

"Yes, I will. Don't worry, Mitzi. This has to happen. I have to let these tears out or they'll drown me. Just let me cry. I'll be okay."

She waited until she heard Mitzi leave, then grabbed a handful of tissues and began cleaning up the mess she'd made of her makeup.

Talking to Mitzi had been the distraction she needed to regain control of her emotions. By the time she came out of the break room, she was carrying a fresh cup of coffee and a piece of chocolate. She slipped into her cubicle, popped the candy in her mouth and set the coffee safely out of reach of her keyboard. She finished up what she'd been working on before Willard's arrival, then began working on the Graze account. After a while, the numbers pulled her in, searching what needed to balance, and getting info ready for final payroll.

It was going to be a long day.

Jack rolled into their neighborhood just after 9:00 a.m., took a quick turn down the alley behind their house and killed the engine.

With privacy fences in the backyards of all these houses, he felt somewhat secure. He knew Shelly would already be at work, and he had stashed his duffel bag in a numbered locker at the bus station until he could find another place to live.

He slipped around to the side gate and then darted into the yard, unlocked the back door and ran to disarm the security panel before it could alert.

The scent of lemon from her shampoo was still in the air as he ran through the living room to the office. He went straight to the wall safe hidden behind the bookshelves.

He already had a different identity stashed here that he could use, but it had come from the Bureau. If he assumed that identity, the social security number would immediately activate, notifying the powers that be he was still alive. Gut instinct told him that would be a mistake. He needed more information about Ito and he had to find out who put Ritter into the bust. It had to be someone from the Bureau who knew Jack had once used him as a snitch, and the only reason for that to happen would be to create a diversion that would give Adam Ito time to escape.

He set the what-ifs aside and went straight to the shelves, removed some of the books to reveal the safe in the wall behind them, then entered the code into the keypad. The lock clicked and the safe door swung open.

Jack pulled out a small bag first and dumped the contents out onto a desk to make sure everything he needed was still there. A different birth certificate, a driver's license for a man named Shane Franklin, passport, social security numbers, an address book and everything else he might need to assume an identity the Bureau knew nothing about.

He put it all back in the bag and then opened the bottom drawer on the desk, rummaging around until he found a larger bag and took it back to the safe. He removed his official FBI badge, and an iPhone registered to Shane Franklin, which would be his new identity. The phone was loaded with Jack's contacts and all the info he'd used in normal life, and at the bottom of the safe, nearly twenty thousand dollars in untraceable bills. He put it all into the larger bag along with a phone charger.

When he left Paul's house, it had not occurred to him to see if they'd kept his shoulder holster, but he had another one on the top shelf of the closet here, so he stuck the loaded Glock 17 in the back of his jeans, bagged two more loaded clips and a box of ammo. The last thing at the bottom of the safe was a license tag for the Indian that matched this new identity.

After he'd taken everything out, it dawned on him that Shelly might need to get into the safe at any time, thinking that money was her cushion until widow's benefits kicked in. He didn't want to scare her, leaving her to believe she'd been robbed, and now he was second-guessing his reasons for not telling her.

He shut and reset the safe and then looked around for his laptop and finally saw it on the top of the bookshelves. He grabbed it and the charger cords and headed for their bedroom.

It wasn't until he walked in and saw the neatly made bed that he was overwhelmed with memories of the last time he'd been here. They'd made love in desperation and without caution. He ached for what she was going through, and being back in their home was swiftly changing what he'd thought of keeping her in the dark. He needed to find a better way to keep her safe without breaking her heart.

A car honked outside, which made him jump. He ran to the window to look out, then saw it was the Realtor and more prospective buyers at the empty house next door. But it reminded him to quit daydreaming and do what he'd come here to do. He went inside the walk-in closet to get his gym bag and the shoulder holster, and dumped the laptop and the bag inside of the gym bag, then grabbed an extra leather jacket that he used when he rode the Indian, and headed out of the bedroom on the run.

He got all the way back to the kitchen when conscience struck him again. Did he leave her to believe she'd been robbed and scare the hell out of her to add to her grief?

"Dammit...no," he muttered.

He thought for just a moment how to let her know without leaving his handwriting on anything, then set the bag on the floor and began opening cabinets until he found the spice shelf, and searched until he found what he wanted.

His stomach was in knots for what he was about to do, but he couldn't do this to her anymore. Shelly knew the ropes. He'd talked to her too many times about the dangers of saying the wrong thing or saying too much to the wrong people. Even if he revealed he was alive, he was satisfied she wouldn't talk.

He got a notepad, a pen and the box of spice and started drawing. When he had finished, he left the note and the spice container on the kitchen table, knowing she'd see it as soon as she got home.

He grabbed his bag, gave the kitchen one last look and then reset the alarm on his way out. He stopped in the garden shed to get a screwdriver and took it to the alley to switch out the license tags. When he had finished, he returned the screwdriver and the other tag to the shed.

Within minutes, he was riding out of the alley and back onto the streets. His next objective was to make his appearance match the picture on his new ID, and he knew where to go to make that happen.

Makeover Magic was a hair salon in a strip mall about a mile from their house. He and Shelly had laughed more than once at the clients coming and going there, most of whom sported hair the color of Easter egg dyes. He wasn't going for purple, but he needed that kind of transformation.

He wheeled the Indian in and out of traffic until he reached the mall, then drove into the parking lot and rolled up to the curb at the salon. He was carrying his helmet as he walked toward the entrance when he caught a glimpse of himself in the window. He would be leaving that guy inside.

A buzzer sounded as he entered, and when the four stylists heard the thump of men's boots up front, they all turned to look and were immediately sorry they had customers in their chairs.

Rhonda Brewer was at the front behind the counter. She'd had clients who were skinheads, bikers, Goths and a multitude of everything in between, but she couldn't remember the last time a man like this had walked into her shop. Her heart skipped a beat as he strode up to the front desk.

"Good morning. How can I help you?" she asked.

Jack read people easily and could tell this woman was living a rough life with no excuses.

"I need a haircut."

"Trim or—"

"No, ma'am. Off," Jack said.

Rhonda grinned. "Are we shaving it?"

"Not quite. More like this," he said, and pulled out his new ID. "I haven't cut my hair in nearly two years and it's bugging the hell out of me. I want me back." He showed her the driver's license picture.

Rhonda noted his name. "Okay, Shane, are you ready to get this party started?"

"Yes, ma'am," he said.

She took him back to her chair and caped him up,

then took him to the shampoo station. She washed his hair longer than she had to, just because she loved the feel of all that thick black hair between her fingers. Finally, she took him back to her chair and combed out the tangles before she started to work.

Jack watched his hair falling to the floor, waiting for the man his enemies knew as Judd Wayne to disappear and Shane Franklin to emerge. It didn't take long for him to realize that Rhonda's shop was aptly named. She was making magic happen. Thirty minutes passed. The length was long gone and she was still shaping and clipping, blending the three-inch length into the beard he was growing.

"Is that short enough?" she asked.

Jack ran his fingers through the spiky strands. "Perfect," he said.

"Great," Rhonda said, and began working product into the short, stubby strands. Then she turned him around to face the mirror.

Even Jack was impressed at the transformation.

"What do you think?" she asked.

Jack grinned at his own reflection. "Hello, Shane. Where the hell have you been?"

Rhonda giggled. "So we're good here?"

"Yes, ma'am. That we are," Jack said.

Rhonda removed the cape and whisked away any lingering hair from his neck, then he followed her back to the counter.

"That'll be thirty dollars," Rhonda said.

Jack gave her forty. "Much appreciated," he said.

"Y'all come back anytime," Rhonda called, as he headed out the door.

He gave her a thumbs-up but kept moving.

Rhonda was still watching as he climbed onto that motorcycle and fired it up. The first rumble of the engine made her girlie parts ache, and when it went from rumble to roar, she squeezed her legs together and moaned.

"Lord have mercy, that is one fine man," she said, and went to get herself something cold to drink.

Unaware he was still the focus of Rhonda's attention, Jack rode away, very much relieved. For the first time in days, he was anonymous again.

All he lacked now was a place to call home.

Eight

Shelly's day at work finally dragged to a halt at 5:00 p.m. She logged out of the computers at her workstation and left the building, hurrying to her car before anyone else was out of the building. She didn't want to talk. She didn't want to listen to music. She just wanted to go home.

About halfway there, traffic began to slow. She groaned.

"Dang it. Not this evening," she said, guessing it was because of a wreck. They happened daily on the Loop and in varying numbers. Depending on the time of day, and despite the five lanes of traffic, it always snarled.

Sure enough, the traffic finally came to a dead stop, which meant the wreck had just happened somewhere farther up, and they were waiting either for rescue or for wreckers to clear bodies and cars before releasing the traffic.

Less than a hundred yards ahead, she saw an exit ramp, and because she was on the outside lane, she had the freedom to take it. It would add a good half hour to her drive to go this way, but she might sit longer than that on the freeway, so she pulled out of line and drove down the shoulder to the exit ramp, grateful she was moving again.

She was so tired and beat down by the day and the extended drive that she began crying a few miles from home. By the time she pulled into the drive and hit the remote to open the garage door, she was nearly blind with tears. She made it inside the garage and then gathered up her things, disarming the security alarm as she went inside.

The house looked the same, but as Shelly went down the hall to her bedroom, the hair crawled on the back of her neck. Something felt off.

She went into her bedroom and immediately saw the closet door open and the light inside it still on. That was unlike her to do that, but it had happened before. She didn't think much about it as she changed out of her work clothes into shorts and a T-shirt, then walked barefoot into the living room, picked up the mail from the floor in front of the front door and moved into the kitchen.

She started to toss the mail onto the table as always, when she saw a notepad, a pen and a box of spice from her spice rack. She turned in sudden fear to see if she was alone, and she was, but it was obvious someone had been in her house.

She moved closer to the table, saw the notepad and what was on it, then saw the box of mustard seed and gasped.

The message on the notepad was impossible to mistake. There were no words. Just a drawing of a woman's lips that had been padlocked shut. She grabbed the mustard seed and clutched it to her heart, trying to remember the verse in the Bible—something about having the faith of a mustard seed, and moving mountains.

"Oh my God, oh my God, Jack! You're alive!"

Then she thought of the safe. That would be the last bit of proof she needed. She ran down the hall and into the office and could already tell someone had been in here. The books were not in order as she moved them aside to get to the safe, and her suspicion was confirmed when she found it empty.

She was crying again, but this time for joy, and shaking so hard she could barely function. She started looking around to see what else he'd come for, but it took her a few minutes to realize his laptop was missing, too.

This was like something out of a dream. She was overjoyed, and at the same time, beginning to realize the seriousness of his situation. If he'd come back to retrieve money and a new identity, and he'd left her a most explicit message not to tell, then he was in danger and didn't know who he could trust...except her. He trusted her.

Shelly began putting everything back the way it was supposed to be, then ran into the kitchen, grabbed that notepad and shredded the drawing before putting her mustard seed back in the cabinet. This was why they hadn't been able to find his body. She couldn't imagine where he'd been hiding, or how badly he might have been injured, but he was obviously well enough to be on the move.

She stood in the middle of the kitchen and then put both hands over her heart and whispered just loud enough for only God to hear.

"Thank You, Lord, for giving him back."

* * *

When Adam was growing up in Tokyo, he wanted nothing more than to one day step into his father's seat at the cartel. The fact that would no longer be possible had eroded his purpose and his plans for the future. In the old days in his culture, a man who has lost face with his peers or shamed his family took his own life. Yuki might be the kind to lean that way, but not him. He was bent on revenge. He needed to make sure Judd Wayne was dead, and then he was going back to Japan to take down the cartel, beginning with his father. And, since he and his brother had come across the border into Laredo, Texas, early this morning under false identities, they were moving on to the next step.

"What are we doing now?" Yuki asked, as they left the café where they'd just eaten breakfast.

"We're going back to Houston," Adam said. "And don't forget…you call me Lee. I'm Lee Tanaka. You are Soshi Yamada. We aren't related, just traveling together."

"Yes, I understand," Yuki said, as they headed North up I-35 to San Antonio.

Adam was taking care not to speed so he wouldn't give the Highway Patrol a reason to stop him, and it was past noon by the time they reached San Antonio. They stopped to eat again and stretch their legs, then took Interstate 10 and drove straight into Houston.

It was night by the time they arrived. Adam chose a La Quinta Inn for the night. His steps were dragging by the time they got into their room. They washed up, then went down to the restaurant to eat dinner.

When the waitress came to take their orders, she gave the men a quick once-over and then started talking.

"Do you guys know what you want?"

"I'll have the blackened tilapia and hot tea," Adam said.

"Y'all want fries with that?"

Adam kept his head down. "No, thank you. I'll have the rice."

"And what about you?" she asked, looking at Yuki.

Uncertain about some of the offerings, he chose the safety of his brother's order.

"I will have the same," he said.

She wrote it all down and picked up their menus, then walked away.

When their meals finally came, they were anything but an epicurean experience. He tried not to think of all the fine dining he was accustomed to, and ate the food for sustenance, signed the ticket to have it charged to his room, and then they left the dining area and returned to their room.

Because he let Yuki shower first, Yuki was already in bed and snoring by the time Adam emerged from the bathroom. It was the quickest shower he'd ever had, and he was just as tired as his brother. He barely remembered pulling up the covers.

The next time Adam woke it was morning, his brother was in the bathroom and a waiter had just dropped a tray of someone's breakfast in the hall outside their door. It was after 8:00 a.m. and time to find a better place to stay and then start his search for Judd Wayne.

He wanted a body, or the man's real identity. If the bastard was still alive and hiding out somewhere, Adam knew the incentive it would take to get him into the open, but first things first. They needed an apartment, and in a part of the city where people could easily lose themselves.

Adam pocketed the room keys as they walked into their new apartment. He'd just set his bag down on the floor when Yuki gasped, then cursed in Japanese.

At the same time, the smell and the condition of the room hit him.

"Are they serious?" he muttered, staring at the sagging furniture and the dirty carpet.

"I will not stay here," Yuki said.

"Wait here," Adam said, and, still carrying his bag, walked into the kitchen. One burner worked. The refrigerator light was on, but it wasn't cold and it smelled bad.

The bathroom was functional. The shower dripped and must have been doing that for some time to produce a rust stain like the one around the drain.

The linens consisted of five towels and two washcloths. A used bar of soap was on the shelf inside the shower and there was no bath mat.

He turned around and walked into the bedroom across the hall and grunted in shock. The mattress was a good five inches lower in the center than it was on the sides. There was what looked like a bullet hole in the headboard, and when he pulled back the sheets, bedbugs abounded.

"Oh hell no!" he said, and stormed out of the apartment with his brother right behind him, making haste back to the manager's office.

The door slammed against the wall as he entered,

and it slammed again as Yuki followed, but the clerk was already wearing a look of defiance.

Then Adam started shouting. "I wouldn't stay in this hellhole if it was the last place to live on earth. Give me back my money!"

Obviously this wasn't the clerk's first displeased renter. He already had the rejection down pat.

"Hell no! This ain't no money-back-guarantee place and—"

Adam leaped over the counter. His hands were around the clerk's neck and squeezing before he saw it coming.

"Either you give it back, or I break your neck and take it," Adam whispered.

Yuki was stunned. He'd never seen his brother act this way and suddenly realized this had nothing to do with keeping books, and how out of place he was going to be on this side of their business.

The man's face was turning purple and he was trying to break Adam's hold.

"Talk or die," Adam said.

"Okay, okay, okay," he said.

Adam turned him loose, and when the man turned around to open the cash drawer, Adam took the gun he saw beneath the counter, and then pocketed the money he was given.

"You're taking my gun?" the clerk cried.

"So you can't shoot me in the back," Adam said. "If you want it back, it'll be in the Dumpster at the end of the parking lot."

"Shit, man, they don't pick up trash here no more! There ain't no tellin' what's in there."

"Matches your accommodations, then, doesn't it?" Adam vaulted the counter, picked up his bag and looked at his brother. "Get," he told Yuki, and he didn't have to say it twice. He stopped in the doorway on his way out and pointed the gun at the clerk, who ducked and ran.

Adam smirked.

The brothers got in the Jeep and started out of the parking lot, pausing long enough for Adam to toss the gun into the Dumpster before he drove away. The incident taught him a lesson. He'd do what he had to do, but he wasn't going to hide in hell to do it.

By the end of the day they were in a nicer complex in a decent part of the city, with a furnished two-bedroom apartment on the ground floor at the back of the building. He'd had to sign a six-month lease, but at this point, he didn't care. The place was clean, although meager in accommodations, and the location of the apartment was perfect for staying under the radar. All he had to do was drive up to the door and they'd be inside in ten seconds, calling no attention to themselves.

"I'm starving," Yuki said.

"So am I," Adam said. "But I have to shower first. That apartment was so terrible that I feel like bugs are crawling on me." He knew a shower was the only way he could get the stench from that dump out of his nose. Afterward, he ordered food, and while he was waiting for it to arrive, he called around to see what he could find out about Judd Wayne.

Newton Rhone was the first person Adam called with his burner phone.

"This is Rhone."

"And you know who this is. Do you know anything more about the subject we discussed?"

"What I do know is they called off the search in the bay. No one's had a funeral or a memorial service.

There's been no obit in the papers, and no mention of a dead Fed on TV. I can't say that means anything, but it's what I know."

"Interesting," Adam said. "One other thing, I now know he was in my crew under an assumed name. Is there any word on the streets about who he really was?"

"None of that. Sorry."

"No need to apologize, and thank you for this."

"Yeah, sure," Rhone said.

Adam disconnected, then thought about his inside contact on arms shipments. Right now, he wouldn't piss him off by calling tonight, but he'd call early tomorrow morning when he was on his way to work, and so he moved down the list of names, but with no success.

Their food arrived, which gave him an excuse for a break. Yuki ate without conversation, which reminded Adam of home, then he was immediately angry with himself. Home did not exist anymore, thanks to their father.

When they finished, he carried their garbage outside to the Dumpster a few yards from the car and then hurried back inside to resume making calls.

By the time he gave it up for the night, he was tired and frustrated, and Yuki had long since fallen asleep in bed with the television on. Before, the power he held over people meant his problems had immediate solutions. Now, it seemed, problems were all he had.

Jack eventually found a furnished apartment less than ten minutes from his and Shelly's neighborhood. He could be close enough to keep her safe, while maintaining just enough distance to remain undetected. He would shop for groceries and the like at night, when he knew Shelly wouldn't. And he didn't think anyone else in their area knew him well enough to recognize him in this disguise.

He ordered chicken wings, coleslaw, and got a couple of cans of Pepsi from the dispenser in the lobby, then went back to his room to wait for the food delivery.

While he was waiting, he thought of Shelly finding the note and was glad he'd made that decision. At least tonight she would not sleep in grief. He wanted to call her but didn't trust that the Bureau would not tap their phone, since his body was still missing.

When the knock came at his door, he had cash ready and gave the delivery man a good tip. As soon as he'd eaten, he went to the nearest supermarket and gathered up enough food for a few days, then took the backstreets to his new home.

Charlie brought Alicia and their son home from the hospital late in the afternoon. They were both excited, but neither one of them had expected the panic they were feeling about how to take care of him.

Alicia knew that, as a newborn, baby Johnny was supposed to sleep a lot, but after two hours of sleep, they both began to panic that he hadn't woken up. She checked in with the New Mommy group she belonged to on Facebook, and once she realized that was both normal and a blessing, she quit worrying.

And then when Johnny did wake up, new fears arose. How to stop the crying? A change of diapers and a warm bottle solved all that. Charlie was so in love that when she put Johnny back to bed, he just stood over the crib and watched him sleep.

Alicia had to come get him by the hand and lead him out of the nursery.

"Come talk to me."

He wrapped his arms around her and kissed her soundly, then kissed her again.

"The first kiss was because I missed sleeping with you by my side, and the second was for giving me our wonderful son."

Alicia smiled. "I don't know how I got so lucky, but you and Johnny are the best things that ever happened to me, and I'm so glad to be home. We'll get this baby stuff figured out. In the meantime, I'm starving and the baby is asleep."

Charlie grinned. "I got your back, darlin'. There's cold fried chicken and potato salad in the fridge."

Alicia smiled. "My favorites! Thank you!"

Charlie kept his arm around her shoulders all the way into the kitchen, then urged Alicia to sit while he got everything on the table. He didn't have to say it twice.

They were through with their meal and just finishing up their Rocky Road ice cream when they heard a tiny, high-pitched squeak on the baby monitor. They looked at each other and grinned.

"And so it begins," Charlie said.

Shelly was sitting alone in the kitchen eating her evening meal, but tonight she could actually taste it. She did dishes with joy in her step. When she sat down to pay bills later, she pulled up the accounts online and paid them with a happy heart. She tried watching TV but couldn't concentrate for the overwhelming joy of knowing Jack was not only alive but on the move.

She got ready for bed, and when she pulled back the

covers to lie down, she just sat on the side of the bed instead and put both hands over her heart.

"Oh, Jack… I don't know what's happening, but I will never complain about you being gone again. Just knowing you're alive is all I need. And thank You, God, for the blessing."

Jack didn't sleep much. He needed to know if Adam Ito had surfaced anywhere, and only someone in the system—most likely the CIA—would know that.

The agencies almost never worked together, and when they did, it wasn't always successful. But he needed help, and right now he trusted them more than he did his own people.

As soon as the sun was up, he took the bag he'd gotten out of the safe and removed a small notebook. Names were all in code only he would be able to decipher, and when he found the one he wanted, he reached for his phone.

The number rang and rang, and just as Jack was ready to hang up, a man answered in a breathless voice.

"Whoever this is, how the hell did you get my number?"

"Lamar, don't talk, just listen. This is Jack McCann."

Jack could hear Lamar gasp.

"You are shitting me!" he said.

Jack's voice deepened. "No, I'm not, but I don't want anyone to know I'm alive."

"What about the Bureau?"

"Not even them," Jack said.

"But why not? What happened?"

"One of my snitches just happened to show up with Dumas's crew on delivery and showed no surprise when he saw me. Only people in the Bureau knew his connection to me. Someone there obviously wants me dead."

"Dammit," Lamar said. "So what do you need from me?"

"I'll never be safe and neither will my family until Adam Ito is behind bars. I need to know if anyone on your team has eyes on him. If he's out of the country, then I need to know where. If he's snuck back into the States, I need to know that, too."

"Give me an hour. I'll call you back… Is this number good to use?"

"Yes," Jack said.

"For the record, I am damn glad to know you're still in the world."

"Thanks," Jack said. "I'll be waiting for your call."

Jack took the phone into the bathroom with him as he showered, and as he was drying off, he glanced at his new look again. It was one of the few times he was grateful for how fast his whiskers grew. He was sporting a true beard that was as black as his hair.

He ate cereal while waiting for Lamar to call back, and again, he thought of Shelly. The urge to take her and run was strong, but gut instinct told him Ito would find out and they'd be running again, and then again, until someone was dead. He'd considered his own death as a possibility many times in the past year. He wasn't afraid to die, but he was concerned with protecting Shelly at all costs. But if she was on the run with him, then she'd be in just as much danger.

He finished his cereal and was sitting on the sofa watching TV with the sound on mute when his cell finally rang.

"Hello?"

"It's me," Lamar said. "Facial recognition at the Laredo, Texas, border caught Adam Ito reentering under the name Lee Tanaka. He's with a Japanese guy named Soshi Yamada, but we think it's his brother, Yuki Ito, although they don't look anything alike. If you have an email address, I'll send you the pics."

Jack gave him the info, then asked, "How long ago?"

"Day before yesterday. He's had plenty of time to get back to Houston…if that's his destination."

"Oh, it's his destination, alright. In his eyes, I brought him down. He needs to see a body, and there isn't one, so he'll be looking for me. Thanks for the info. Now I have to find him, before he finds me."

"Good luck," Lamar said, and disconnected.

Nine

Knowing Ito was back was one thing. Finding him and his brother in a city the size of Houston without any starting point was another. It would take time he and Shelly didn't have to waste.

He needed the Bureau. They wanted Ito. But who could he trust? Charlie was his best friend. For sure he could trust Charlie. But once one agent knew, they would all know, and it seemed pretty obvious that someone there was leaking secrets.

And then it hit him. He could sic the Bureau onto Ito anyway by sending them this information about his whereabouts on a flash drive. They didn't have to know where it came from or who sent it.

He dug through his stuff for an empty flash drive and, when he found one, uploaded the file that had been sent to him and dropped the flash drive in his pocket on the way out the door.

A quick ride down to an office supply netted him a small padded envelope that he addressed to Special Agent Charlie Morris, then he added the word *Confidential*. He wiped his fingerprints off the flash drive

and sealed the envelope. The next stop was Houston's
Courier, a service he'd used before. It was all the way
over on Alabama Street, but he wanted this delivered
today and trusted them to do it.

It took almost an hour through traffic to reach the
courier office, and when he got off his bike, he tucked
his helmet under his arm and kept his sunglasses on. He
walked in and slipped into the shortest line, patiently
waiting his turn.

One man kept changing his mind.

The next customer couldn't find the address in her
purse.

Jack was trying not to fidget, and finally patience won
out.

"Next," the clerk said, and Jack moved up to the
counter.

"This is a rush, as in within the next hour," Jack said.

The clerk glanced at the address, quoted a price and
then said nothing when Jack counted out three hundred
dollars in twenties.

"A little something extra for the courier," Jack said.
"And I'll know if it doesn't get there on time, so don't
screw this up."

The clerk paled. "No, sir, we wouldn't do that. I'll
instruct the courier myself."

Jack nodded, then turned around and walked out.

Morning arrived before Adam was through sleeping,
but there was too much to do to give in to the urge to
sleep all day. Yuki was still asleep when he got up, but
after he walked into the kitchen, he remembered they
hadn't shopped for food, and there was nothing for their
breakfast, not even tea or coffee.

He grumbled beneath his breath about what Judd Wayne had cost him in lifestyle and respect, but before they went out to eat, he needed to call the go-between who always set up the arms deals. He knew people. He had connections. He would also have the answers Adam wanted, but he wasn't sure if he would divulge them. Selling arms was one thing. Selling out a specific man was another. He pulled up the number on his phone and hit Dial, then waited for someone to answer. When the man did answer, it was with shock.

"Are you kidding me?"

Adam's eyes narrowed. "What happened to hello?"

"What the fuck do you want?"

"I want the mole...the spy...the man who gave me up. He called himself Judd Wayne, but we both know that wasn't his real name. I want to know what it was, and where he's at."

"You mistake my presence within our deals as someone who works for you, and we both know I don't, so don't go there. Why would you assume I would have that kind of knowledge?"

"Don't play dumb with me. We both know why. I want his name."

"That's not part of our deal."

"It is now," Adam said. "It's up to you. If I can't have him, then I'm coming after you and yours, so don't lie to me about anything, because I can find you far faster than I can find Judd Wayne." The silence was long and telling. "Are you still there? No matter... I'll just invite myself over to dinner one night. It'll be a surprise. Is your wife a good cook? Oh...wait...here's a thought. Just give me the real name of Judd Wayne, and give me the address of his wife. I'll dine with her instead,"

Adam said, and then waited. When the man spoke, the rage in his voice was unmistakable.

"You are despicable," he whispered.

Adam smiled. Now he was getting somewhere. "Well, yes, I know that, but it's obvious you've been kidding yourself about your part in our business association. This is not my country, it's yours, and you sold her out."

"Get a pen and paper. I'm only going to say this once."

Adam grinned. "Start talking. I have a good memory." He listened intently as his go-between unloaded. "Is that all?" he asked.

The man hung up on him.

His smile grew. "I guess it is."

But now that he had the information, he needed coffee.

It took an hour for Adam to get Yuki up and dressed before they went to get breakfast.

Yuki wasn't picky. He just wanted food. Adam chose an IHOP because he liked waffles, then Googled the closest one and put the address in the GPS on his phone. After all the years of having a chauffeur, and a few white-knuckle moments in Houston traffic, Adam was proud of himself when he drove straight to it.

Just before they entered, Adam glanced at his brother. He was so nervous he was shaking.

"Calm down. You won't be on anyone's radar. Just be yourself," Adam said, and as they went inside and approached the hostess stand, he yanked the cap from his head and waited for her to look up.

"Good morning," she said. "Is it just the two of you?"

"Yes," Adam said softly.

"Follow me, please," she said, and grabbed a couple of menus on her way toward their table. "Enjoy," she said, and laid the menus on the table as they slid into the booth.

Adam glanced up, furtively checking out the customers before he decided they were of no consequence.

His waitress appeared. "Y'all want coffee?" she asked.

Yuki started to order hot tea, then saw his brother choose the coffee, so he did, as well. He watched apprehensively as she filled his cup so full that he knew it would slosh when he picked it up.

"Do you need a few minutes more with the menu?" the waitress asked.

Adam shook his head no. "Belgian waffle and bacon."

"I will have the same," Yuki said.

"Comin' up," she said, and went to turn in their orders.

Adam was breathing easy as he waited for his coffee to cool a bit, then happened to glance out the window and saw two police cruisers pulling up at the same time. Both officers got out and walked into the restaurant with such purpose that it immediately unsettled him. To his relief, they had only come to pick up to-go orders and were back in their cars and gone in under five minutes. Adam relaxed and reached for his coffee. It was finally cool enough to drink. A couple of minutes later their food was delivered, and they settled in to eat. The waitress came by, refilled their coffee cups and left the ticket.

"Thank you," he said.

She smiled and then surprised him with a wink.

He buttered his waffles, taking delight in the butter melting into the crusty little square pockets, then chose straight maple syrup and poured until the butter floated up and pooled on top. His first bite was nothing short of ecstasy.

Yuki wolfed his down, then sat watching the precise way in which Adam cut the waffle so that each bite consisted of two squares.

"Hey, Adam?"

Adam frowned. "Do not call me by that name."

"Sorry," Yuki whispered.

"So what do you want?" Adam asked.

"It was nothing," Yuki said in a soft, quiet voice.

"No…ask. We're brothers," Adam said.

"I guess I was going to ask what gives you pleasure. I watch the precise way in which you prepare a bite and wonder if you are as controlled in everything you do. Is there never a time when you give yourself permission to let go and enjoy?"

Adam thought about it a few moments. "I think the proper answer would be that I enjoy being in control. Can you understand that?"

Yuki nodded, still watching as Adam cut another bite, then swished it through the syrup in his plate two times before popping it into his mouth.

"Do you ever think why we are so different?" Yuki asked.

Adam shrugged. "No."

"I do," Yuki said. "You are handsome. I have the features of a peasant."

Adam glanced up, studied his brother's eyes, the big jaw and wide nostrils, and his ears—so tiny against his big head they seemed as if they would be incapable of aiding him in hearing.

"You look like our grandfather," Adam said.

"I look nothing like him!" Yuki argued.

"I mean our mother's father. He died before you were born. I barely remember him, but you look like him."

Yuki smiled, showing tiny, even white teeth. "I do?"

Adam nodded and took another bite.

Yuki sighed. "I used to think I was a foundling that our parents took in. I didn't see myself in either of them."

Adam was shocked. "Why didn't you ever say something?"

Yuki shrugged. "I was afraid of the answer."

Adam sighed. The eight-year difference in their ages had probably caused part of his brother's feeling of not belonging. He had never paid much attention to Yuki other than acknowledging him as family.

"I am sorry you have felt this way," Adam said. "We are brothers. We will stick together, no matter what."

The vow made Yuki happy. He needed to belong.

Adam finally finished eating, and when he got up to go pay, he left a ten-dollar tip.

Once inside his car, he entered the address of the Mc-Cann residence into the phone's GPS. He didn't have a clue where that was and pulled up a city map of Houston. When he found it, he frowned.

"This is a very long way from here, and I suddenly realize I should have asked if the wife had a job. I would hate to drive all that way to find her not at home," Adam muttered.

Yuki glanced at his older brother. "If I had a laptop, I could find out where she works," he said.

"How?" Adam asked.

"A simple search will probably do it," Yuki said.

"This sort of information isn't difficult to track down online."

"I have a computer back in the apartment," Adam said.

"Then we go there first. Be wise with our time."

Adam couldn't disagree, even though he wanted to.

"Then we go back," he said. "Better safe than sorry."

Yuki gave him an odd look.

Adam shrugged. "It is an American expression."

"I understood the meaning," Yuki said.

Adam frowned. "Then what was that look about?"

"I have no wish to involve a woman. I do not like this side of the business."

"She means nothing to us. Her husband does. Whatever happens makes her collateral damage."

"What if this Jack McCann is truly already dead? What do we do with her?"

"Leave the body behind and go home."

Yuki's eyes widened. He didn't want any part of killing, especially a woman. And going home? What was Adam thinking?

"But we are forbidden," he said.

Adam turned on him in rage. "They disowned us. We are no longer bound by their orders."

Yuki had seen that look on his brother's face too many times not to recognize the danger.

"Then if we go home, what do we do?"

"We take them down, one by one, beginning with our father."

Yuki sighed. "Do you really intend to kill our father?"

"He was willing to kill us," Adam snapped.

"What about our mother?"

Adam shrugged. "More collateral damage, and we do not discuss this again."

The drive back to their apartment was in silence.

Yuki felt like he was living a nightmare. He wanted so desperately to wake up. His brother was a monster—like their father—like the rest of the cartel. He wanted out but was now aware that would never happen. Adam would no sooner let him go than he was going to forgive their parents. The breakfast they'd just eaten felt like it was going to come up.

As for Adam, he had come back for one thing and one thing only. He didn't know if Jack McCann was alive or not, but snatching his wife would drastically shorten the search.

Once the Ito brothers got back to their apartment, Yuki began searching sites.

Adam was pacing the floor behind him to the point that it was making Yuki nervous. He kept glancing over his shoulder, thinking Adam would get the hint, but all he did was move closer until he was literally breathing over his shoulder. Finally, Yuki shoved his chair back in anger as he spun around.

"What's the matter with you? Do you know how to do this?" he yelled.

"No, but—"

Yuki poked a finger in Adam's chest. "Then get off my back. I can't concentrate with you hovering."

"Fine," Adam said, and he reached for the TV remote.

Yuki sat back down and resumed his search. About an hour later, he shoved the chair back again, but this time calmly.

"Shelly McCann is an accountant at Bates and

Davis Accounting Firm. I have an address in downtown Houston."

Adam glanced at the clock. It was almost 4:00 p.m. He pulled up the home address his snitch had given him and entered it into the phone's GPS system.

"Are we going to her house now?" Yuki asked.

"Yes. We will take her as she arrives."

They went out the door and were soon back in traffic and heading for the 610 Loop.

Charlie had some personal business to attend to after he left home. He'd missed a couple of car payments because he'd been out of the city on a case and simply forgot. He went to the bank to pay in person and explain what had happened, which got him to work a couple of hours late, but instead of an apology, he walked into the office whistling. "Who wants to see baby pictures?" he asked.

Fred Ray was the first to get up. "I do."

Charlie pulled them up on his phone and then began flipping through a good two dozen, explaining something about each one. Fred just nodded and smiled, because the only differences were the colors of the blankets. The baby was asleep in all of them.

"Alicia says he looks like me," Charlie said.

Fred grinned and patted him on the back. "Congrats again, Charlie. I better get back to work. I'm still sorting mail."

Charlie's partner, Nolan Warren, was at his desk.

"I better see those pictures so I can check out my new partner. Maybe I'll get to train him before I retire."

Charlie laughed. The thought of his son following in his footsteps made him proud. He went through the photos over and over as the other agents came to see. A couple of them even had the good sense to ask about Alicia.

"They're both doing great!" Charlie said. "I am one lucky man." Then he glanced up at the clock. "Looks like I need to get busy. The morning is going to be over before I even get started."

The agents scattered, some leaving to work on cases and others, like Charlie, were catching up on paperwork.

Charlie had just pulled up the case on Jack McCann's disappearance, when Fred came over to his desk and handed him an envelope.

"This was couriered here to you," he said, and went back to his desk.

The first thing Charlie noticed was no return address. He felt the padded envelope and knew within seconds that it was a flash drive or something like it inside. He opened it carefully and, as suspected, a flash drive slid out onto his desk. He looked inside for a note of explanation, but there was nothing. He put the flash drive into a USB port in his computer and then pulled up the file. When the photo popped up on his screen, his heart skipped a beat.

From the signs in the picture, it was obviously at a Mexico/Texas border crossing. People were leaving Mexico and crossing the border in Laredo, Texas. Then he focused in on two men caught in the image taken from the security camera and realized he was looking at Adam Ito. He saw the time and date on the bottom of the photo, then frowned as he pulled up the second picture, which was a screenshot of the passports. Ito was traveling under the name Lee Tanaka and the other man was Soshi Yamada. They didn't look alike, but Charlie wondered if he was the younger brother from Japan.

"Nolan! Come look at this," Charlie said.

Nolan got up, grinning as he walked over. "Are you on that porn site again?"

Charlie snorted. "Be serious for a second, will you? Who does that look like to you?"

Nolan leaned closer. "Oh hell! That's Adam Ito, isn't it? Who's the dude with him?"

Charlie clicked on the next picture that showed their passports.

Nolan's eyes widened. "Those documents look forged to me. He has a brother, right?"

"In Japan. Maybe that's where he went. But why come back?"

"My first guess would be revenge…or to make sure the man he knew as Judd Wayne is dead."

"I'm showing this to Wainwright," Charlie said, and grabbed the flash drive as he headed for the boss's office.

This picture was taken a couple of days ago and proof that Ito was back in Texas. He didn't know who sent it, and right now it didn't matter. They just needed Ito behind bars or dead. The choice would be up to Ito once they ran him down.

Within the hour, the scramble was on. Snitches were on alert. Agents were calling in favors. All they needed was a starting point.

Agent Fred Ray was at his desk pulling up all property in the city that was registered under both Adam Ito's name and the import/export business. Once he had the list, he sent the file to Charlie, who was lead on the case. From that point on, they had locations to search.

* * *

Jack rode past Shelly's place of work to make sure she was there. Once he spotted her car in the parking lot, he knew she'd be safe until quitting time. He would just hang around this area and make sure to follow her home, and he trusted she would reset the security alarm once she was inside. Now that he'd alerted the Bureau to Ito's presence, he felt confident they would be after Ito, which would leave him free to focus on nothing but keeping Shelly safe.

Unaware of the danger she was in, Shelly clocked out as usual and headed for the elevator. Mitzi was right behind her on her phone, and from the sounds of the conversation, she was in an argument with one of her two teenagers.

"You heard me," Mitzi said. "You will not be leaving the house tonight and we'll discuss your punishment at dinner…What are we having? Oh, I don't know what the rest of us are having, but you're eating crow!…What? You have to be joking! Oh! Although you're the one who had the wreck, got the ticket and put an elderly woman in the hospital, you hate *me*? Ha! Just wait until your father gets home. I'm going to be your next best friend."

Mitzi rolled her eyes and dropped her phone back in her purse as they reached the elevator.

Shelly pressed the button and then turned around and leaned against the wall as they waited for the car to arrive.

"I'm sorry," she said. "Sounds like dinner will be interesting tonight."

"Don't ever have children," Mitzi muttered.

Shelly wanted to laugh, but it wouldn't fit in with

being a newly grieving widow. Then she could tell by the look on Mitzi's face, she'd just realized what she'd said.

"Oh, honey, I'm sorry. I wasn't thinking about anything but my dumb-ass daughter. Today, because she was texting and driving, she put a woman in the hospital. Thank God the hubster has full coverage on all of our vehicles. If we're sued, we're still protected. We may never be able to afford food again when the rates go up, but oh well."

The door opened. A man got off, nodded at them in passing as Shelly and Mitzi got on.

"Is your daughter hurt?" Shelly asked.

Mitzi's eyes welled. "Not yet," she said.

Shelly gave Mitzi a quick hug.

"I'm sorry, honey!"

Mitzi sighed. "Thank you. You just never know, do you?"

"No, you don't," Shelly said, then picked her things back up and moved aside as another half-dozen people got on.

Two more stops and they were finally at the ground floor. They walked outside together, and then Shelly went one way and Mitzi another to get to their cars.

Shelly thought about Mitzi as she drove. It wasn't just about a wreck. Her daughter had been at fault and a woman was injured. That was very serious business. She said a quick prayer for the injured woman's healing and then took the on-ramp onto the 610 Loop, so ready to be home.

Jack was sitting on the Indian less than a block away from Shelly's workplace, waiting for her to exit the building. He had eyes on both the exit and her car, so he knew he wouldn't miss her. And when he finally saw her walking out beside Mitzi, his heart skipped a beat.

"Love you so much," he said softly, and then put his helmet on and started up the bike.

When Shelly left the parking lot, Jack was four cars behind her. He followed her up the on-ramp to the 610 Loop, then got in another lane to keep a better eye on her.

They'd been on the loop for a good twenty minutes and were less than a mile from their exit when the driver of the car just behind Shelly suddenly swerved into the lane to his left, colliding with the car beside him and shoving it over another lane. Jack was frantically weaving his way through traffic to get to the other side of the road before he got nailed, too. Cars behind the initial wreck were all slamming on their brakes as the chain reaction grew and grew. He had one last glimpse of Shelly driving safely away, while he got stuck on the other side of the freeway, blocked in by wrecked cars and smoking debris as he rode his bike to a halt.

The man in the truck in front of him was climbing down from the cab. He had a small cut on his forehead as he turned around and looked behind them, and then looked at Jack.

"Ain't this a fuckin' mess! What do you want to bet someone was texting?"

"The odds are that you're likely correct, so I'll pass on that bet. Did you call this in?"

The trucker blinked. "I didn't even think about it."

"911 is probably getting dozens of calls, but I'm not going to assume. I'll call it in, too, and then I've got to find a way out of here."

"Good luck," the trucker said, eyeing the motorcycle. "You have the best chance, that's for sure."

Jack called 911, reported the accident and the location and then started his bike back up and began slowly winding his way through the piled-up cars until he reached the exit and took it. He wasn't all that far behind Shelly, but the fact that he'd lost sight of her made him nervous. He wouldn't rest easy until he knew for sure she was safe inside their house.

Ten

Shelly saw the wreck happening behind her and sped up, grateful she hadn't been caught in the chaos. When she finally reached her exit, she left the 610 with relief. It wasn't long before she began seeing Aerocare helicopters and hearing ambulance and police sirens.

"God bless all who are in need," she whispered, and then stopped for a red light, which gave her a moment to think about Jack. "I know you are in need, too, my darling. I am praying for your safety."

The light finally turned green and she accelerated through the intersection. Only after she drove into their neighborhood did she allow herself to relax. She made a conscious effort every day not to become a statistic, but twice a day on the 610 Loop was always stressful. Today had been a horrible reminder of how swiftly life could change.

As she drove through the streets, she began noticing a couple of new for-sale signs. It was the same Realtor as the one showing the house just north of their house. And as she drew nearer, she noticed there was a car parked at the curb in front of the vacant house. She frowned. Getting new neighbors was always stressful.

The windows in the car were dark, but she didn't think anyone was inside.

"Likely interested buyers," she decided, and hit the remote as she turned up her driveway. She braked, waiting for the garage door to go up, and then pulled inside.

She was still rolling forward when she caught a glimpse of something in the rearview mirror, but then when nothing appeared, she decided it had simply been a glimpse of a passing car out on the street, and hit the remote to lower the door. As soon as it was down, she got out and went inside.

Her routine never changed as she pushed the door shut behind her, and paused in the hallway to disable the alarm. It wasn't until she heard the squeak of a hinge that she realized the door from the house into the garage was opening again.

Thinking she hadn't pushed it all the way shut, she was turning around when a man appeared in the doorway. Before she could react, he hit her in the face with his fist. Blood spurted from her mouth and nose, but she didn't feel it. She was unconscious before she hit the floor.

Adam turned and pressed the button to raise the door back up for Yuki, who had already pulled their car up and was running inside.

In less than a minute, Shelly McCann was gagged, her hands and feet tightly bound, and her body wrapped up in blue plastic tarp. She was beginning to come to when Yuki scooped her up into his arms and carried her to their car.

The door to the back of the Jeep Cherokee was already up. He dropped her inside and slammed it shut, then leaped into the passenger seat. Adam was already backing out as Yuki buckled up.

"Drive!" Yuki shouted.

Adam glanced up, saw that the garage door was still open, and cursed, but there was no time to go back and close it. And then he saw a neighbor from across the street running out of the house toward them with her cell phone to her ear, looking at them and screaming.

"Dammit!" Adam said. He rolled down the window enough to fire off a shot, and saw the woman hit the grass facedown as he sped away. Her arrival was nothing but a little hitch to his plan, because he finally had the bait he needed.

From her living room window, Barb Hightower noticed Shelly coming home from work, just as she did this time every day. She was about to turn away when she saw a man come out from the bushes behind Shelly's house and roll under the garage door as she was driving inside. Her heart started to pound. Shelly was inside that garage with a bad man! She was about to run for her cell phone when she saw the garage door going back up, and the dark car that had been parked at the curb next door was now pulling into her drive. The driver braked, killed the engine, and when he ran inside the McCann house, too, Barb ran for her phone.

By the time she got back to the window, one man was heading for the driver's side of the car, while the other was carrying something wrapped up in blue plastic to the back. It wasn't until he dropped it inside that Barbara saw long blond hair fall out of the tarp.

"Oh my God, oh my God," Barb moaned, and was already calling 911 as she bolted out of the house, screaming for them to stop. The driver's-side window began to slide down. She saw the gun a fraction of a second before the shot was fired, and dropped facedown in the grass as the car accelerated and sped away.

By the time she looked up, they had already turned a corner and disappeared from sight. Still screaming for help, she got up on her hands and knees to look for the phone she'd dropped. But when she found it, she soon learned the dispatcher was still on the line and had already dispatched the police.

"Ma'am, ma'am, are you alright?" the dispatcher kept asking.

Barb took a deep breath. "Yes, yes, I'm okay. They shot at me but missed. I just witnessed two men kidnapping my neighbor Shelly McCann. They carried her body out of the house wrapped in blue plastic tarp and dumped her in the back of their SUV. I didn't know it was Shelly until I saw her long blond hair hanging on the outside of the tarp."

"Did you know them?"

"No, never saw them before. They were driving a late model gray Jeep Cherokee."

"Can you describe them?" the dispatcher asked.

"They were late thirties or early forties, and both were Asian. One was taller and slimmer. One was a bit shorter and heavyset. You have to hurry! Shelly is such a dear. I can't believe this has happened!"

Jack made good time once he got off the Loop, and sped toward home. It didn't take long before he began meeting rescue vehicles—ambulances, fire trucks and police cars. He saw the choppers flying overhead and saw that a few were from television stations, but the majority were from Aerocare companies.

By the time he finally drove into their housing addition he was beyond anxious. It had taken longer to get here than he first thought, but when he finally turned down their street and saw police cars everywhere, his heart sank. He didn't want to believe it, but they were at his house.

The area was roped off with yellow crime scene tape and not an ambulance was in sight. Then he saw Barb Hightower sitting in a chair on her porch. When he realized she was crying, the feeling that swept through him was pure panic. He rolled the Indian to the curb and killed it, then got off running.

Barb saw a stranger coming toward her and jumped up in fear. She was about to call out to the police across the street when she realized she knew that voice, and he was calling out her name.

"Barb, Barb, what's going on?" Jack asked, and then yanked off his helmet so she could see his face.

She paused. "Jack? Is that you?"

"Yes, ma'am. What happened to Shelly? Where is she?"

Barb let the door swing shut and grabbed his arm. "Oh, honey! I am so sorry to tell you, but I witnessed her being kidnapped."

"No," Jack groaned, as his legs went weak. "Did you see the kidnappers?"

"Yes. They were driving a late model gray Jeep Cherokee. I couldn't get a tag number because the driver shot at me as they drove away."

Jack grabbed her by the shoulders. "Are you okay?"

"Yes, but Shelly...they had her rolled up in one of

those blue plastic tarps… You know, those cheap ones like you can get at Walmart? I didn't know it was her until I saw her hair. It was hanging out the end."

Jack shuddered. "Faces! Did you see their faces?"

"Yes…they were Asian."

"Would you know them again if you saw them?"

"The big one for sure because I clearly saw his face. The slimmer one, yes, maybe."

Jack pulled up the email on his cell phone that Lamar had sent him, then opened the attached file to the picture of the two men at the border crossing.

"Do you see the men anywhere in this picture?" he asked.

Barb peered at the screen and then pointed. "Those two. It was those men. Do you know who they are?"

"Yes, I do," Jack said, and then hugged her. "If I can save her, I will have you to thank."

"Oh lord," Barb said, and was in tears all over again as she watched him running back to the motorcycle. Within seconds he was speeding away.

Jack was sick to his stomach. He knew the level of depravity hidden within Adam Ito's cool demeanor, and he knew Shelly was going to be tortured. There was no time left for secrets. He needed the Bureau's help and reluctantly pulled over. He was so scared and so mad that he had to take a couple of deep breaths before he could speak in a calm enough manner to be understood, and then he made the call.

Charlie answered on the third ring. "This is Special Agent Charlie Morris."

"Charlie, it's me."

He couldn't see his friend's face, but he heard joy in his voice.

"Oh sweet holy Jesus! Jack! You're alive!"

"Yes, but there's nothing to celebrate. Adam Ito just kidnapped Shelly."

"No! Oh my God! What can I—"

"Shut up and listen. I need a list of every piece of property he owns in this city, no matter how inconsequential. Email it to my personal computer. A neighbor witnessed it go down. It's the same two men who were in the file I sent you."

"I should have known that was you! The other guy is his brother," Charlie said. "We've already had Fred compile that list. I'll have him send it directly to your personal email. You also need to know that we have men out checking every address on the list, looking for them. What else can I do?"

"Find out which locations have already been checked, because the kidnapping happened less than thirty minutes ago and he might backtrack on you and head for one that's already been cleared. That's all, just find them, but know that if I find them first, you only get what's left of him. Oh. One more thing. You have a leak somewhere in the Bureau. When Dumas and his men came in with the goods, Ritter was with him…and he was looking for me."

The tone of Charlie's voice deepened in anger. "Ritter—as in your snitch?"

"Yes."

"How do you know? Maybe it was just an accident and—"

"No. I saw him first. When he saw me, it was as if he expected me to be there, which means someone with access to that information told him. Make sure Wainwright hears about this."

"Son of a bitch," Charlie muttered. "I'll inform him myself."

Jack ended the call, put the helmet back on and pocketed the phone before he took off. He wanted to get back to his apartment first and gather up some equipment. With the Bureau checking the properties, he needed another plan.

Back at the Bureau, Charlie was on his feet and shouting.

"McCann is alive! Ito! Ito!" He barked out orders to the agents around him, then bolted out of the office to fill Wainwright in on what was going down.

Shelly regained consciousness in the dark, choking on her own blood and wrapped up like a burrito. It didn't take long to figure out she was in the back of some kind of speeding vehicle. She knew it was a hot day, but in the back of this vehicle, wrapped up in plastic, she was smothering. Whoever had done this was going to get a surprise when they discovered her dead body. Her nose was throbbing. That man had probably broken it when he'd hit her, and despite the gag, she could also taste the blood in her mouth. Her heart was racing and her panic was rising—the thought of not being able to breathe was horrifying. All she could think of was Jack. She didn't have to know the details to understand this had happened because of him. It was what he was trying to fix…maybe even what he'd been trying to prevent.

Oh God…this will destroy him, knowing I died because of his job.

He would have survived his own ordeal, only to wind up having to bury her. She hoped God was listening as she began to pray.

* * *

Adam Ito was driving too fast and he knew it, but they needed to get off the streets. It was only a matter of time before every cop in the city had, at the least, a description of their car and maybe the tag number. And that witness had been on the phone when she came out screaming, which could mean she'd seen them come out of the house with the woman's body. And that meant she could possibly identify them.

None of this had gone as he'd planned, but it was the first time he'd pulled any kind of job without paying people to do it for him and protect his identity. He was getting a dose of how small-time criminals worked. Sometimes they pulled it off. Most times they got caught.

"Where are we taking her?" Yuki asked.

"One of my properties out near Houston Hobby Airport, but it's not in my name. It's listed as belonging to one of my shell companies."

"What if the Feds know about it?" Yuki asked.

Adam glared. "Just shut up and ride. Everything is going as planned."

Yuki glared back. "You *planned* to shoot at a witness and alert the whole neighborhood to our crime?"

"Don't piss me off right now!" Adam shouted.

Yuki's heart was pounding now. This was the brother he remembered from his youth. The one he'd hid from. But he wasn't afraid of him in this moment. He was too angry.

"You would be wise to remember that while I am your younger brother, I'm still the one who's stood by you all these years. I'm still the one here helping you now. And I haven't been a small, helpless child for many years. You've needed me this whole time, and you still need me now, so how about *you* don't piss *me* off?"

Adam was shocked, but he was also calming down. Yuki was right. Adam needed him. But when he didn't need him anymore, that might be another story...

"I'm sorry, brother. That was just frustration talking. You are correct. I did not plan for a witness. Now, no more fighting between us. We have to stick together. I'm sorry. Forgive me?"

"Of course," Yuki said, but he wasn't going to let down his guard again.

It took an hour for Adam to reach his destination.

Planes were landing and taking off beyond the chain-link fencing between the warehouses and the runways. He circled to the back of his building, put the car in Park and jumped out running. When he reached the keypad, he punched in the code, then got back in the car as the doors swung outward. He drove between the gap, stopping long enough to go back to close the doors, then drove all the way to the far end of the building.

"Get her out!" Adam said.

Yuki popped the hatch from the front seat, then went around to the back to lift her out. But when he felt the heat emanating from the back of the vehicle and realized how limp she was, he began tearing away the plastic from around her head and shoulders.

"What the fuck are you doing?" Adam said. "I told you to get her out!"

"The heat...all that plastic. I don't think she's breathing," Yuki said.

Adam saw his plan falling apart before it began, and started pulling at the plastic, trying to free her.

Her clothes looked as if they'd taken her out of a swimming pool. There wasn't a dry thread on her, and her skin was dripping in sweat.

"Shit," Adam muttered, feeling the woman's neck for a pulse. His relief, when he found one, was huge. "She's alive. Get her and follow me," he said, and then hurried into what had once been the warehouse office.

The door was unlocked, which didn't really matter, because all of the windows facing the interior of the warehouse were missing their glass. It was a wide-open space, but the shabby furniture that had been there when he'd bought the property—a chair, a cot and an old desk—still sat untouched.

"Put her down there," Adam instructed, pointing at the floor inside the door, "then untie her hands and secure her to the bed."

"She needs water," Yuki said.

"And I need answers!" Adam snapped.

"If you want her to talk, then give her water. Otherwise, we can sit and watch her die," Yuki said.

Adam gestured to a bathroom. "Fine. See if the water is still on."

Yuki stopped inside the small room, then jumped when a rat ran out between his legs. Those disgusting creatures gave him the creeps. He tried the light switch but noticed there was no bulb in the fixture anyway. He turned around to the sink and tried the taps, but nothing came out.

"No water," he said, as he walked out.

"Go check the car. See if there are any bottles of water."

Yuki went back to the car and began searching. He finally found one unopened bottle of water that had rolled beneath a seat.

"Found one," he said, and handed it to Adam as he returned.

Adam opened the bottle and started to pour it on her face when Yuki snatched it out of his hands.

"Inside her, not on her!" he said.

Adam said nothing but stood and watched as his brother lifted the woman's head just enough to pour a little water into her mouth.

It dribbled back out.

"Lady! Lady! You need to swallow," Yuki said, and tried it again. This time, when he poured a tiny bit into her mouth, he saw her tongue move and watched the water go down.

Little by little, he got almost half of the sixteen ounces in the bottle down her throat before he began to see signs of waking.

"She's regaining consciousness!" Yuki said.

"It's about time," Adam muttered, and then kicked the side of the bed, jarring it and her. "Wake up, Shelly McCann!"

Shelly moaned. She was so hot she couldn't breathe, but someone was calling her name. Her lips parted, but she couldn't make a sound.

Someone lifted her head. "Drink," he said. She felt water on her lips, then her tongue, and swallowed.

"Wake up, Shelly McCann!" Adam yelled again.

She tried to lift her hand to her mouth, only to realize she was tied up at the wrists. Her heart started to pound. Something was wrong! What had happened to her? Who were these men?

"Give me that damn water!" Adam shouted, and snatched it out of Yuki's hands and turned it upside down, sloshing it all over her face, in her eyes, up her nose, down her throat, then threw the empty bottle into the corner of the room and yanked her upright by the hair on her head.

Shelly screamed, then choked as she was dragged into a sitting position. She kept blinking, trying to clear her vision, and then when she did, she wished she was still unconscious. She didn't know these men, but they knew her, and likely they knew Jack.

"Who…are you?" she whispered.

"I ask the questions!" Adam said, and slapped her, which started her swollen lip to bleeding again.

Shelly moaned. *God give me strength.*

"Where is your husband, Jack McCann?" Adam asked.

Shelly started crying. "Dead… He's dead."

Adam frowned, then slapped her again. "You lie. Tell me where he is or I will kill you."

Shelly looked up, straight into Adam Ito's face. Blood and tears were flowing.

"Then kill me. At least then I'll be with him," she whispered, and felt the room beginning to spin. "Hot… too hot. You can't kill me. Heat will kill me first," she mumbled, and fell forward off the bed onto the floor, unconscious once more.

"Worthless bitch!" Adam screamed, and kicked her in the ribs. "Put her back on the bed, and this time, do what I say and tie her up."

"I need rope. These ties are too short," Yuki said.

"There's rope in the car and you know it! Go get it!" Adam shouted.

Once more, Yuki went to the car, returning with a yellow nylon rope.

He untied the cloth rags from around her hands and

ankles and used the rope to tie her to the bed. Now she was spread-eagle upon the thin, filthy mattress, as helpless as a woman could be.

Yuki saw her as the victim she was and looked away, ashamed of his part in this farce. His brother was crazy if he thought this was going to work, but he didn't know who was crazier—Adam for thinking he could get his revenge without getting caught, or him for being a part of it.

"You! Guard her!" Adam said.

Yuki grabbed Adam's arm as he started to leave. "Where do you think you're going? You will not leave me stranded here. You will bring food and water for the both of us now, or I'm walking and she can die in here on her own. Then you will have accomplished nothing! I know how to get myself on a plane."

Adam yanked his arm free and stormed out of the room with his cell phone in his hand. Right now he hated his brother almost as much as he hated his father, but he couldn't do this alone. So he would get food and water.

Once he'd left the property, the urge to keep driving and leave all of this behind was real, but his need for revenge was stronger.

He drove to the first truck stop he came to, fueled up the car and then bought a sack full of snack foods and a case of bottled water. All of this food was disgusting to him, but he knew Yuki would eat it. By the time he left the truck stop he'd also had the foresight to purchase toilet paper, a roll of paper towels and a cheap Styrofoam ice chest that he filled with three bags of ice.

He had a heart-stopping moment on his way back

when he looked up in his rearview mirror and saw a police car behind him coming fast with red lights flashing.

Then when everyone else began pulling over to the outside lane and stopping, he did the same. To his relief, the police car flew past on its way to an emergency elsewhere.

When the rest of the traffic began moving again, so did he, and the next time he stopped, it was to open the doors to his warehouse to drive in.

The sun was moving faster toward the horizon. It would be dark within a couple of hours, maybe less. He had no intention of spending the night in this filth, so he needed McCann's wife to start talking.

Eleven

Yuki was miserable in this heat. He'd already shed all of his clothing except for his undershirt, shoes and pants. Sweat was pouring out of his thick black hair and running into the rolls of fat on the back of his neck. His clothes were sticking to him, and the filth in this place disagreed with his sense of propriety.

He felt sorry for the woman tied to the bed. Her breathing was shallow and he could barely see the pulse in her neck. She was a beautiful woman, and she was likely going to die.

When he finally heard the doors opening again, he ran out to meet his brother.

"Stuff is all in the back. I'm going to close the doors," Adam said, and ran back to the entrance, while Yuki began carrying the food and the sack of paper goods into the office.

Adam grabbed the case of bottled water and followed.

"Did she wake up?" Adam asked, as he set the water down.

"No. She's barely alive. Something is wrong with her.

She said the heat would kill her. Maybe it will save you the trouble," Yuki said.

Adam cursed in his native language, opened a bottle of water and shouted, "Wake up, Mrs. McCann," then poured enough water on her to bring her to consciousness.

Shelly choked, then gasped, then opened her eyes. *Oh God. I thought this was just a dream.*

Adam leaned over the bed. "Where is your husband?"

Looking for me, I hope. But she didn't say what she was thinking. Instead, she let her eyes tear up again before she answered. "They said…his body washed out to sea."

Adam drew back and slapped her so hard it popped her neck. Her eyes rolled back, and she was out.

Yuki laughed.

The sound startled Adam enough that he stopped and turned around.

"Why are you laughing?"

"All these years and I thought I was the stupid one."

Adam doubled up his fists. "Are you calling me stupid?"

"You tell me! You want this woman to talk, and every time she regains consciousness, the first thing you do is knock her out again. That is very stupid behavior, big brother."

Adam flew at his brother, but Yuki grabbed his wrist, yanking him around and pinning his arm against his back until Adam was shrieking in pain.

"You do that again and I'll break it," Yuki said.

"I'm sorry. Let me go!" Adam said.

"Since I'm *not* the stupid one, I think you should

know that I don't believe you are sorry on any level. Now wake her up, question her until you are satisfied she is either telling the truth or she's lying and isn't going to talk, so we can leave here."

"Yes, alright," Adam said, then when his brother turned him loose, he grabbed a handful of ice and packed it around her throat, then rubbed ice on her face before pouring more water on her face and neck. Finally, she began to stir and move her head from side to side.

"Don't…" she mumbled.

Adam grabbed her by the hair and yanked her head around to face him.

"Don't hit…" she begged.

Adam hated to admit it, but his brother was right. The woman was barely here…one eye was swelling shut. Her mouth was so bloody and swollen that he barely understood what she was trying to say, and her nose was obviously broken.

"Where's Jack?" he asked.

"Under…sea. Gone from me…" Huge tears rolled down her face.

Adam pulled a knife from his pocket and cut her blouse straight up the middle, then cut her bra in the middle as well, revealing a wealth of bare flesh. He ran the point of the knife from her collarbone all the way to her navel, cutting just deep enough to make it bleed.

Shelly arched up off the bed, screaming.

"That was just a taste of what's coming. If you're lying to me, you're about to pay for it dearly," he sneered, and dug the point of the knife into her flesh while she howled in pain.

Yuki dived toward them, grabbed the knife out of his

brother's hand and threw it across the room, embedding it a good three inches into the wall.

"Not only are you stupid, you're a monster," Yuki said. "If you weren't my brother, I would have already snapped your neck."

Adam stood up, his hands fisted as he stared into his brother's face. There were no words for what he was feeling, but he knew he was losing control. He turned around and grabbed one of Shelly's breasts and pinched it until she screamed again.

"You want me to stop?" he asked.

Light was flashing behind Shelly's eyes and she could feel herself fading.

"Stop…" she mumbled.

"Then answer my question! Where is Jack?"

"Dead…like me."

Adam cursed. She was either telling the truth or willing to die to protect him. He'd leave her to think about it awhile.

"We go!" Adam said, and headed for the car. "If she's still alive in the morning, we'll talk to her again. If she's dead, then that is the answer I get."

"Wait. I want to give her another drink," Yuki said.

He opened another bottle of water, drenching her face and hair, and then lifted her head and poured some down her throat. She swallowed enough to satisfy him, and then he straightened up and looked around.

"Stay strong, lady," he said softly, and got back in the car.

When they shut the warehouse doors before driving away, Yuki felt bad. The rats… Oh no! He hadn't thought of them. Now he was going to imagine the worst, but Adam was philosophical about the woman as they drove back to their apartment. If she was dead in the morning, then it was meant to be. If she stayed alive, maybe a night alone would change her mind about talking.

"I'm hungry. Keep an eye out for a place that cooks hibachi. I want sake and beef. What about you?" Adam asked.

Yuki stared at him. "Her blood is on your hands," he said, and turned away.

Adam glanced down, surprised he had not noticed that himself. "Thank you. I will make sure to clean up before we go inside."

Yuki shuddered. His brother was crazy. "Why do you call yourself Adam? Why not use your Japanese name?"

Adam frowned. "Because this is America. *Sota* is not a name of power in their eyes."

"And Adam is a name of power?" Yuki asked.

"In their Christian religion, it is the name of the first man their God created. Adam was the first man. Eve was the first woman."

Yuki nodded. It didn't make sense to him, and he was glad he did not live in this country. But the moment he thought it, he sighed. He no longer lived in his country, either. He had no home.

"What if the rats get to her?" Yuki asked.

Adam turned to him in anger. "Stop talking about her! I don't want to hear it again."

Yuki frowned, but he didn't argue. And when they finally found a Japanese restaurant that satisfied Adam's sensibilities, they parked and went inside.

Adam and Yuki went straight to the men's room to clean up, and then back to the hostess stand to be seated. The whole ambiance was what Adam craved. The decor was cheap, but the aroma from the food cooking was enticing. They were seated at a table with a hibachi grill, introduced to their chef and then entertained for the next hour by the chef's knife skills and the tasty food he turned out.

Yuki was drawn into the experience to the point that for a while he completely forgot about the woman he had tied to that filthy cot.

It was late by the time they got back to their apartment. Showers and rest were in order, and Yuki went first without asking. But the ride back had resurrected his guilt about the woman they'd abandoned, and he was wondering if he would be able to sleep.

Adam could tell Yuki was still upset, and he wisely chose not to engage him in conversation. He watched him from the corner of his eye as he stripped beside his bed, slinging off his clothes and shoes in angry gestures, then walked into the bathroom and shut the door.

Adam thought about his brother's corpulent body. It disgusted him, but there was nothing to be said. Yuki wasn't the kind of man interested in staying fit or eating healthy. His wants were few and his ambitions barely above menial positions. If he did not look so much like their maternal grandfather, he would think his mother had mated with a gorilla.

In a good humor about the joke he'd just made, he aimed the remote and turned on the TV before kicking back in bed to wait his turn in the shower.

Shelly was in and out of consciousness but never knew when it was reality and when it was dream-based nightmares. She believed the men who had kidnapped her were hiding now. She felt like if she made a sound, they would come running back in anger and beat her again. It was dark…so dark. Sometimes she heard sounds she recognized, like the pop of a settling building, or a loose piece on the roof above her banging in the wind. If there was wind, that might mean a storm was coming. And planes…all she kept hearing were planes. Some landing, some taking off. She must be near an airport, but where? The wind was stronger now.

If it stormed, maybe it would cool off.

Please find me, Jack. I am so scared.

"Help! Help! Water… Please bring me a drink. I need a drink," she said, mustering all her strength.

It felt like she was screaming, but most of the words were only in her head.

Something dropped from above onto her leg. She screamed and screamed again as she tried to kick it away, but she was tied down so tight all she did was make the cot jump up and down. She was crying again, but quietly. She didn't want the men to see her weakness if they returned.

Then she heard something rustling beneath the cot— like the sound of tiny nails—and thought of rats.

Oh my God! That's what was on my leg!

She screamed again, "Help me! Please help me!"

Then the rustling sound grew louder, then louder still. She heard squeaking, and scrambling, then the sound of ripping paper and more squeaking. Then chewing… gnawing…

She tried so hard to see, but her eyes were so swollen, and it was too dark.

Find me, Jack. Please find me.

The wind was picking up. The loose pieces on the roof were flopping back and forth. Then she heard what sounded like a whisper of flapping wings, then a loud thud, the rapid scramble of things running…and one gut-wrenching squeal. A death scream. Something had died. Thank God it wasn't her.

Jack was riding the Indian from one address to another on the list of Ito's holdings.

He'd searched two warehouses on the list before dark caught him, then rode to the next one on the list beneath streetlights, wondering if this was how Shelly felt as she drove home every night thinking he was dead. The irony of the way fate had switched their places in this nightmare held its own kind of horror.

A streak of lightning flashed again. Jack watched, in awe of the power of the storm to have the energy to produce something like that. And when the shaft of lightning suddenly split into two at the bottom, it felt like the universe was mirroring what was happening to them. He and Shelly had been split apart, and it seemed just as violent.

He'd always thought he'd know if anything ever happened to her, and right now he couldn't feel her life force anywhere. Maybe it was because of the sickening guilt of being too late. He'd known the danger she was in and still hadn't been able to keep her safe.

Was this how Shelly felt when he was missing? Was this dark hole inside of him real, or was it just fear? When she thought he was dead, did she think her life was over? If he lost her, his life would no longer hold meaning.

"I won't believe I was saved just so I could feel what losing you was like. I didn't die. You won't, either. I'll find you, Shelly. Don't give up on me. I will find you or die trying."

* * *

The baby was crying.

Alicia groaned and started to get up when Charlie stopped her.

"Stay here, darling. I'll change him and bring him to you."

"Thank you," Alicia said, and got up to go to the bathroom as Charlie ran across the hall to get the baby.

"Hey, buddy," Charlie said softly, as he picked the baby up and carried him to the changing table.

Little arms flailed in the air. His tiny little feet and legs were in constant motion, making changing a diaper more than a feat of dexterity, especially since there was baby poop to go with it.

Charlie had a strong stomach. He'd smelled dead bodies. Baby poop was nothing. He grabbed a handful of baby wipes and started cleaning him up, talking and laughing, until the baby finally focused on the deep rumble of his father's voice.

"Now that you're clean as a whistle, it's time for a fresh diaper. Hmm, I don't know what to think about these baby critters on here. Not quite what a little man would be wearing, but hey…one of these days you'll be choosing your own duds." He fastened the tabs on the diaper, then laid him back down in bed long enough to bundle him up in his blanket.

"Just like a peanut in a shell," he said, and when he picked him back up, he kissed that little sweet spot behind the baby's ear. "You smell so good, little man. Daddy is the luckiest guy in the world."

He carried him back across the hall to where Alicia had propped herself up against the headboard in a mound of pillows, waiting to let him nurse.

"Your prince awaits," he said, and laid the baby back in her arms.

Charlie stood a few moments, watching the baby latch on and start nursing. The soft shadows thrown by the lamplight fell across mother and child, and for a few moments Charlie felt as if he'd stood this way before, maybe in another lifetime, watching this very same scene, and with the same overwhelming feeling of witnessing a miracle. Being a part of creating new life made him humble, and made everything he did for them worthwhile.

"I'm going to the kitchen. Want anything to drink?" he asked. "Maybe some water?"

"I'm good, darling, but thank you for asking."

Charlie blew her a kiss and then left the bedroom, feeling the cool tiles beneath his bare feet as he moved from room to room.

He couldn't help but think of what Jack must be going through. The last thing he'd heard, they had no leads on Ito, which didn't bode well for Shelly McCann. For all they knew, she may already be dead. But there were search crews still going through property listings. Hopefully they'd know something positive by morning.

Shelly woke up peeing the bed and still unable to move.

There was a moment of pure embarrassment, and then she remembered where she was and why. In the grand scheme of things, a wet bed meant nothing.

She tried to open her eyes, but they were too swollen.

"Help!" she cried, but the word came out like a whisper. Her mouth was so dry and her lips so puffy it felt like they might explode.

Would those men come back? Or had she been left here to die?

"Water, please, I need water," she begged, but no one answered. She had no idea how long she'd been passed out.

She heard the scurry of tiny feet again and knew now it was the rats. The horror of being eaten alive by them was real and she started crying.

"Please, God, don't let this be the way I die. I am asking You to help Jack find me before it's too late."

Then she heard the tiny feet again, scratching, climbing, gnawing. And there was another smell now that hadn't been here before. The smell of death.

That was when she remembered the high-pitched animal scream from last night. Something had died in here. But what was big enough to kill rats, that wouldn't try to kill her, too? The answer was too horrifying to consider.

Then she felt something against her leg, moving down toward her ankle.

"No, oh my God, no," Shelly moaned. "Please don't let this be real. Don't let this be real."

Then something bit her, then bit again, then tried to tear away flesh. Her ankle was on fire, and she was screaming, screaming, screaming. Kicking and jerking, begging and crying.

In the morning, Adam's behavior toward his brother seemed more congenial. They shared breakfast in a good mood and then headed back to the warehouse in comfortable silence.

"Adam, do you think she is alive?" Yuki asked, as they drove toward Houston Hobby Airport.

"I don't know, and if she's not, then she's not."

"We should not have left her alone last night," Yuki added.

Adam laughed. "I have no intention of babysitting someone to keep them alive when I fully intend for her to die anyway. If last night alone in the office didn't kill her, maybe it scared up new information. And if she still tells me the same story, I'll kill her myself."

Yuki looked away.

When they reached the warehouse, Adam gave the code to Yuki to open the doors. Yuki exited the air-conditioned car into the sweltering Houston heat and punched in the code, then stood aside for Adam to drive through.

He heard her screaming even before the doors were open, and the sound curdled the food he'd just eaten. Without waiting for Adam to drive through, Yuki took off running to the old office at the far end of the warehouse and entered to the sight of rats scurrying out of sight. The woman was bleeding from rat bites on her ankles, and she was in true hysterics. What was left of a dead rat was scattered among the opened snacks on the table that Adam brought last night. He didn't know what to say or how to soothe her.

And then Adam pulled up in the car and got out running.

"What happened? What's wrong?"

Yuki pointed at her ankles.

"Rats were all over her." Then he pointed at the table. "And something killed a rat here last night."

Adam grabbed another bottle of water and poured all of it on her face and head. She couldn't breathe without choking, which stopped the screaming. Exactly what Adam had intended.

"I came to talk to you again, Shelly McCann."

She turned her head toward the sound of his voice.

"Drink...need drink," she said.

"Not until we talk."

She turned her head away.

"Where's your husband?"

Her silence angered him. He pinched her breast again to get her attention.

"Drink of water," she whispered.

"If I give you a drink, will you talk to me?" Adam asked.

She turned her head back toward the sound of his voice.

Adam pointed to the case of bottled water. "Would you please give this woman a drink?"

Yuki nodded, relieved that the shouting and beatings weren't happening. He opened a fresh bottle and lifted her head. Shelly drank greedily, choking more than once, desperate to get as much in her before he withheld it again.

"Now then. I did you a favor. You do one for me," Adam said. "Where's your husband?"

"Dead."

He opened his fist and slapped her. It would hurt, but it wouldn't knock her out.

"You lie."

Shelly's mouth was bleeding again. She was crying, but making no sound, and the whole side of her face felt like it was on fire.

"What if he really is?" Yuki asked.

Adam glared at him and, to prove he was the one in charge, slapped her other cheek.

Shelly moaned, turned her head enough to spit out the blood in her mouth.

"Tell me the truth and I'll stop hurting you," Adam said.

"I wouldn't tell you if he was alive," Shelly mumbled. "Beat me until my heart stops."

Adam stood up in a rage. This wasn't going the way he wanted. But after what she'd just said, it made him think McCann was alive. And if he was alive, she needed to be, too.

"Maybe you need to spend another day with the rats. I do not like liars, but apparently these vermin aren't so choosy. You think about it. I may be back later, and I may not."

Then he poured the rest of the bottle in her face and walked out.

Yuki was in a panic. He didn't want to leave her alone with the rats. Now that he'd seen what they did, he didn't think she'd still be alive when they came back.

"Adam, I will stay with her," Yuki said.

Adam stopped, then turned around, staring at his brother in disbelief.

"Look around you!" he shouted. "It is disgusting! You would stay here in this mess with her, rather than go with me?"

"I don't want to stay here, but this mess is yours, not hers. I would not want to live knowing I had let a person die from rat bites."

Adam's face flushed a dark angry red. "What makes you think I'll come back for you?"

Yuki shrugged. "If you don't, then I'll just call the police and save the both of us."

Adam reached behind his back to get his gun, but it wasn't there.

"Looking for this?" Yuki asked, holding up his brother's weapon.

Adam froze. "Give it back," he said.

"You'll get it when you come back for me," Yuki said.

Adam started to charge him, and Yuki calmly pointed the weapon at his brother's head.

"Don't try me. I have a strong sense of self-preservation. I would choose me over you every time."

Adam stopped, then held up his hands.

"Sorry. Lost my cool again. I'll be back around noon. You have water. I'll bring fresh food."

Yuki shrugged. "If you're late, then know I've already called for medical attention for her and turned myself in."

Adam backed away slowly, shaking his head. "You are a coward. You aren't tough enough to be a leader."

"And yet I'm the one with the gun," Yuki said. "Stop insulting me and go fuck yourself. That will take the edge off."

Adam couldn't have been more shocked if Yuki had bitch-slapped him where he stood. He got back in the car and left.

Yuki didn't relax until the doors swung shut, and even then, he ran up front to make sure he saw Adam driving away, before he went back to the office and felt the woman's pulse.

She was still alive.

He wasn't ready to completely defy Adam, but last

night he'd dreamed of being chased by rats. Seeing the truth of what happened when dream became reality had been too much. The least he could do was make sure she wasn't eaten alive.

He wanted to remove all the guts and garbage but had nowhere to put it. But he could get it out from under their noses, so he picked the table up and threw it through the openings where the windows used to be. The water was here. He had a chair in which to sit, but not in these clothes, so he started removing clothing again, beginning with his shirt. He started to remove the undershirt, too, then left it on—not so much for propriety, but to catch the sweat.

He saw the package of paper towels, unwrapped it and tore off a few sheets and then folded them up, soaked them with water and laid them on her forehead, then poured a little bit between her lips.

"Don't die, lady. I don't want you on my conscience."

Jack had ridden the streets of Houston all night, even when it was raining, chasing down the addresses on the list, then searching the premises of each one for signs of habitation. There were a few that were being used as legitimate businesses, and short of setting off security alarms, he was going to have to leave those to the police. He swung by his place long enough to shower and get into dry clothes before going back out again. He put his phone on the charger and started a pot of coffee before going to shower. Less than an hour later, he was ready to pick up where he left off.

He took his phone off the charger, dropped it in the outer pocket of his jacket and put his Glock in the shoul-

der holster. He was on the way down to get the motorcycle when his cell phone rang. It was Charlie.

"Hey, Jack! I'm on my way to the office and just
got a call from Fred. One of the search crews thinks
they've got a lead. They are on their way to a property
on the east side of the city. Two stoners were spending
the night in an empty building and said they heard a
woman crying but couldn't find her. They called it in,
and the cops are already on the scene looking. I'll let
you know if we find her."

"I'm already on the move. What's the address?"

Charlie told him.

"I'll meet you there," Jack said, and accelerated. It
was their first break in the search.

Twelve

It took Jack almost forty minutes before he rolled up on the search in progress and saw both the Houston PD and the FBI were on the scene. When he realized it was an abandoned hotel, the scope of the search just got bigger. He parked in front of one of the Bureau's SUVs and flashed his badge at a couple of officers standing guard at the entrance.

"Who's in charge?" he asked.

"You guys are," the officer said. "Special Agent Warren is in the lobby."

"Thanks," Jack said, and saw Nolan Warren almost immediately.

Nolan looked up, saw the stranger coming toward him and frowned.

"You're not allowed to—"

"Nolan, it's me, Jack."

Nolan did a double take. "Whoa! I did not see you in that face."

"That is the idea," Jack said. "What do you know? How many floors in this building?"

"Fifteen floors, six hundred and twenty-five rooms. They're less than halfway done."

"I want to help. Where can I start?"

"Feds started at the top and are working their way down. PD began at the bottom and are working their way up. We're on the twelfth floor. I'll radio them to let you know—"

Before he finished what he was saying, one of the search teams suddenly checked in.

"Search to Command Post. Come in!"

"This is Command. Go ahead."

"We found a woman on eight. She's too old and she's homeless, so she's not your missing woman, but she's ambulatory and we're coming down."

"Ten-four. Command out," Nolan said, and then looked at Jack. "Dammit. I'm sorry. I was so hoping this—"

Jack was too disappointed to comment. He just turned around and walked out of the building, got back on the Indian and took off for the next address on the list. He kept telling himself it didn't mean she was gone. It just meant she was somewhere else.

And so the morning went. Jack rode from property to property, marking them off after he'd searched, and moving to the next, and the shorter the list became, the more desperate he felt.

Noon came and went, and the heat continued to rise. He kept bottles of water in his pack, and around 3:00 p.m., he finally stopped long enough to get something to eat.

The food was tasteless and every bite stuck in his throat. He finally gave up, threw the rest of it away and got back on the Indian. He put on the helmet and fired up the engine.

Fear rode behind him.

Panic sat on his shoulders.

But quitting wasn't an option.

"Don't give up on me, baby. I haven't given up on you."

Adam came back to the old warehouse with food at straight-up noon. Yuki heard the car circling the building and grimaced. Just like his brother to leave him guessing. He got here on time, but not a moment early.

He glanced at the woman as he stood up. The hotter it got, the weaker she had become. Despite the water he had poured down her throat and on her, she'd passed out almost two hours ago and he hadn't been able to rouse her since. He was afraid for her. Adam would kill her if she didn't tell him what he wanted to know, or she would die anyway before he got the chance. He watched the car coming into the warehouse and Adam getting out to shut the door behind him.

When Adam realized Yuki was watching him, he stopped in midstep and stared back, expecting Yuki to be the one to look away first. But he didn't move.

Adam got back in the car, aimed the car right at the office and stomped the accelerator. The SUV fishtailed, leaving rubber on the concrete floor as he raced toward them.

Yuki's heart began to pound. What was this crazy man trying to do—kill them? What would he gain if they were dead? He wanted to run, but something told him that showing fear was exactly what Adam wanted to see, and so he stood in the doorway with his hands in his pockets, calmly watching the event unfold.

Adam was aimed straight at his brother and expect-

ing him to panic, to run, or at the least get out of the
way. But he didn't, and Adam was forced to turn away
at the very last moments, which sent his car into a spin.
He hit the brakes, leaving dark stripes on the concrete
floor and the scent of burning rubber in the air.

When the car finally quit spinning, Adam got out
with a sack of burgers and cold beers and stomped toward the office. It took everything he had not to throw
the food at Yuki.

"Why didn't you move?" Adam shouted.

Yuki made himself look surprised. "What? Move?
You mean you were actually going to run me over?"

Adam sighed. He'd asked that wrong, and now anything he said would make him the stupid one.

"I brought burgers and beer—the dark ales that you
like."

Yuki smiled. "Thank you, brother! That was very
thoughtful of you."

Adam handed him the sack and two bottles of beer.
"The woman…has she said anything more?"

Yuki shook his head. "I kept giving her water, even
pouring it on her, too, but she's really out of it and hasn't
regained consciousness in over two hours. Look at her.
As hot as it is and she's barely sweating. I think she's
dying, Adam."

Adam ran toward her, grabbed her by the shoulders
and started shaking her, then slapped her face on one
side, and then on the other, but there was no response.
He glanced down at the rat bites on her legs. They were
red and looked like they were getting infected. Her eyes
were swollen shut and her lips were twice the normal
size and glued shut with dry blood. Even the cut down

the middle of her chest had caked. Yuki was right. She looked bad.

"This pisses me off," he muttered.

"You beat her," Yuki said. "What did you expect?"

The hair rose on the back of Adam's neck as he turned and stared at his brother. Yuki had grease from one of the burgers running down the side of his mouth, and a splotch of mayo and tomato had fallen onto his sweat-stained undershirt. The gun Yuki had taken without his knowledge was lying on the window ledge, and he could see the package of toilet paper had been opened. He didn't want to know where he'd taken a dump, but guessed he had.

He didn't understand this man. At all. And he damn sure didn't like him. What was that saying that Mahalo Jones used to say? Oh yes. Worthless as tits on a boar hog. That was Yuki.

And then all of a sudden, the whole filthy scenario disgusted him. He couldn't stand being in this building, with these weak people, for one more minute.

He walked over to the ledge, picked up his gun and shot his brother in the back of the head. Yuki fell face forward onto the floor near the cot, his body completely still.

Adam hovered over him for a moment but couldn't muster any feelings of regret or sorrow. He was merely relieved not to have to listen to his brother's nagging anymore. Lifting the gun once more, he pointed it at the woman passed out in the cot. He held his aim for at least a minute before he lowered the gun again.

"No. Killing you would be a kindness, and I do not feel kindly toward you," he said. Adam turned and left the warehouse without even a glimpse back at his brother's dead body. He got back in the car, drove out the front gate and never looked back. Between the heat and the varmints, he felt confident there wouldn't be any bodies left to find.

He glanced at the time. It was almost 1:00 p.m. as he headed back to the apartment to pack his things. He needed a new place to hide, but the usual traffic delayed him. By the time he arrived, it was almost three.

He grabbed his suitcase and started packing up his things, making sure he left nothing of himself behind. He went through the rooms, one by one, picking up a nail clipper here and a tin of breath mints there. He made his bed, took all of the wet towels and washcloths into the bathroom Yuki had used, and made it appear as if only one man had been in residence.

There was that six-month lease that he'd signed to get the place, but it was under the name Lee Tanaka, so he still felt somewhat anonymous.

Now he had to decide what he wanted to do. Since it appeared Jack McCann was really dead, and his wife about to be, his business in Houston was over. Tomorrow, he'd book a flight back to Japan, but not to Toyko. That was too close to home. He needed time and distance to figure out how he would go about destroying the cartel, and he needed to switch out the license tag on his vehicle, just in case that witness had seen it.

But what he did want tonight was a woman. Ling was his favorite. He needed to place an order before it got any later, and he made a call to Angelique.

"PreJean Escorts, Angelique speaking."

"Hello, Angelique, this is Adam Ito."

"Mr. Ito. It is always good to hear your voice. How can I be of service?"

"I want Ling tonight."

"Oh, I'm sorry, Mr. Ito, but she's on a date. Would you like another girl?"

"No. I want Ling."

Angelique stifled a groan. "Please, Mr. Ito. You know I don't send my girls out on two dates the same day. She is free tomorrow afternoon until the next day. Could we set that date for you instead?"

"Nine p.m. tonight. Five thousand dollars."

"You are very persuasive. I will make an exception this time, but this time only. Shall we deliver her to a specific place?" Angelique asked.

"Yes, but my estate is not available for guests at this time. Take her to the alternate address. You know, the one on the outskirts of Pasadena."

"Yes, of course. I have the address right here," she said, and quoted a street and house number.

"Yes, that's the one. Ling knows. Nine o'clock tonight and prompt."

"Yes, sir," Angelique said. "Will there be anything else?"

"No," Adam said, and disconnected.

He grabbed his things and walked out, leaving the apartment unlocked and the key on the floor by the door.

It was after seven when Jack unlocked the door to his apartment and walked inside. He'd been to every address on that list without a hint of the possibility that Ito had even been there. He was sick at heart and scared. The day had been sweltering and it was still like a sauna, even in the shade. But clouds were building up on the horizon. Likely it would rain sometime tonight, and on the way here, he'd had an idea. It was a wild shot, but worth the try. And, if he caught the woman in the right mood, there was a good chance she could help him pinpoint Adam Ito's current location. He made the call, then leaned back against the table as he listened to it ring.

Angelique PreJean had been born in a pirogue beneath a three-quarter moon down in a Louisiana bayou. Her daddy had been poling as fast as he could, but her mama's time to birth her hadn't been waiting on home and a bed. The story went that she came out of her mama's womb so quiet that they thought she was dead. But when they looked down and saw her eyes wide-open and staring up into the dark, star-studded heaven, they cried from the relief. Her daddy cut the cord with his fish-skinning knife and her mama tied the knot, then held the bloody baby against her breasts.

"Take us home, *Prayjohn*," she'd whispered.

Francois PreJean had smiled. He loved the way Carla said his name…all soft-like, in the proper French way.

"What do we name her?" Carla had asked.

"Angelique, ma chère, because she is an angel to me."

"Then Angelique it is," Carla had said, and held her first child just a little bit closer.

Forty years of a hard life later, Angelique PreJean's inauspicious entry into this world hadn't stopped her from garnering something of a reputation. She ran an escort service in Houston for the rich and famous, and knew many people on both sides of the law.

When her phone rang and came up with an Unknown on her caller ID, she answered with caution.

"Hello?"

"Angelique, this is Jack McCann."

She breathed an easy sigh of relief. They had no quarrel with each other.

"Jack McCann, what is it that brings you to make this call?"

"I need a favor. Adam Ito is one of your clients, yes?"

Angelique frowned. "You know I don't divulge my clients' names."

"These aren't normal circumstances. He kidnapped my wife yesterday. You and I both know he will torture her before he kills her. I love her, Angelique. With all my heart. And any information you have might help me save her. Please, don't make me have to bury her."

It was the fear and passion in his voice that touched her most.

"Yes, he is a client."

Jack exhaled slowly. "Okay. When was the last time he called you?"

"Not too long ago, actually."

"What did he want?"

"A date with Ling," Angelique said.

"When and where is this date taking place?"

"He has a place…like a bunker beneath a property he owns. Ling says it is quite beautiful. They are meeting there tonight at nine."

"How does she get into this bunker?" Jack asked.

"The property…the building, is a small, modest home. One bedroom, one bath. He had the bunker built belowground in the backyard, but the entrance is inside the house. He often uses it for his little parties. The entrance is inside the bedroom closet. Twist the clothes rod. After the door opens there are stairs, but move quickly. I would assume he has security cameras, too, since he has all that other security set up. But hear me say this… Ling says no one can go in before Ito is on the premises. I guess there's some kind of a booby trap. She is free to enter the house only at her appointed times."

"Do you know the address?"

"Of course. My driver takes girls there on a regular basis." She told him the address and then sighed. "This mess is going to cost me five thousand dollars."

"My wife is my life. I will give you five thousand dollars for this information," Jack said.

Angelique's eyes welled. She'd lost a chance to be loved like this.

"No. A life is worth far more than any amount of money. I am ashamed I even mentioned it. Mr. Ito does not tolerate anyone being late. If you are lucky, he won't know it isn't Ling arriving until you are in the bunker."

"Thank you. Your help means more to me than you will ever know."

"Go with God, Jack McCann."

And the line went dead.

Jack dropped the phone back in his pocket. He was grateful for the information, but frustrated he couldn't go any earlier. The longer it took to find Ito, the more danger Shelly was in.

Rats had already been through the food that had been thrown out of the office. But they kept coming, because they smelled blood. Yuki's blood.

It was a blessing for Shelly that she didn't know it, even though it was Yuki's dead body that was saving her from them.

Only rarely did she surface from the darkness that

held her down, and when she did rise above it, she was out of her head from the growing fever and pain.

While the heat began to fade with the setting sun, even the doors Adam Ito had left open didn't help the cloying, airless feel inside the building.

An owl perched high in the rafters didn't mind the weather. It was eyeing the buffet of rats below, and the lack of ceiling between them. The owl stayed motionless, watching for the right moment to go in for another kill. But it was hunger and the easy prey below that overrode its wariness to fly into an enclosure. The owl aimed for the rats as it came off the rafters, soaring silently with talons outstretched, and swooped down amid them. The owl's talons curled into the spine of the rat it just caught, piercing the body and breaking the bones in its back. Once again, the rat's final death squeaks sent the others scrambling for cover, running deep into the darkness, back into the rubble.

Shelly was spared the frantic squeaks and the death throes of the owl's catch tonight, as well as the disemboweling of its prey. She was somewhere between worlds, unaware of the angels around her bed, waiting to see if she chose to stay, or chose to go. And then the sun finally dropped below the horizon, putting an end to this day.

Charlie had been at the computer all afternoon updating the files from the hotel search, and coordinating the agents' continuing searches of Ito's properties from the office. Every time a team of searchers cleared a property again, they sent in the information and he recorded the time and charted it.

Knowing Jack was alive was nothing short of a

miracle. Nolan told him the story of Jack showing up at the search site, and then leaving within minutes of his arrival. Charlie regretted the fact that he hadn't seen him. Nolan couldn't quit talking about what he'd done to disguise himself. He couldn't wait to hear the details, but Shelly's kidnapping had put a damper on any joy he might have had at hearing about Jack. He kept thinking about that bust. It should not have gone down like that. He was entering the last of the data for the day when he got a phone call from Alicia.

"Hey, babe," he said, as he answered the call.

"Hi, honey. I have a favor to ask. Would you please stop at the store on your way home and bring home a carton of cream? I'm making Stroganoff and need it to finish off the sauce."

"Yes, and yum," Charlie said. "How's Johnny?"

"Sleeping. He's been such a good baby today."

Charlie couldn't wait to get home and hold him. "Takes after his old man."

Alicia laughed. "That's possible. You're really good at sleeping, too."

Charlie grinned. "Guilty. So, I'm about ready to leave. Trust that your carton of cream is on the way."

"Thank you so much. Love you and drive carefully," Alicia said.

"Will do, and I love you, too."

Charlie was still smiling when he logged off. Unless they got a break in the case and Ito was located tonight, he got to spend the whole evening with his two favorite people.

Jack found the house just before 8:00 p.m., then circled the blocks around it, looking for a place to wait.

He guessed that Adam Ito was already there, but there was no way he could test the theory, so he was forced to wait another hour. He chose the parking lot of a small strip mall nearby and settled down to wait.

His heartbeat accelerated as it always did when something was about to go down. He patted the feel of his shoulder holster through the jacket to make sure the Glock was there. He had already checked it at the apartment to make sure it was loaded, and he had a couple of backup clips in an inner pocket to go with it. He had a length of rope and a roll of duct tape, and if he needed anything else, he would improvise.

His shoulder was aching. He'd been on the bike too long. He rolled his shoulder muscles to ease the tension. The next time he checked his watch, a wave of relief washed through him.

It was time.

He started the engine and headed back to the neighborhood, making the ride back with a couple of minutes to spare. He eased off on the throttle as he rolled up behind Ito's car, and was on the porch in seconds, entering the house through the unlocked door. With only four rooms, there was no searching to be done. The bedroom was down a small hall and across from the only bathroom. He ran into the bedroom and then into the closet, grabbed the clothes rod and twisted it, but nothing happened.

"Son of a bitch," he muttered, then thought to turn it in the opposite direction.

The moment he did, a door swung inward at the back of the closet. He palmed the Glock, took it off safety and took the steps down two at a time. He was half expecting Ito to be waiting for him below with some kind of weapon, but there was no one there, and he was hearing music instead. After a quick survey of his surroundings, he moved through the rooms, following the sound.

Adam was anticipating Ling's approach. She always chose a new way to excite him, and he had prepared accordingly. He was nude and facedown on the massage table, wanting that rush of lust—that moment of what the French called "the little death"—when he was no longer in control. It was a weakness—a release that he rarely allowed himself to experience. But the tension within him was overwhelming. He needed this.

A tiny alarm went off on the table beside him. It was time. When he heard the door open, his body physically tensed with excitement.

So, my beauty, prompt as always, he thought to himself.

He heard footsteps behind him and shivered in anticipation. "Hurry," he said aloud.

"As you wish," Jack said, and hit him over the back of the head with the butt of his pistol, sending Adam's world into darkness.

Adam woke as a great gush of water hit him square in the face. He was blinking trying to clear his vision when he realized he was in the kitchen by the sink, tied to one of his own wooden dining chairs with his arms secured behind him. But when he saw Jack McCann standing in front of him with a Glock pointed right between his eyes, he crowed.

"You're alive! Oh, that bitch! No matter how many times I threatened and asked her, she swore you were dead. But I knew it—I knew she was lying."

The thought of what Shelly must have endured every time she told him "no" made Jack sick. And the asshole just howled about it. Without thinking, he lowered the gun and fired a bullet straight through Adam Ito's right foot and into the floor, cutting through his flesh like a hot knife through butter.

Blood splattered. Bones shattered.

The shriek that came up Ito's throat was ear-splitting.

Jack stuffed a kitchen towel into Adam's mouth and then leaned down until they were eye to eye.

"Where is my wife?" Jack asked.

Adam shook his head, and when Jack pulled the towel out of his mouth, he moaned.

"I asked you a question," Jack said.

Adam raised his head and then grinned.

Without hesitation, Jack aimed the Glock at Adam's other foot and fired a second shot.

Again, flesh parted for the hot lead, revealing shattered bones and adding more blood to the pool beneath his chair.

The shock on Adam's face morphed to a horrified grimace as he screamed—adding shriek after shriek as his body began to shake from the pain.

Jack watched the blood running across the floor toward the corner of the room. He stuck the towel back in Adam's mouth, waiting until his shouts died down to moans.

"Where is my wife?" he repeated, removing the towel.

Adam's chin dropped to his chest. He kept shaking his head back and forth like a bull trying to work up the courage to charge.

Jack put the gun against his right knee and fired again, and Adam's body jerked as if he'd been electrocuted.

"Tell me where my wife is *now*, or I will gut you where you sit and leave you to die here, naked, alone and pathetic."

Adam shook his head. "You murder me and you'll never find her!" he cried.

Jack pulled his knife and slit the end of Ito's ear.

"And no one will find you, either," Jack said calmly. "You will rot here. The Feds will think you escaped, and the world will forget you. Tell me where my wife is, or your balls are next."

Adam looked down at his naked body, then at the blood beneath his feet.

"If I tell, you'll just kill me anyway, won't you?" he asked.

"Only one way to find out. Is Shelly alive?" Jack asked, and aimed the gun at Adam's nude crotch.

And that was the moment Adam Ito knew that if he didn't cooperate, his life was over.

"No! No! Don't—don't shoot," he screamed. "She was alive when I left."

"Where is she?"

Adam only moaned.

Jack put the muzzle of the gun against Adam's penis and Adam immediately started talking.

"In an empty warehouse near Houston Hobby Airport. There's a long chain-link fence separating the warehouse area from the runways, and the warehouse she's in has a Hostess Twinkies logo painted on the side of the building. Now, call an ambulance for me."

"You get nothing until I find her. And if she's dead, so are you. If she's alive, I'll send the Feds here to collect you. Don't bleed to death while I'm gone, because if she's not there, I'm going to come back, and if you're not already dead, you're going to wish you were."

Jack punched Adam in the face hard enough to knock him out, then grabbed his helmet and ran back up the steps. He reset the secret door and ran out of the house. Seconds later he was on his bike, heading to Houston Hobby.

He knew the Feds could beat him to the site, but if she wasn't there, then they'd take possession of Ito, and wherever Shelly was, she would die. He needed to make sure she was where Ito said she was before he called in the cavalry.

He'd put his job before Shelly for the very last time.

Thirteen

It was dark now, and yet Jack rode through traffic like a madman—weaving his way in and out of the cars, risking everything as he flew through intersections. Once he got on the 610 Loop, he opened up the Indian, and then everything around him became a blur of lights. Every heartbeat he prayed a mantra. *She's alive. She's alive.* He needed to believe that, if he gave that intention to the universe, then it would be so.

Just when he was beginning to think he'd never get there, he saw the exit sign to the airport. He shifted lanes and then rode the shoulder of the highway, passing traffic as if it were standing still. He slipped off the Loop onto the exit ramp and shot down the incline, downshifted gears and began passing any car that was in his way until he finally saw the buildings in the distance beyond the runways. But how the hell did he get to them?

Fate answered as he rode up on an open gate and shot through it without stopping. It took him straight onto the blacktop running parallel to a couple of miles of chain-link fencing. The runway lights beyond the fences were bright enough that he could see the buildings, but none of them had any kind of Hostess Twinkies logo painted on the side.

Then he rode up on a property at the same time he saw the logo and took the turn into it in a slide, righted the bike and accelerated.

As he neared the building, he began to worry. He didn't see any open doors, but his headlights did flash on a gravel road that appeared to encircle the building. He took it fast, sending gravel flying in his wake, and the moment he turned the corner, he saw the huge doors open to the night, just like Ito said they would be.

"Please, God, let her be here," he said, and rode straight into the warehouse.

At first he saw nothing but what was directly lit by the headlights on his bike. He braked for a few seconds to survey the area, then began slowly riding the bike around the interior. It wasn't until he turned a corner and headed to the other end of the building that his headlights flashed on some kind of structure. He accelerated, and as he rode up to it, he aimed his headlights into the interior before he dismounted. He toed down the kickstand, leaving it idling as he ran inside.

He saw a man's body on the floor, rats crawling all over it, unbothered by the light and sound cast from his bike. The he saw Shelly on the cot and screamed out in horror and rage.

Rats began scattering at his approach, but not fast enough. He sent one flying with a kick of his boot, which aided in the others' rapid disappearance.

The headlights from his bike illuminated the worst of her injuries, and she was so hurt he was afraid to touch her. When he felt for a pulse at the base of her neck and it was there, a faint but steady throb, he choked on a sob. Now he had to get her free.

Something squeaked in the dark behind him, but he ignored it as he began cutting away at the ropes.

"Shelly, it's me, Jack! I found you, baby. Stay with me. Stay with me. I'll get you out of here."

A few quick slashes and her hands were free, then he freed her legs. Rage billowed inside him when he touched the bloody cut down the middle of her chest. If he'd known what Ito had done to her, he would have killed him where he sat.

He felt the heat of her body, but the fact that she was no longer sweating scared him. She was so dehydrated that there wasn't enough water left in her body to sweat. He pulled out his phone and dialed 911.

As soon as the dispatcher had the location, Jack began grabbing unopened bottles of water and poured the first one all over her face, then down her neck and all the way down the bloody cut. Then he opened another bottle and lifted her head a few inches before he put the bottle to her lips.

"Shelly, it's water. Swallow it, baby!" He let a few drops trickle into her mouth, but they ran back out.

"Please, God, help me," he whispered, and then held the bottle to her lips again. "Shelly, it's Jack. Open your mouth and swallow." He let a few more drops trickle in and thought he saw her throat move. "One more time, sweetheart…for me. It's water. Swallow it."

And this time when he poured in a few drops, her mouth opened and she drank.

"That's my girl! Here's some more," he said, and poured a little more into her mouth, making sure she didn't choke.

When he laid her back down to get another bottle, he heard something scurrying beneath the cot, and so did she. She let out a scream that would haunt him for the rest of his life, and that was when he knew she'd been terrorized by more than Adam Ito in this dump.

"I'm here, baby. You're safe now," he said, and picked her up in his arms and carried her out of that room, away from the rats, the decomposing body and the stench.

He got on the bike with her, then draped her upper body across his left arm and the handlebars, and the rest of her across his lap, letting her legs dangle as he rode with her toward the doorway.

As he neared the opening, the faint sound of sirens could be heard. Clearing the doors, he rolled out into the night and looked up just as the first flash of lightning from the approaching thunderstorm streaked across the sky. The storm was coming, but so was help. The sirens were getting louder and louder.

He needed to notify the Bureau about Adam Ito, and as soon as he had her safely balanced across his lap and her head pillowed against his shoulder, he made the call.

Charlie was holding his son when his phone began to vibrate, and when he recognized the number, he quickly answered.

"Jack?"

"I found her," Jack said. "She's alive but in bad shape. I'm waiting on an ambulance, so I'm giving you a heads-up that if the Bureau wants Adam Ito alive, they need to rescue him fast."

"What the hell happened?" Charlie asked.

"He needed persuading. I left him bleeding."

"Shit, Jack…"

"No...he's the shit in this scenario. He's at a place he calls his bunker, so—"

"I'm on it!" Charlie said. "You go take care of Shelly. I'll catch up with you later."

Lightning flashed again—this time a little closer.

And just like that, the breath left Jack's body, his heart pounding so fast he thought he might die.

There were tears in his eyes as he pulled up his Contacts and then hit Call on yet another number that was answered on the second ring.

"Hello?"

"Deputy Director Wainwright, this is Jack McCann."

"Jack! I heard the good news that you are alive. We are all elated."

"Yes, sir, and thank you, but we have a problem."

The delight in Arch Wainwright's voice shifted to all business.

"What's going on?"

"My wife was kidnapped from our home yesterday afternoon by Adam Ito and his brother. I've been looking for her ever since. I found Ito first and persuaded him to tell me where she was. I just found her, and the body of Ito's brother beside the cot she was on. She's alive but in serious condition. An ambulance is on the way. I can hear the sirens, but I already called my contact, Charlie Morris, and told him I had found Ito."

"Wonderful! I'll check in...but I'm sure he's already working on getting him into custody."

"No, sir... I don't think he is."

"What are you saying?" Wainwright asked.

"I told him he needed to get to Ito fast, because he might not be alive and that he was bleeding when I left him. I told Charlie that if the Bureau wanted him alive, they better hurry. I told him Ito was in a place he called 'his bunker,' when Charlie suddenly interrupted me, said he'd get right on it and hung up."

"I'm sorry. I'm not following you," Wainwright said.

"I've already reported to Charlie that there is a leak in our Bureau and how I knew it. But when I called Charlie just now, I did not give him an address for Ito's location. He should have no way of knowing the address of that bunker, because that address is not on the list of properties we have. Unless he's affiliated with Ito, he should not know where that bunker is. I'm telling you now that if Ito isn't dead when Charlie gets there, he'll be dead by the time our Bureau boys show. Charlie has been my best friend for years, but…I can't deny how this looks. I strongly suspect he's the leak—the leak that nearly got me killed, and the reason my wife was kidnapped. Stop him."

"Give me that address," Wainwright said, and Jack did, along with the instructions on how to access the bunker. "I hope you're wrong," Wainwright said. "But this shit doesn't go unpunished on my watch. I'll be in touch."

"Thank you, sir," Jack said, then looked up just as the ambulance took the turn into the gate, spotlighting Jack and Shelly in the oncoming headlights.

The ambulance came to a sliding stop, and then paramedics seemed to spill out of the ambulance from every direction. Behind them, a police car raced through the gate, coming toward them with lights and siren.

The paramedics took Shelly from Jack's arms and laid her down onto the gurney. Jack leaped off his bike and followed them as they pushed her toward the back of the ambulance.

Just before they put her in the ambulance, Jack leaned down and whispered near her ear.

"You're safe, baby. I'll see you at the hospital. I love you so much, and everything's going to be okay."

Then the paramedics lifted her and the gurney into the ambulance so they could assess her beneath the lights.

"What happened to her?" one asked, as another was trying to put in an IV. But she was so dehydrated they couldn't find a vein. They started looking for one down around her ankle when they saw the infected wounds.

"What the hell is this?" the paramedic asked.

"Rat bites," Jack said. "Her name is Shelly McCann. She was kidnapped yesterday evening. I'm her husband, FBI Special Agent Jack McCann. I just found her. Where are you taking her?"

"Memorial Hermann Southeast Hospital on Astoria."

The paramedic tried her arm again for the IV and then suddenly shouted. "I got a vein! Load up. We can move."

"I'll be right behind you," Jack said, and ran back to his bike as a cop approached him.

"What happened here?" the cop asked.

Jack pulled his badge.

"I'm Special Agent Jack McCann. That's my wife in the ambulance that just left. She was kidnapped yesterday afternoon from our home. There is a dead man inside the warehouse at the far end."

"Did you kill him?" the cop asked.

"No. He's been dead for hours. Rats were all over him when I got here. I'm guessing his brother did it."

"His brother?"

Jack sighed. "Look, it's all part of an ongoing FBI case, although I understand the dead body being found on this property falls under your jurisdiction. I have to get to the hospital. If you want answers, call Deputy Director Wainwright at the State Office of the FBI. I'll be at Memorial Hermann Southeast…on Astoria."

He took off after the ambulance as the cop ran back to his car and drove inside the warehouse, then down to the office. One look inside and he was back in the cruiser, calling dispatch to notify Homicide that they had a new crime scene.

Charlie was already gathering up his weapon and his ID to head out when Alicia returned.

"I put Johnny down. What's happening?" she said.

"Jack found Shelly. They're on the way to the hospital. I've got to call in the crew so we can pick up Adam Ito. I don't know when I'll be back, but I think this is finally winding down."

"Be so careful," Alicia said.

Charlie wrapped his arms around her and pulled her close.

"I love you so much," he whispered. "You and Johnny are my world. I don't ever plan for trouble, but just know that if anything ever does happen to me, I've made sure you two will be fine, money-wise. The info is in our safety deposit box."

"Don't talk like that," Alicia said. "You'll be fine. Johnny and I need you, okay?"

He leaned down and kissed her, then moments later he was out the door. He took off toward Pasadena. As soon as he made a quick reconnoiter, he'd call in the troops.

It was pain that shifted Adam from an unconscious state to being alert with pure fear. He knew from the looks of his feet and knee that if he lived through this, he might not walk again. He had never been this afraid. Not even standing before his father and the cartel thinking they would kill him. It was eye-opening to be on the other side of violence. Before, he had dished it out, but now he knew what it was like to receive it.

He rocked back and forth in the chair, moaning beneath his breath as wave after wave of pain rolled through him until there was no beginning and no end. He didn't know what he wanted more—for the Feds to come save him or to let him die. What he did know was that he didn't want to see Jack McCann's face again. Adam's only hope at survival was McCann finding his woman alive.

He tried to think of something else besides the pain and focused on the faucet over the sink. It leaked. He began watching the drips, counting the time between each one. He was getting weaker. Losing too much blood. He was wishing for a drink—a drink and pain pills, lots of pain pills—as the room began to spin, when he suddenly thought he heard footsteps coming down the stairs. For a moment, the steps ceased, and then started moving again. The fact that there was only one set of footsteps was bad news. The Feds came in packs. Oh hell, McCann was back.

And then a man he didn't know walked into the kitchen, and he saw a ray of hope.

"Please help me. I've been robbed," Adam said. "Untie me and call an ambulance. I need to go to the hospital."

The man didn't comment. He just kept staring, almost as if he wasn't sure what he was going to do.

Adam moaned. "I hurt…so bad. Have mercy."

The man pulled a weapon from a shoulder holster beneath his jacket.

"What the hell?" Adam shrieked. "I don't even know you."

"Uh, no, you *do* know me, and that's the trouble here."

It was the voice that gave him away. "You!" Adam gasped. "How did you know this was here?"

"I know everything about you," Charlie said. "And yes, it's me. You weren't supposed to get away. You were supposed to go to prison along with everyone else, which would have put an end to our tenuous relationship. I wanted out and arresting you was tying up loose ends."

"Who are you?" Adam asked.

Before Charlie Morris could answer, a team of FBI agents swarmed in behind him, with Deputy Director Wainwright in the lead.

Charlie sputtered as the deputy director issued an order.

"Agent Warren, go back up and get the paramedics. Tell them the site is cleared and safe to proceed."

Warren was staring at Charlie as if he'd never seen him before, and Charlie was in shock. This shouldn't be happening. And then he saw the looks on the other agents' faces and gave in to the bone-deep misery of knowing it was over.

"How did you know?" he asked.

"Jack figured it out," Wainwright said. "You didn't wait to ask for an address to this place when you hung up on him. The only way you'd know where it was is if you're the leak…the man connected to Adam Ito."

"Tell him I'm sorry," Charlie said, and before he could be disarmed, he put the gun to his head and pulled the trigger.

Chaos erupted.

* * *

Jack rolled up to the ER entrance in front of a security guard and parked off to the side of the doorway.

"Hey, you can't park there," the guard yelled.

Jack flashed his badge. "FBI," he said. "That was my wife they brought in."

The guard waved him through, but Jack was already inside with his helmet in one hand and his badge clutched in the other as he ran up to the desk.

"Shelly McCann. Where did they take her?" he asked, and flashed the badge.

The receptionist checked her computer. "Exam room five," she said, and then pointed at the double doors. "That way."

Jack could hear someone crying as he entered the ward. He knew without asking that it was Shelly and started running.

He entered as they were trying to take blood. A nurse was trying to hold her shoulders, and the lab tech was struggling to get a needle in her arm. It was obvious that she was disoriented and afraid. He pushed past the nurse trying to hold her down and glared at the lab tech.

"Both of you! Just a second, dammit."

He sat down on the side of the bed and gently lifted her from the bed into his arms.

"Hey, baby, it's me, Jack. You're in a hospital. You're safe."

She was still sobbing and trying to talk, but her words were unintelligible.

"I know, I know," he said, and started rocking her. "I caught the bad man. I saw the rats. I know what he did to you. I'm so sorry. I'm so, so sorry."

She kept shaking and clutching at his clothes and

feeling for hair that was missing and feeling a beard that didn't used to be there. It sounded like Jack, but she couldn't see him and couldn't believe he was real.

"Jack?" she kept saying.

"Yes, Shelly, it's me."

"Jack? My Jack?"

Tears were rolling down his face and he didn't know it.

"Yes, your Jack…forever yours."

Then she went limp in his arms. "I didn't tell," she said softly.

Jack laid his head against her hair. "I know. You are the bravest woman in the whole world. The lab tech needs to take a blood sample to help you get well. Is that okay with you?"

"I can't see. You see for me," she mumbled.

"I'm looking right at him and he looks like a very nice man." Jack saw the name tag on his lab coat. "His name is Justin." Then Jack gave the lab tech a pointed look. "She's dehydrated. The medics had a hard time finding a vein in her arm."

Justin nodded, then started talking.

"Shelly, I'm Justin. I've been a lab tech for almost fifteen years. My hair is growing gray and I'm a bit overweight, but I do know my stuff. I'm going to put this band around your arm for just a minute to see if we can find a vein. If not, we'll try elsewhere. So there will be a little stick. I will try my very best not to cause you more pain."

She pressed her face against Jack's chest. "You're watching?"

"I'm watching," Jack said.

"Okay," she said, and didn't move.

A few moments later, a doctor walked in. He eyed

the lab tech and motioned for him to continue, then focused on Jack.

"I'm Dr. Habib."

"I'm Jack McCann, Shelly's husband. What can you tell us?"

"I just saw her X-rays. She has a cracked rib and a concussion. She is very dehydrated. The good news is that the cut on her chest is shallow enough that it will heal without stitches. As soon as we get the area cleaned up, we'll glue it together. She has rat bites, so we'll clean and treat them accordingly. She has a couple of loose teeth, but I think they will reseat themselves. We also need to put some stitches in her upper and lower lip."

Shelly shuddered.

Jack kept rubbing her arm in a slow, gentle motion. She was silent, so horribly silent, and he wondered if she was reliving how she got the injuries as the doctor named them.

"I wanted to ask if there was anything in her medical history that we should know," Dr. Habib said.

"She had a severe heatstroke when she was younger, and has never been able to tolerate extreme heat since," Jack said.

The doctor nodded thoughtfully. "Yes, that is good to know. We'll start pumping fluids and keep an eye on her organs."

Jack wasn't satisfied. "What about her eyes…and her face? Her jaw isn't broken, right?"

"No bones broken in her face, but she was badly beaten, as you can see. We'll have to wait and see about her eyes as the swelling goes down, and as soon as we get her mouth stitched up, we will be admitting her, at least for a day or so."

"Okay," Jack said, "but I'm requesting a private room with a place for me to sleep. I'm not leaving her alone again."

Dr. Habib didn't hesitate. "I will let them know. I was filling in at ER for a colleague tonight, so she will still be my patient in the morning as I resume my normal duties. I make rounds in the mornings around seven." He moved a little closer to Shelly and gently touched her hand. "Shelly, you will be safe here. I am so sorry about what happened, but we're going to take good care of you."

She didn't answer, but she also didn't flinch from his touch.

"Thank you, Doctor. How about pain meds?" Jack asked.

"I left orders," he said. "We'll keep her comfortable as she heals, have no worries about that." Then the door opened behind him. "Ah, here comes the nurse. She's going to clean you up, and as soon as she has finished, I'll be in to take care of closing up those wounds."

The doctor went out as the nurse came in. Jack saw the washbasin and washcloths. He was going to have to turn her loose.

"Shelly, I need to lay you back down so the nurse can clean you up, okay?"

"You'll stay?" she asked.

"Right beside you."

The nurse glanced up at Jack. "I'm going to have to remove her clothing."

"She's my wife," Jack said. "Do what you have to do, but I'm not leaving her."

The nurse pulled the curtain around her bed. "We need to get her clothes off first. I can cut them—"

"No knife. Jack can do it," Shelly gasped.

"It's not a knife," the nurse said. "They're scissors, and they do not have sharp points."

"Jack can do it," Shelly said again.

"Please," Jack said. "It won't take long. I've been doing this for years, but for a much better reason, right, babe?"

Shelly sighed. "You do it."

And so he did. They raised the head of the bed up enough so that she was reclining, and then he removed her blouse and what was left of her bra.

"Okay, honey, now we're gonna lower the bed so I can pull off your pants without you having to stand up."

So he pulled the sheet loose from the end of the bed and covered the top half of her body before he undid the zipper in her pants.

"I'm going to pull them down now," he said, and began to ease them down her hips and out from under where she was lying.

As he pulled her clothes, the nurse pulled one end of the sheet with them so that Shelly would not feel exposed. Within a couple of minutes she was completely nude beneath it.

"Thank you," Jack said.

The nurse nodded and then touched Shelly's arm to let her know where she was.

"I'm going to give you a bath. We'll start with your face and clean up the dried blood, then I'll work my way down. If at any time I hurt you or frighten you, just say stop, okay?"

"Okay." Then her arm suddenly flailed outward in a frantic motion. "Jack?"

"Right here," he said, and laid a hand on her hair.

"Feel that? It's me. I'm trying to stay out of the nurse's way, but I'm right here."

Shelly sighed again. "Awful feeling…can't see."

He patted the top of her head. "Let the nurse do her job so the doctor can finish his."

"Yes," she whispered, and then lay perfectly still for about three minutes. Then out of the blue, she jerked and reached for Jack's hand. "I didn't tell," she said again, unaware she was repeating herself.

Jack lifted her hand to his lips and kissed the bruises on her knuckles. "I know. You are so very, very brave."

She relaxed again and was completely silent until the nurse pulled the sheet up to her chin, then uncovered the lower half of her legs. The moment the washcloth touched her skin there, she screamed.

"Get it off! Get it off!"

The nurse jumped and pulled back the cloth. "What's wrong?"

"There were rats," Jack said. "I think she thought it was them again."

The nurse stared at Shelly's face and then the wounds on her legs while the water from the cloth she was holding dripped onto the floor at her feet.

"Who did this to her?" she finally asked.

Jack sighed. "A very bad man."

The nurse nodded, then started over by talking. "Shelly, I'm going to wash your legs. What you feel is me and a washcloth dipped in warm water, okay?"

"Yes. Sorry. Okay."

"Honey, you don't owe anyone an apology," she said. "Now here we go. Starting on your upper thigh and working down to the bottom of your feet."

"Yes," Shelly said.

And then there was a knock at the door.

"Hang on, Shelly, I need to see who that is."

"Don't leave!"

"No, baby. I'm just going to the door. You can hear my voice."

"Your voice," she echoed.

The nurse made sure that Shelly was completely covered up now except for the one leg.

Jack pushed the curtain aside and went to the door. When he saw it was Wainwright, his heart sank.

"Was I right?" Jack asked.

Wainwright nodded. "He didn't even try to cover it up."

Jack scrubbed at his face with both hands, unable to accept this was happening. "I don't get it."

"We are guessing desperation, with a touch of greed. It appears he was in debt in a lot of places. We had to notify his wife. She came undone. We stayed until her parents arrived."

"Man, he isn't ever going to get out of prison. He'll never see that baby grow up."

Wainwright put a hand on Jack's shoulder. "He won't go to prison. He's dead. Shot himself before we could disarm him."

Jack shuddered and then looked down at a spot on the floor for a very long time, before he looked up.

"You told Alicia what he did?"

"You know how this stuff goes. It will be in all the papers. We had to."

Jack nodded. "And Ito?"

"He's undergoing surgery, then straight to lockup facility until he can be sentenced by the court. We re-covered a gun in the bunker. I'd lay odds it's the one he used to kill his brother. Houston's Homicide Department will be handling that. Murder on their turf and all. And thanks to you, we have him dead to rights on all the black market gun running. As for running, he'll be lucky if he ever walks again."

"Good," Jack said, and then turned and pulled the curtain back so Wainwright could see. "That's what he did to Shelly, then left her tied to a cot beside his brother's body. He left them both for the rats to eat."

Wainwright blanched, then made the sign of the cross. "Sick bastard," he said softly.

Shelly jerked and then grabbed at the sheets, looking for Jack.

"Jack! Jack!"

"I'm right here," he said, and then reached out and shook Wainwright's hand. "Thank you for telling me in person. And just so you know, I'll be resigning from the Bureau in the coming weeks."

Wainwright was shocked and it showed. "You don't have to do that, Jack. Forget the undercover work. You can go back to—"

But Jack interrupted. "No. No more."

"What will you do?" Wainwright asked.

"Something else," Jack said. "Anything else. But for now, Shelly has a long way to go with healing from this, and I need to be there for her."

Then he turned away, pulling the curtain shut as he went back to her bed.

Wainwright was saddened as he left the hospital. This was going to be a hell of a report to write up. He didn't lose just one man today. He was losing two.

Fourteen

They moved Shelly to a room around midnight. They'd wrapped her rib cage to reinforce the cracked rib. She had two stitches in her upper lip and four in her lower. The rat bites were being treated and she was getting meds to treat the infection. Her eyes had been cleaned and doctored, and her body was regaining some normal readings as rehydration continued.

Several nurses had found fleas in her hair and had offered to shampoo and treat the scalp before moving her upstairs. Shelly was so horrified throughout the process that she couldn't stop crying.

Jack stood by her side, holding her hands and talking to her throughout the whole process about the stakeout he'd been on when he got bedbugs.

He had the nurses laughing about all the treatments he did on the rooms trying to get rid of them, and how he finally gave up, shaved his head and walked out of the stakeout apartment, leaving everything behind. He elaborated enough about some guys from the Bureau picking him up and dropping him off at an ER wrapped up in a sheet one of them had brought from home that they were all laughing in hysterics.

Shelly was even distracted enough by the story that the nurses were completely through with the third shampoo and the scalp treatment before she knew it.

She squeezed Jack's hand. "You never told me about that."

"I was afraid you'd never let me back in the house," Jack said.

Shelly moaned, stifling laughter, as Jack lifted her hand to his lips and kissed it.

Now they were upstairs, and the overstuffed recliner the orderly just brought to her room was for Jack. They added a pillow and a blanket and showed him how it reclined all the way back for sleeping.

Nurses came and went. The pain meds they had given Shelly finally began to take effect as she fell asleep. Finally the room was in shadows, except for a small light on the far side of her bed, and the lights on the machines hooked to her body.

Jack shoved the recliner close enough to the bed that he could hear her breathing, and only then closed his eyes.

Shelly's kidnapping was on the early-morning news, along with an interview of their neighbor Barb Hightower, who'd witnessed it happening. No one knew Jack's part in her recovery. Only that she'd been rescued by members of the FBI. There was mention made of closing the case on the stolen military weapons, and the last man connected to the case being in custody and charged with his brother's murder.

It was the subject of conversation for many Houstonians over their breakfasts, but no one was more horrified than Mitzi Shaw.

After the mess their daughter had gotten them into, she was certain their life was never going to be the same. And now this happened. Suddenly, their troubles seemed petty and small.

She called her boss, Willard Bates, to tell him what she'd learned.

"Thank you for the heads-up," Willard said. "But I'm already on it. Her husband actually called me this morning. Can you believe this? He's actually a federal agent! He survived being shot and went into hiding, trying to find the man who got away from that weapons bust last week. The man wanted revenge against Jack and kidnapped Shelly to draw him out."

Mitzi gasped. "Oh my God! That sounds like something out of a movie. Not a thing that happens to people we know."

"Life always imitates art. This is no exception," Willard said. "I've already called in a temp to cover Shelly's clients, but from what I understood, her healing involves time and way more than physical injuries."

Mitzi started crying. "I'm so glad this is over and they're both still alive."

"Yes, well, I'll see you at work?" he asked.

"Yes, of course. I'll be there," Mitzi said, then hung up and went to blow her nose.

Then she called the hospital, only to learn there had been a No Visitors order put on Shelly's care. Mitzi cried all the way to work and kept thanking God that her husband sold shoes in a department store for a living.

Angelique heard about the arrest on the news as well and was greatly relieved to know that Adam Ito would be in prison for the rest of his life. She would not have wanted him to know she had anything to do with getting him caught.

She was also thrilled to find out that Jack McCann's wife was alive and in the hospital. It pleased her greatly that she'd helped make that happen.

So she began the day in her office by removing Adam Ito's name from her records, along with expunging all of the information she'd kept on him. She didn't trust the law or the government, and she feared if they found out she'd done any kind of business with him, that it wasn't above them to somehow include her in the indictments against Ito, just because they could.

By noon, she was puttering about in her kitchen, making herself a cup of tea to go with a cold shrimp salad, when her doorbell began to ring. She wiped her hands and then fluffed up her hair as she moved through the penthouse apartment. Once she got to the front door, she peered through the peephole. It was Henry, the downstairs doorman, holding a huge bouquet of flowers.

She turned the dead bolt, removed the chain and then opened the door. "Good afternoon, Henry. You shouldn't have."

He grinned. "Afternoon, Miss Angelique. This just came for you, and the instructions from the florist said to put these in your hands only."

Angelique smiled and grabbed a ten-dollar bill from a jar of money on the hall table that she kept for tips.

"Thank you for bringing them up."

"Yes, ma'am," Henry said, then handed her the vase and pocketed the tip. "Have a nice day," he added, and went back down in the elevator.

Angelique kicked the door shut behind her, turned the dead bolt and put the chain back on the door.

"Now, let's see what we have here," she said, as she carried them to a side table in her living room to remove the card.

Thank you, lady.
J.

Angelique smiled. It had been a while since anyone had called her a lady.

"You are so welcome, Jack McCann."

On the morning of Shelly's second day in the hospital, the phone rang in her room. The swelling was going down in her eyes enough that she could see a little bit from one eye, and even more from the other, and when Jack didn't immediately appear, she managed to answer the phone.

"'Lo," she said, then winced as the skin pulled around the stitches on her lips.

There was a brief moment of silence, then a voice in whispers, sounding as raw as hers felt.

"Shelly? This is Alicia. Please don't hang up."

The skin crawled on Shelly's head. She was still trying to come to terms with how horribly their friend Charlie had betrayed them, when it dawned on her that he had betrayed his wife and child even worse.

"I…here. Can't talk much…stitches."

Alicia moaned. "Oh my God, I am so sorry, Shelly. I don't even know what to say except that my heart is broken for what you and Jack endured. I need you to know that I didn't know this was happening. I would have told. I would never have been a part of such treason."

"Unnerstood," Shelly said. "Not your fault."

Alicia was crying softly now, trying to talk through tears.

"I'm moving back home with Mom and Dad for a while. They live in Pasadena. I doubt we'll ever cross paths again, but I couldn't bear for you to think I just skipped out on you guys without calling. It would seem like I didn't care about what happened, and at the same time, I am ashamed to show my face."

"So sorry," Shelly said. "No…blame."

Alicia sighed. "Thank you! You guys have a long and happy life. You deserve it."

The line went dead before Shelly could say goodbye. She replaced the receiver and then leaned back. Maybe *goodbye* wasn't a word that worked between them anymore.

But it made her remember something that happened to her when she was young.

She had just turned seven when she learned her best friend had moved away over Christmas vacation, and she came home from school in tears. Her mother sat down in the rocker and lifted Shelly into her lap and wrapped her up in their old green-and-yellow grannysquare afghan. The comfort of her mother's arms, the afghan tucked around her and the lull of the rocker was the medicine she needed. She remembered feeling her mother's hands smoothing the curls away from her face, and how she leaned down and kissed her.

"You'll make new friends," her mother said. "That is how life works. Some people are meant to be in your life for a while, and then they leave, while others will be with you always."

Shelly remembered falling asleep within the warmth of her mother's arms, and the smell of camphor from the afghan up her nose. That was how she felt right now. Sad, but accepting that Alicia had been a passing-through friend. Not the kind meant for staying.

Then the door opened, and Jack walked in. She was still getting used to the short hair and dark beard, but he could never disguise his voice and those eyes from her.

"Hey, baby. I was at the nurses' station. The doctor left orders that if you don't have any kind of setbacks today, he will let you go home in the morning."

Shelly clapped her hands. It hurt too much to smile, and Jack was still talking.

"Barb Hightower called the nurses' desk while I was there. She was going to leave a message for me to call her, but as luck would have it, I was already there." He sat down on the side of her bed. "She wants you to know that she and her neighbor Ginny went over to our house and cleaned up the blood from where you were attacked. Your purse and keys were on the floor where you dropped them. Barb took your stuff, locked the house back up for you and is keeping them safe until you come home."

"Oh...never thought! Thank her?"

"Yes, I did, and I don't think I told you yet, but Barb witnessed your abduction. She saw it from the beginning, when Ito rolled under the garage door as it was going down, to them driving away. She was on the phone with 911 when they began backing out, and when she ran out shouting at them to stop, Ito shot at her."

Shelly's eyes widened in disbelief. "Hurt her?"

"No, she hit the ground before he fired, but if it hadn't been for her, it might have taken us longer to find you. She gave us the identities and the getaway car."

Shelly patted his hand, then touched her heart.

"Yes, I'm grateful, too," he said. "I'll tell her for you."

Shelly nodded, then took his hand and laid it against her heart.

"Love you," she said, then winced again as the stitches pulled.

"I already know how much you love me," he said. "You suffered all of this because you wouldn't tell him I was alive."

She reached for his hand. "God gave you back. Couldn't lose…again."

Jack groaned and lifted her hand to his lips.

They had been given a second chance. He would never put her in danger again.

It was the duty of Homicide detectives to notify next of kin when a body was discovered, and it had fallen to Homicide Detective Ryan Trotter of the Houston PD to locate and notify Yuki Ito's next of kin, even if it meant a phone call to Toyko, Japan. Just getting the number had been a hassle, and he also had to find a Japanese translator to deliver the news. Then Trotter looked up from his desk. That someone had just arrived.

"Detective Trotter?"

Trotter stood up to greet him. "Yes, I'm Trotter."

"Officer Michael Mendoza, Pasadena PD. My mother is Japanese. I speak it fluently. They said you need a notification of death made to Toyko?"

Trotter nodded and handed him a typewritten page of info.

"Take my seat. I'll stand by in case they have questions for you."

"Yes, sir," Mendoza said, and sat down in the detective's chair to make the call.

Ken Ito was spending a rare night at home with his wife. Ever since the renunciation of his sons, she had taken to her bed in grief. She wouldn't talk to him and was refusing to eat. At first he'd ignored it, thinking she would come to accept what must be, but it was becoming apparent that he'd been wrong. She was all the family he had left now, and he could not bear to lose her, too.

He'd spent the evening at her bedside, trying to coax her to eat, then reading to her from *Kokoro* by Soseki Natsume. It was one of her favorites, but he didn't think she could hear him over the scream in her heart.

He heard their phone ringing but ignored it, knowing one of the servants would answer. What he hadn't expected was the sound of running feet and then a quick knock at their door. He frowned. They'd been told he was not to be disturbed.

He laid the book aside and went to the door, ready to chastise whoever dared defy his orders.

Their maid was rattled, her voice was shaking as she continued to apologize over and over for disturbing them, and then she got to the point. There was a call for him from the Houston Police Department in the United States of America. He must come, she said. "It is urgent," she said. "They are on hold," she said.

"Stay with her," Ken said, and went to his office to take the call.

He answered the call in English, then got his message in Japanese.

He stood without moving, hearing the words and knowing this news would end his wife's life. And then he asked his first question in English.

"Where is his brother?"

"One moment, sir. I will let you speak to the homicide detective who worked the case. His name is Detective Trotter."

Mendoza handed the phone to Trotter. "He wants to talk to you. He speaks English."

Trotter took the phone. "This is Detective Trotter."

"Detective, I have a question. How did this happen, and where is his brother, Sota?"

"Who?" Trotter said.

Ken sighed. For a moment he'd forgotten. "Adam. He calls himself Adam Ito."

Trotter grimaced. This wasn't going to make them happy.

"For the time being, Adam Ito is in a prison hospital. The brothers kidnapped a woman. We don't know why it happened, but we do know that your son Adam Ito killed his brother, Yuki."

Ken closed his eyes, but he couldn't shake the image of what he was being told. He knew why the kidnapping had happened. Because he ordered it when he'd demanded Adam find his betrayer. And now one of his sons was dead. He took a deep breath.

"You said Sota killed him. How was Yuki killed?"

Trotter sighed. This man wanted all the ugly details.

Some families did. Some families didn't, but when they asked, they got the truth.

"He was shot in the back of the head."

"And the woman they kidnapped?"

"She was left for dead with him. However, she did survive."

"You said Adam is in a prison ward, recovering from his surgeries?" Ken asked.

"Yes, sir," Trotter said. "They were wounds incurred when the FBI found him."

"Of course," Ken said.

"I am very sorry for your loss," Trotter said. "Will you be claiming the body?"

Ken almost said no, and then it dawned on him that this might be what his wife needed. Even if Yuki was dead, she could still bring him home.

"We will be flying in within a day or so. Are you the one I contact when we come?"

"Yes, sir. I'll help you through the process. If you give me an email address, I can send you the information."

Ken gave him a household email and ended the call, then walked straight to the wet bar and reached for the bottle of sake.

He downed the first drink like medicine, tossing it back and swallowing without tasting. And then he poured a second drink, walked out to the koi pond bubbling near the stand of bamboo and stared down into the shadows.

The koi were in hiding. Just like his sons had been. The demand he'd made of them had ended Yuki's life, and probably Sota's, as well. His heart was aching as he looked up. The night sky was clear. The stars were bright and dazzling, as his sons had once been to him.

Then he shook his head, accepting the weight of his decision.

"You were both men. You knew the consequences of your actions when you stole from me—from the cartel—and yet you did it anyway. You brought shame into this house...shame to me...shame to your mother...to the family name. But I am remembering you now as children who gave me such delight. It is the child I will visit in the hospital. It is the child whose body I will recover." Then he lifted the glass of sake to the moon and poured it out onto the grass.

His steps were slow, his conscience heavy with the guilt of bringing them into the cartel life. Even though they had shamed their name, part of the shame was his.

He went back into the house, then returned to their suite. The maid left as soon as he returned, and he sat back down beside his wife's bed. But he did not pick the book back up from which he'd been reading.

She'd given birth to them. It was her right to know their fate.

"Beloved, I have news I must share. It is about our sons."

For the first time in days, she rolled over and met his gaze, her dark eyes questioning the look on his face. "That phone call was from the police in Houston, Texas. Yuki is dead."

Silent tears rolled from her eyes. He saw the blame she directed at him, but she deserved to know all.

"The police did not kill Yuki. Sota did."

She threw back the covers and sat up as the tears continued to fall. "They always fought. Adam was cruel as a child. Something is wrong with him."

Ken did not disagree. "Adam is in a prison hospital,

recovering from wounds gained during his arrest by the FBI. I must go to the States to claim Yuki's body. I do not want to do this alone."

She reached toward him, and when she did, he clasped her hand. "I will go with you," she said. "We will bring our Yuki home together."

He sat down beside her and took her in his arms, holding her as she cried. The weight of her long hair was heavy on his arms, but not as heavy as the guilt within his heart.

Adam had not expected to recover from his wounds like this. He had envisioned a sparkling facility with the latest in medical marvels that Texas had to offer. Not this drab prison hospital.

After he came out of surgery and had come to himself enough to know what was going on, he'd sent for his lawyer, only to be told the man wanted nothing to do with him. It had to do with the fact that the lawyer's son was a soldier, and he wasn't going to represent a man selling stolen military weapons on the black market.

Then he learned that Mahalo made a deal with the Feds and told them everything he knew about Adam Ito and his business, and in turn received a lighter sentence and a transfer to another facility.

No only did that piss him off, but it also left Adam with nothing. When you're the top dog, you have no bargaining power. There was no one else to give up—not even the cartel. Other than the names, he knew nothing about their operations or how distribution was made, even though they ran everything from drugs and guns, to child prostitution and money laundering in places all over the world. They were already known by what they did, but hadn't been caught in how they did it. That was him, before Jack McCann aka Judd Wayne showed up in his world, and look what happened.

Being flat on his back in a hospital bed left him plenty of time to think, but all he could focus on was the reality of spending the rest of his life behind bars.

Fifteen

The swelling in Shelly McCann's face was finally receding, leaving her with two black eyes. The rat bites on her legs were healing faster than anything else and had already scabbed over. Her broken nose was in a splint, and the stitches in her lips were still very painful. The first time she saw herself in a mirror, she cried.

It took a while for Jack to calm her down, though he finally made it happen by reminding her how rare it was for people who'd been in situations like theirs to have been given a second chance.

"Bruises will fade, bones will heal and scars are just proof of being a survivor. When I found you in that warehouse still breathing, I thought you were the most magnificent thing I'd ever seen. You didn't quit, Shelly. You just didn't quit, and because you were so strong, I still have you to love."

She put her arms around his neck.

"You always say the right thing."

"The smartest thing I ever did was ask you to marry me. My blessing was that you said yes."

* * *

That afternoon after she fell asleep, he took the opportunity to call Nolan Warren. He needed help getting his transportation traded so he could get Shelly home tomorrow.

"I know it's the weekend, but I need a favor," Jack said, when Nolan answered.

"Anything, buddy. Just ask."

"Looks like Shelly is going to go home tomorrow and I got here on my motorcycle. I need her car to bring her home, which is at my house. I know you ride, and I wondered if—"

"Oh hell yes, I want to ride that Indian. I'll have my wife, Linda, bring me over to the hospital right now. What room are you in? I'll come up and get your helmet and keys."

"Sixth floor. Room six twenty-six."

"Hot dang...this is seriously more fun than mowing the yard."

Jack grinned. "Linda won't be too happy with me if I'm taking you from a job."

"I have a teenage son. He can get off his butt and do it for me," Nolan said. "See you in a few."

"Thanks, I really appreciate this," Jack said.

Shelly wanted to go home and sleep in her own bed, and Jack wanted to go home and shower and shave. It was time to lose the Shane Franklin look and put Jack McCann back in existence.

When Nolan arrived, he was grinning like a teenager who'd received the keys to his first car. He tried on the helmet and gave Jack a thumbs-up when it fit. He listened to instructions, then returned a couple of hours later, quietly knocking on the door.

Jack answered, then stepped outside into the hall so they could talk.

Nolan gave Jack's keys back as well as the keys to Shelly's car. "I left your helmet and the Indian in your garage. Man, that is one sweet ride. And I got a chance to talk with your neighbor Barb. She's a hoot. She's talking about organizing a neighborhood watch, and she gathered up a change of clothing for Shelly to wear home. It's all in this sack, she said."

"Oh man, I didn't think of that. Good for Barb," Jack said, as he gladly took the sack.

"That's what I thought," Nolan said. "Anyway, the car is in valet parking. Here's your ticket."

"I sure appreciate this," Jack said.

"I was happy to help you, man. We're all still in disbelief about Charlie. I mean…we know he did it, but it's just hard to rationalize his actions with the man we knew."

"I know what you mean," Jack said.

Nolan gave him a sideways glance and then came out and said it.

"Wainwright said you're resigning. Are you firm on that decision?"

"Very firm," Jack said.

Nolan sighed. "What are you gonna do?"

"Like I told Wainwright, just something else. I don't know what, but we'll figure it out."

He nodded. "I can't fault you. It's one thing when it's us. We chose this life. But when a perp messes with our families, that's a whole other issue." He looked a little embarrassed and then grinned. "I'd better hustle. Son is otherwise occupied, I learned, so I'm still mowing, and Linda is waiting outside."

Jack grinned. "Then don't keep the boss lady waiting."

Nolan nodded. "That's for sure." And then he was gone.

Jack went back into the room. One more night and they'd be home.

They passed the night the same as before, with Jack stretched out in the recliner beside Shelly's bed. She fell asleep easily, but within an hour she had already begun to dream. Jack knew when he heard her crying that she was reliving something bad.

He woke her gently.

"Shelly, Shelly, this is Jack. Wake up, baby. You're having a bad dream."

She woke up in the room's half-light with tears on her face, struggling to sit up.

"Wait, honey. I'll raise the bed."

She eased back against her pillow, trembling from head to foot, rubbing the wound down the middle of her body.

"I thought he was going to rape me when he cut my clothes. He cut me instead. He is in prison, right? They won't let him out, will they?"

Jack couldn't bear hearing the tremor in her voice and slid onto the bed beside her and pulled her close.

"No, he won't get out. When you go to a federal prison, you serve your time. He committed murder. He sold stolen military weapons on the black market. And I'm sure there are a good dozen more charges they've tacked on. Besides, he has to get well enough to go before a judge, and I don't think he'll be walking anywhere ever again."

"What do you mean?" Shelly asked.

"He didn't feel inclined to tell me where you were, so I tied his naked ass to a chair and started shooting."

He heard her swift intake of breath and worried that he might have upset her.

"I'm sorry, baby. I didn't think how that might sound to you. I was desperate to find you and—"

The warmth of his body and the strength in his arms kept the bad dream at bay.

She was whispering now. "Um...Jack?"

"What, baby?"

"What did you shoot first?" she asked.

"His right foot. He yelped a little, then had the audacity to grin, so I shot his other foot. Changed his attitude pretty fast, but he still wasn't motivated to tell me where you were. That's when I shot his right knee. But it wasn't until I stuck the gun barrel in his crotch that he remembered where you were."

Shelly sighed. "Thank you."

"For what?"

"For taking the monster out of my memories and leaving me with that image."

Jack swallowed past the lump in his throat. "You're welcome. Close your eyes now and try to get some rest. Monster killer at your service."

The next morning a nurse was helping Shelly dress while Jack went down to the nurses' station to sign release papers. He came back with an orderly pushing a wheelchair.

"We're ready to go. Are you ready, honey?"

Shelly was sitting on the edge of the bed in a pair of blue Bermuda shorts and a button-up, blue plaid shirt. A pair of backless sandals were the final touch. Thanks to Barb's thoughtful choices, it had all been easy to get on.

"I'm so ready," she said, then winced. Her stitches pulled like heck when she talked.

"If you want, you can go ahead and drive the car up to the front entrance, then I'll wheel her out," the orderly said.

Jack eyed the anxious look on Shelly's face and turned him down.

"Thanks, but the car is in valet parking and I'm going to walk down with her."

The tension Shelly was feeling immediately eased, knowing she wouldn't be going down in an elevator with a stranger, and she wondered if this fear of everything would ever pass.

They walked the hall in silence, then rode down the elevator without talking, but Jack was holding her hand. When they reached the lobby, Jack got the valet receipt from his pocket.

"Wow, it appears there is a breeze today," Jack said. "Do you want to wait inside until they bring up the car?"

"I'll wait with you," she said.

"Then we're all going out," Jack said.

Within a few minutes Shelly was buckled into the front seat and Jack was rolling down the windows to blow the hot air out of the car.

"You okay? I didn't think about the heat. Maybe I should have—"

"I'm fine," Shelly said, and reached across the seat and clasped his arm. "The air conditioner is already blowing cold air in my face."

Jack lifted her hand to his lips and kissed it.

"I can't remember the last time I was in a car with you."

"It's been a while," Shelly said. "I'm going to enjoy

having you home in the daytime, even if it's only for a little while."

Jack rolled all the windows back up and the journey home began.

Shelly took a deep breath and exhaled slowly. Finally, they were together again, which at this point seemed like a miracle. She had fully expected to die tied to that cot.

Jack turned the radio on and then turned it down low. The constant swirl of traffic, the profile of her husband's face, the bruises and skinned knuckles on his hands, the way his eyebrows always knitted when he encountered reckless drivers.

She didn't know she was crying until she felt tears on the backs of her hands, then began scrambling for tissues.

Jack glanced over and saw she was crying.

"You okay?"

She nodded.

"Most of the time I don't know why I'm crying. I'm sorry."

Those dark eyebrows knitted again, but this time at her.

"Don't you ever apologize to me again. You damn well cry when you want to, when you need to, when you have to. It's PTSD, sweetheart. You are entitled."

"Women are taught at an early age to apologize, even when what's wrong is someone else's fault. It's a kind of brainwashing, I think. Something left over from the old times to keep women under their thumbs."

Jack grinned.

"You're not under anyone's thumb, but you have certainly wrapped yourself around my heart."

Shelly sighed. Jack did have a way with words.

"How long do you get to stay home with me?" she asked.

"Actually, I'm not going back to work," he said. "I gave Wainwright notice the night I found you. I'll have to put it in writing, but I'm not setting foot back in that building again."

Shelly was shocked and it showed.

"Is this because of me? Because of what happened? I don't want to be the reason you quit a job that means so much to you."

"You're not, and that job doesn't mean so much to me anymore. It nearly cost me my life, and it came close to killing you. I want to live my life with you, not for others."

"I'm not going to pretend this isn't good news. It's hard loving someone who puts their life on the line day in and day out. But since this is your idea, it makes me happy...so happy."

Right now, the weight of the world was off Jack's shoulders. All he had to do was get her home.

By the time he finally drove into their neighborhood, Shelly was asleep. It was when he began moving at a slower speed that she woke, and then she saw where they were.

"Oh! We're almost home! Look! One of those houses sold."

Jack turned down their street. "The one by our house is still for sale," he said, and then hit the remote to raise their garage door.

As it was going up, he saw Barb coming out of her house in the rearview mirror. She was carrying a covered dish, and then one by one, four more of their neighbors fell into step with her, carrying their dishes.

"Look!" Shelly said.

"I see them. Looks like Barb organized a little welcome home for you. I'll make sure they don't stay long."

"It's okay," Shelly said. "It just shows me that they care."

He killed the engine and then ran around to the other side to help her out as Barb stepped into the garage.

"We aren't staying," she said. "We just wanted to welcome you both home and deliver a warm meal, then we'll be gone."

Shelly was suddenly self-conscious of her appearance, but she needn't have worried. The women followed her and Jack into the house, praising how brave she'd been, left their food on the kitchen counter and blew her kisses.

"We're so glad you're home," they said, and then they were gone.

But Shelly stopped Barb's exit. "I heard what you did," Shelly said. "You went a long way in saving my life. I'm so… I'm forever grateful."

Barb hugged her gently, then looked at Shelly's face and dissolved into tears.

"I know you suffered terrible things and I'm so sorry. You are quite a warrior woman. Promise if you need anything that you'll let me know."

"Yes, I will, and thank you again, Barb. You're pretty amazing yourself."

Barb patted her arm and let herself out. The little swarm of neighbors had come and gone so fast Jack might have thought he'd imagined it but for the food on the counter.

Jack hugged her gently. "I love you, baby, and you need to be in bed. Do you want to lie down in the bedroom, or do you want me to make a bed for you in the living room?"

"The bedroom. There's a TV in there if I want."

"Then that's where you'll be," he said, and picked her up in his arms and carried her all the way down the hall into their room.

She slid out of his arms and undressed, then put on one of his old T-shirts as he turned down the bed.

"In you go," he said, and tucked her in.

"Will you lay down with me for a bit?" Shelly asked.

"I want to shower first, but I'll leave the bathroom door open so you can hear me."

"Is the house locked?" Shelly asked.

"Yes, and I'll set the security alarm, too. Okay?"

"Yes, thank you," she said, and pulled the covers up beneath her chin.

He stepped out in the hall to set the alarm there, then readjusted the thermostat so it would be cooler, before he ran to the kitchen to see if any of the food needed to be refrigerated.

He put a pasta salad into the fridge along with a casserole and left the bread and dessert on the counter and the pot of soup on the stove. By the time he got back she was already asleep, but he closed their door and locked it anyway, then stripped and headed for the shower.

When he came out later, the black beard was gone. Jack McCann was back. Then he looked at Shelly, asleep in their bed, and thought, *Right where I belong.*

Shelly woke abruptly, her heart pounding. The dream was already fading as she found herself in Jack's arms. She stretched gingerly, then turned over to face him. She gasped, then cupped his cheek.

His eyes opened instantly, and then he saw her and relaxed.

"You're back," Shelly said, feeling his clean-shaven cheek.

"I'm sure I look better," he said.

"You feel better, too," she said, rubbing her hand against his skin.

Jack looked up, glancing at the clock on the wall. "Oh wow, it's after one o'clock. We missed lunch. Do you feel like trying to eat something? Remember, the neighbors brought food. There's a pot of vegetable soup, which should be easier for you to eat."

"Yes, okay, but I want to sit in the kitchen, okay?"

He raised up on one elbow and kissed her forehead.

"Anything you want is okay with me," he said, and threw back the covers. "Need help?"

"I can manage," Shelly said. "I need some shorts, though. Something with elastic in the waist. Will you look for me?"

"Absolutely," Jack said. He got up, then helped her scoot to the side of the bed.

She went into the bathroom, while he began going through the middle drawer in their dresser where she kept gym shorts and socks. He pulled out the pink ones from Victoria's Secret, just because he loved the way they fit her backside when she walked.

She came out, pointed a finger at him as she shook her head.

"You just like the way my butt looks in these," she said.

"Guilty," Jack said, as he held them open for her.

She held on to his shoulders to brace herself, and

when he bent over to pull them up, she saw the new pink scar from the bullet wound on his shoulder.

"Oh no!" Shelly said.

He straightened up with a jerk. "What's wrong? Did I hurt you?"

"Your shoulder! I just now saw where you were shot. In all the awful things that happened to me before I saw you, I completely forgot this had happened."

She threw her arms around his neck. "I am so sorry. I can't imagine what you went through. I don't know anything and you have to tell me. It's what we do, remember? No secrets."

He gave her a gentle hug. "I remember. But we'll talk about it later, okay?"

"I hate not being able to kiss you," she said.

"Then I'll kiss *you*," he said, starting at her chin and kissing all the way down to the hollow at the base of her throat.

Shelly sighed as she ran her fingers through the short black spikes in his hair.

"Love you," she whispered.

"Love you more," he said, then took her hand. "Kitchen. With me."

She clasped his hand, grateful in so many ways. He sat her at their kitchen table, and as he began heating up soup and getting things on their plates, he opened up about what had happened the night of the bust, from being made by a snitch, to being pulled out of the water by two random fishermen. He told her about the army medic who'd dug the bullet out of his back, the giant mastiff named Dwayne. How he wouldn't tell them his name or what had happened to him, and they still didn't care.

He told her about a man named Paul, who named him

Dude and took him home to heal, and how, when the time was right and without knowing the reason, Paul took him back into Pasadena, let him out at a gas station without a question.

Shelly was stunned by the story, and so grateful to those men.

"I need to meet them," she said.

"I promised them we'd meet again under better circumstances. When you're better, we'll make it happen."

"I can't wait to thank each of them in person for saving you."

He grinned. "They'll probably all fall in love with you, which is fine. Just remember, I have known and loved you longest."

Then he carried a bowl of soup and a plate of food to the table for her and went back to get his.

"Sweet tea?" he asked.

She nodded.

As soon as they were both seated, Jack reached across the table and clasped her hand.

"We're blessed, baby. I feel the need to bless the food, too."

Tears welled as Shelly bowed her head, listening to the deep rumble of Jack's voice all the way to Amen.

He looked up, saw her tears and then winked.

Her heart lifted as she reached for her soup spoon.

"Soup's hot, don't burn your mouth, and it needs salt."

Shelly grinned. Even if the stitches pulled, she didn't care. Jack was home.

Sixteen

Two days later, Ken Ito and his wife, Kaho, were exiting their plane and following the signs to luggage claim. Ken had traveled extensively in his life and thought nothing of all the protocol it took to get in and out of airports, but Kaho was overwhelmed. She'd traveled some, but never before to North America. There were so many rules in a language she didn't always understand that she was getting frustrated.

"When we get our luggage, where do we go from here?" she asked.

Ken was grateful to have his wife talking to him again, and even more solicitous than normal.

"You do not worry, beloved. I have arranged everything. We'll talk more after we get our bags and get to our hotel."

Kaho stuck close to him. It wasn't the crowds that bothered her. All places in Japan were crowded, but people behaved differently there. Here, there were rude people pushing past, cutting in front of them, treating them as if they weren't even there. She was not pleased.

Once they reached their luggage claim, Ken hailed

a redcap to help them and then pointed out the pieces as they came around the conveyor.

As soon as they'd all been claimed, they followed the redcap to where they could hail a cab, then unloaded their luggage. Ken tipped him generously and was then approached by another man who flagged a cab for them, which required yet another tip to reload luggage into the cab. Kaho didn't miss a thing and complained quietly in their native language as they were seated inside the cab.

"It's the way the world works now," Ken said, and patted her hand. Then he gave the driver the address to their hotel, asked for the air-conditioning to be turned up and settled in for the long ride.

It was almost sundown when the driver finally pulled up to the Four Seasons Hotel.

Kaho rolled her eyes. "It's about time," she said, again in Japanese.

Ken chuckled, and then the flurry began of getting baggage out of the cab and getting it into the hotel, which involved paying off the cabdriver, tipping one man, then another, and then another before they finally got to their rooms with their luggage.

Kaho made a quick sally through the suite, then smiled at Ken as she came out of the bathroom.

"It is clean and well-appointed," she said. "You have chosen well."

"Thank you, beloved. We will rest now. We have dinner reservations for 9:00 p.m. Lie down. Take a quick nap if you wish. I have some calls to make, so I'll watch the time for both of us."

She nodded, slipped off her shoes and lay down on the edge of the massive bed.

Ken laughed out loud. "You are going to fall off the edge. There is plenty of room."

She looked over her shoulder at the space, then giggled a little and scooted back from the edge. The bed was comfortable. Different from what they slept on, but comfortable, and she was tired. Her eyes closed, and within minutes she was dreaming of Sota and Yuki as boys, sitting on the grass beside the koi pond, feeding the fish.

The mood the next morning was anything but jovial. Today was about reclaiming Yuki's body. His remains had been sealed within the shipping casket, too damaged for viewing, and unavailable for any of the normal rituals Kaho would have observed as was their custom. That alone was troubling to her heart. But she could dress in an appropriate color for grieving.

She was a tiny woman, so no matter what she wore, it was always tailor-made for her. This morning, she had chosen a black dress with a hem just below her knees. It had a V-neck, which she usually preferred, and in deference to the heat, one with short sleeves. She often wore heels to her husband's formal gatherings, but today she chose flat slippers without any decoration. The single strand of white pearls she wore were even more accentuated by the black fabric of her dress.

Her hair was wound up on top of her head in a neat twist and fastened down with a mother-of-pearl clip. Had it not been for the gray strands in her hair, Ken Ito might have been forgiven for thinking she had never aged since the day he first saw her.

They had weathered many storms together, and just as many apart, fighting about why it was happening, but they were still together. Today she was sad. It was to be expected. One of their sons had killed the other—a story as old as time.

"You look beautiful," Ken said, as he walked up behind Kaho and kissed the back of her neck.

She glanced up in the mirror at their reflections. Ken's hair was completely gray, but at night in their bed, age did not show. She turned around and stroked the side of his cheek.

"Thank you, my love. I am ready."

"The car is waiting downstairs," he said.

They walked together to the elevator, then together across the hotel lobby and out to their waiting car—a new black Lexus, shining like a mirror in the morning sun.

The driver opened the back door as they approached.

"Mr. Ito?"

Ken nodded.

"My name is William. I will be your driver today."

"This car is beautiful," Kaho said, as she and Ken were seated.

"Only the best for you," Ken said, then gave her hand a gentle squeeze. "Stay strong for me. Today will not be easy."

"I am prepared," Kaho said, but her voice was trembling. "Where do we go first?"

"To the police station to sign papers for Yuki's body to be shipped home."

Ken handed the driver the address.

"Please buckle up," the driver said. "Traffic is bad."

Kaho reached for her belt with shaking hands, but Ken fastened it for her, buckled his own, then, for privacy's sake, spoke quietly to her in Japanese.

"We are together."

She nodded but threaded her fingers through his, just as a reminder.

When Detective Trotter received the text that Ken Ito and his wife were on their way to his office, he sent a quick text back to let them know the message was received, and that there would be an officer in the lobby who would bring them to his office.

But then he looked around at his office, realized what it really looked like and grabbed a handful of paper towels and began dusting off his desk, then dusted off the guest chairs.

Then he noticed the dust on the floor, cursed beneath his breath and stepped outside his office and yelled across the room at the other detectives.

"I need a dust mop! Anyone?"

One of the detectives looked up from her desk and grinned.

"Who's coming, the Queen of England?"

"No, grieving parents from Japan," he said.

The smirk died on her face. "I'll find one. Be right back," she said, and left the office at a lope.

Less than five minutes later she was back with a dust mop and a can of air freshener. "Get out! I'll do it, but keep in mind I'm not doing it for you. I'm doing it for the parents."

A second detective got up. "I'll help you," he said. She handed him the dust mop. "Sweep behind me as we go."

"Will do," he said.

Trotter exited without arguing.

It didn't take them long to clean up, then she sprayed the room with air freshener before they exited.

"There, and it smells better, too," she said, as Trotter started back inside his office "What the hell is in your desk? Last week's tuna fish?"

Trotter's eyes widened, and then he loped into the office to check his drawers. He didn't see or smell anything, and when he turned around and looked back across the room at the detective, she was grinning.

He resisted the urge to flip her off and yelled, "Thank you," instead.

Within minutes, he got a call from the lobby that the officer was on his way up with the parents, then smoothed his hair down and straightened his tie. The file on Yuki Ito was in front of him, along with the release papers they would need to sign. He had already gathered up all the information they would need to get his body out of the country.

Adam Ito had given up the temporary address of the apartment where they'd been staying to the Feds, so they could recover Yuki's personal belongings.

Trotter had to admit this had been one of the more gruesome cases he'd worked. Between the kill shot and the rats, it wasn't something he would easily forget.

Then he looked up and saw the officer coming with the family in tow, and got up to meet them at the door.

The officer paused.

"Detective Trotter, Mr. and Mrs. Ito are here to see you."

"Thank you," Trotter said, and then stepped aside. "Please come in. Have a seat. Can I get either of you anything to drink?"

Kaho glanced at her husband and shook her head.

"Nothing for us, but thank you," Ken Ito said, as they sat down. "We want to get this over with. I'm sure you understand."

"Yes, of course," Trotter said, then got down to business, explaining the process of releasing a body for transport to another country. Ken signed his name on a variety of papers, then received a file with instructions as to how to proceed.

"I'm sorry this is so complicated, especially in a time of grief," Trotter said. "I have one other thing for you," he said, and picked up a large manila envelope. "These are Yuki's personal belongings. They were retrieved from the apartment where they had been staying."

For the first time since the whole conversation began, Ken seemed shaken by the offer. Because he hesitated, his wife, who had not uttered a word since their arrival, suddenly made her presence known.

"My son," she said firmly, and extended her hand.

Trotter gave her the envelope, which she clutched firmly against her breasts. He was beginning to think they were unmoved by the whole process, until he saw a tear rolling down her cheek. He started to offer a tissue and then feared she would not appreciate him calling attention to her grief, so he did nothing.

"That finishes up my part," Trotter said. "Do you have any questions?"

"Yes. How do we get to the prison hospital where Adam is being held, and what do we need to be allowed to visit?" Ken asked.

Trotter blinked. He hadn't thought about them wanting to see the murderer, then realized from their point of view, he was another son. One who had committed an unforgivable sin, but their son, just the same.

"I'll give you the address and will call the warden myself to clear your arrival. Be prepared to have your person and your belongings checked. It is a prison, after all."

Ken nodded once. "Understood. The address, if you please?" And this time, he had no trouble holding out his hand.

Detective Trotter double-checked the address to make sure he wasn't sending them to the wrong location and then wrote down the warden's name, as well.

Ken took the information and slipped the paper into the pocket of his suit coat.

"Thank you for your help," Ken said, as he and his wife stood in unison.

"Of course," Trotter said. "I'll walk you to the door. The officer who brought you up is waiting to escort you down, and again, my sympathies for your loss."

As he'd promised, the officer was just outside the door. They were on their way to the elevator when Trotter hurried back to his office to call the warden.

Adam Ito was shaking and crying from the pain as the doctor on duty peeled back bandages to check the surgery areas. The gauze had stuck to the stitches and staples, and to the bolts holding the bones in his feet together, and at this point, there wasn't an easy way to do it.

Adam was also handcuffed to the bed with chains long enough for him to feed himself, but not long enough to do anyone damage, including himself.

Dr. Grimley had seen frightening men with far worse injuries than these, but there was one thing they all had in common. Without drugs and the weapons that made them feel tough—that gave them what they perceived as a "license to kill"—they all bled the same, and they all cried from the pain, and most of them cried for their mothers when they were dying. This one was doing enough crying, but he had yet to cry for Mama.

"Stop! Stop!" Adam wailed. "Can't you see that's stuck? Isn't there a way to remove that gauze without taking scabs with it?"

"I'm sorry," Dr. Grimley said. "It's unfortunate that you are in this condition, but healing from injuries is not a painless process."

"Then give me some drugs to dull the pain!" Adam begged.

"I'm almost through here," Grimley said. "And as soon as I confirm there's no infections, we'll bandage you back up again."

"This is torture. Is it because it's a prison? That's it, isn't it?" Adam shouted. "We're not good enough for humane treatment."

Dr. Grimley's eyes narrowed. "I know how you got here. Do not utter the word *humane* in my presence again, understand?"

Adam thought about what this man could do to him, and without anyone being the wiser. So he entertained himself by thinking of how many ways he could kill this man without anyone knowing it was a murder, and pretended he was not lying in a prison ward with at least a dozen other men.

He was still plotting the deed when he heard voices, and then he saw the warden entering the ward, talking to the people walking behind him.

Now what? Adam wondered, as the warden stopped at the foot of his bed.

"Dr. Grimley, this is Mr. and Mrs. Ito. They have come to visit their son Adam. Since they came all the way from Japan, I have given them permission to visit for an hour…if they wish to stay that long."

Adam's heart almost stopped when he saw his father's face and his mother standing beside him.

"No! I don't want them here!" Adam shouted. "Make them leave!"

The warden frowned. "First, you don't shout at me. You got yourself in here, and since there's no likelihood that you will ever get yourself out, and they have come such a long way, surely you can spare a few moments to hear them out, don't you think?"

"My father hates me! He'll kill me," Adam said.

"Nobody is dying in here today," the warden said. Then he looked down at the couple standing by in silence. "Do you still wish to visit? It's understandable if you want to change your mind."

"We have things to say. It will not take an hour. We will notify your guard when we are ready to leave."

The warden nodded and then shook Ken Ito's hand. "If you have any further questions, the guard will bring you to my office. Otherwise, have a safe journey home." He bowed awkwardly to Kaho Ito and walked away.

Ken looked at his son, and then the doctor. "Please finish your work quickly. We wish to speak to him in private. We won't take long."

Grimley was happy to accommodate. "Yes, sir. Give me five minutes."

For the next five minutes, Ken never took his eyes off Adam's face, and Adam was finally silent, paralyzed with fear.

As promised, Dr. Grimley finished and then even

helped the nurse replace bandages. "We're through here, and my apologies for keeping you waiting."

"What about my pain pills?" Adam asked.

"I'll write the order on your chart," Grimley said, and left the ward.

The closest patient was three beds away, which was all the privacy they needed, but when Ken moved to the side of Adam's bed, Kaho stayed at the foot of it, her gaze fixed on her son's face.

Adam was pissed at being at a disadvantage. Being flat on his back in front of them was disconcerting. "After disowning Yuki and me, I'm curious as to what the fuck you two are doing here."

"We were summoned," Ken said. "We came to claim Yuki's body."

Adam's face was flushed, first with guilt, then with anger. "Well, obviously Yuki isn't here. And I am no longer your son, so that doesn't answer my question."

As Ken watched the rage moving across his son's face and coloring the timbre of his voice, it occurred to him that if he was not incapacitated by wounds and handcuffed to his bed, he and Kaho could both be dead by their own son's hands.

This, too, was his fault. What he should have done was refuse the cartel's offer to get involved and shot Adam himself. Ken took a deep breath and glanced down at Kaho. It was for her. He'd taken their offer for her.

"Well, I'm waiting!" Adam said.

"You're not going anywhere and we have an hour," Ken snapped. "I have nothing to say to you, but we are here because of your mother. She is the one who has grieved her sons being banished."

Adam shifted focus from his father to the woman standing at the foot of his bed. She was too quiet. He didn't want to look at her, but he couldn't look away. He felt like he had the day she'd caught him strangling their cat.

"Well, then, Mother? What is it you came all this way to say? You are part of the reason I'm here. Part of the reason Yuki's dead. You chose *him*—" Adam gestured with his chin to his father "—over us, or you wouldn't have let him banish us."

"Stop talking!" Kaho said.

Adam opened his mouth, ready to defy the order, when the floodgates opened. Kaho Ito came at her oldest son with a fist upraised. Ken caught her before she could hit him.

Adam was in shock. She had never raised a hand to either of them. Ever. Then she began to whisper.

"Liar. Evil. Cunning. Soulless. Murderer."

Adam felt the skin on his face growing hot, pulling taut across his bone structure, as if he'd moved too close to a flame. He tried to respond, but words wouldn't come. Then she leaned closer.

"You are an abomination. You kill your own blood. I should have thrown you in the river once I'd realized what you were capable of, even as a child. I knew that you were bad, but I thought I could love the evil away."

Adam heard the words coming out of her mouth as though he were in the bottom of a well. He was growing smaller and smaller and the well was getting deeper and deeper beneath her rage.

"I curse you. What days you have left on this earth, may you spend them in total agony, with fear as your pillow, and pain the blanket that smothers you in your sleep."

Adam was beginning to shake. Ken Ito was almost as shocked as his son. Never had he heard Kaho utter words like this. Never would he have believed she even had these thoughts. He was staring at her like he'd never seen her before.

Kaho was oblivious to her husband's shock, but it wouldn't have stopped her. She'd stayed silent too long. She pointed to her son's feet. Without touching them, she could see the wounds and the metal pins beneath the bandages. She could see the shattered knee and feel the broken bones beneath the skin as surely as if she'd run her fingers across their surfaces. Her voice grew softer, then softer still.

"Your feet will not heal. They will rot, like bad fruit on a vine. Your knee will fester, like the blackness in your heart. Like the demon in your brain. You no longer have your power. You no longer have your voice."

Then she took a deep breath. It rattled like chicken bones in a dish as she inhaled. And then she pursed her lips and blew the breath out across the bed, across him, across his face, while the skin tightened even more.

Adam's heart was racing. It felt like it was going to burst.

"I am done here," Kaho said, and then walked away from Adam's bed, leaving her husband to follow as he wished.

Adam started to yell at her. To call her foul names. To deny he ever loved her, but the words wouldn't come. He took a breath and tried again, and then something inside him gave way. The left side of his face began to sag, as if it no longer had bones. Then he lost feeling in his left arm, all the way down his left leg to the foot.

He tried to cry for help, but the words…his words…

his voice. He no longer had his voice. His mother had taken it away. She had neutered him with her curse.

But it was his own grief, his own guilt and shame and anguish that were undoing him.

He was struggling to breathe now, choking on the secretions of his own spit.

Help! Help me!

But no one heard, because the voice was only in his head.

A door slammed.

His eyes rolled frantically toward the exit, but the guard was gone, walking them back out of the prison. He could hear the nurse in the other room, still talking on the phone. The other patients in the ward were too sick to care, or unaware because they slept.

The first voice that popped up in his head was startling. He'd always known they were there, but they'd only been whispers. This one was talking to him in his native language. Then another joined in, talking back in English, then in French.

Adam shuddered. *Go away. Crawl back under the bridge. Go away.*

One of them cackled.

Adam closed his eyes, begging in a silent plea. *Somebody kill me now.*

Then the first voice said, *We cannot leave now. We've just arrived.*

Ken helped Kaho into the Lexus, then directed their driver to take them back to their hotel.

"Please buckle up," the driver said.

"Yes, because the traffic is terrible," Kaho said.

She buckled herself in and then leaned her head against her husband's shoulder and closed her eyes.

Ken buckled his own seat belt, made sure that Kaho was comfortable and then held her hand as she slept, but his head was spinning. He didn't know whether he was holding on to her because she'd frightened him, or because he needed her to know he was not the enemy.

The drive was made in silence. Kaho slept. Ken spent the time gazing out the windows into the city that had been his first son's world. On the surface, it was just another metropolis. But nothing was ever as it seemed. Not even the people you thought you knew.

Kaho mumbled something beneath her breath. He looked back out the window. Part of him wished he had left her at home, but at the same time, he acknowledged that he would have had to bury her upon his return. She needed to face all in order to get through it. To hide from it back in Japan would have meant collapsing underneath all the grief.

He wondered now, as the distance grew between them and Adam, if this was to be his punishment for the life he had led. Losing both sons, and then learning his wife held more power in the breath from her body than he did with his vast fortune and the men and guns at his constant disposal.

Was this what the Americans called "up the creek with no paddle"? Had he, too, lost control? He was as afraid as he'd ever been. Even more afraid than the day he killed his first man.

Kaho pretended to sleep. She and her husband had to discuss what happened, but not here in this car. In private, back in their room. She felt his fear, but it would pass, once he understood that what he'd witnessed was grief and rage. She had sensed far more than they were told about the condition of their son's body, and was greatly saddened about how Yuki's life had ended. Her only comfort was knowing he did not suffer a moment of pain.

And so the wheels beneath them continued to roll, and the comfort of Ken's shoulder finally lulled her past pretense to actual sleep. When they finally reached their destination, she was refreshed.

"Kaho, we have arrived," Ken said, and gently shook her awake as the car rolled to a stop beneath the entrance to the Four Seasons.

She sat up, blinking slowly, trying to acclimate herself to this place, when she'd been so far away in her dreams.

"I dreamed we were in the snow at Yuzawa. Remember when we took the boys? It was their first time riding the rails. Adam didn't like it. It was too cold and uncomfortable, but Yuki loved it. How old was he then? Four, maybe five years old?"

Ken smoothed a strand of her hair back in place as he watched her lips forming words, then realized he was meant to give an answer.

"Ah...I think he was four. It was the year before Sota became a teenager. At that age, he didn't like anything."

Kaho nodded. "Yes, you are correct."

Then the driver was at their door, helping them out, and thanking Ken for the generous tip.

"If you have need of a car again during your stay in Houston, I am available," William said, and handed Ken his card.

Ken dropped it in his pocket. Right now he was more

concerned with getting his wife up to their room. They needed to talk.

They were mostly silent during the elevator ride because they were never alone in the car, but once they reached their room, all bets were off. Ken hung his suit coat over a chair and removed his shoes.

Kaho removed her shoes and moved to the sofa. "Ah, this quiet soothes me," she said.

Ken was more forthright, and the fact that he chose to sit on the opposite sofa so that he could see her face was telling.

"We need to talk," he said.

Kaho smiled. "I know."

"What happened back there? I never saw that side of you before."

His wife shrugged. "I said what had been in my heart for years. I did not make him evil. That is who he is. I did not make him a liar, or a murderer. That is what he did. Calling him cunning only means he is sly, like the fox. Calling him soulless only put a name to what he's always been."

"But you said you cursed him."

Kaho shrugged. "Those are only words. They are vocal ways of making someone look into a mirror. Words have no power unless the receiver hears them and recognizes himself in the accusations."

Ken frowned. "You are talking around my questions. You are trying to fool me. I do not want to see you this way!"

She stared at him across the coffee table, then began slowly shaking her head. "Stop talking. I have never hidden a thing from you. You only chose to ignore it.

Maybe you weren't listening, husband! Maybe you saw only what you wanted to see!"

Ken's hands were sweating like they used to when he was still in school, afraid he was going to fail a test.

Kaho stood abruptly. "Remember your first big deal? The one that set us on the road to success?"

"Of course I remember," Ken said. "I got the art pieces I wanted and the contract allowing me to reproduce them in mass quantities, and negotiated the artist down to one percent of the gross."

"But the contract stated one half percent on the contract he signed. I noticed it but said nothing. It was his mistake, not ours."

Ken's mouth dropped. "You never said anything."

She shrugged. "Call the accountant. Have him look it up for you. It won't take long, and while he's looking, I will tell you now the things I have overheard the servants say and passed on to you, have kept men from betraying you, from stabbing you in the back, from wanting your seat on the cartel bad enough to take a contract out on your life."

Ken turned away from her and strode to the window in anger, but she kept talking.

"Have you ever been sick since we married? No, you have not, because I have always had your health and best interests at heart and made sure you received only the best care. You never told me about the skiing accident you had five years ago…the one where you grabbed hold of that bush just before you fell over the cliff, but I found out anyway. I did not chastise you for keeping secrets from me. You were alive and that's all that really mattered to me. I believe you are successful because we are a team!"

"And what happens if I anger you? Will you speak a curse on me like what you did to Adam?"

Breath caught in the back of her throat as tears suddenly blurred her vision. She held out her hand, as if warding off an approaching enemy.

"How soon you forget," she whispered. "You angered me beyond words when you banished our sons. I went to bed to die. That's what happens when you break my heart."

Ken gasped and then ran across the room and took her into his arms.

"My beloved…forgive me. That was hurt speaking. I felt you had been keeping something from me all these years, when it was I who refused to see you for who you are."

Kaho wiped away tears. This was too important to interrupt with weeping. He was such a stubborn, proud man, but she wouldn't have him any other way.

"What you must understand is that I am as knee-deep in the cartel as you are, but they don't know it. And as long as they see me as nothing but the dutiful wife, I am safe, and so are you. We are not innocents in the world. What's happened to us now is part of our punishment. We let ourselves be corrupted, albeit overtly, but it marked our sons to fail. There is always a price to be paid."

Seventeen

Jack was sitting in their porch swing, watching Shelly hose off the patio. It was something she liked to do because she could get into the shade whenever she wanted, and still be able to enjoy the warm day and the cool water. And she looked hot as all get-out in the cutoff jean shorts and a halter top, even though it left the wrap on her cracked rib showing.

Shelly was enjoying the day. She was feeling better and stronger every day, and her black eyes were fading into faint purples and greens, which she mostly ignored until she saw her reflection in the shimmer of their pool.

"Just look at me! I look like a kid who got caught playing in her mother's eye shadows."

"Stop fussing," he said. "You look beautiful in all that purple and green…like the Northern Lights."

Shelly laughed, then turned the hose on his bare legs.

"The Northern Lights? Really?"

He grinned. Making her laugh was what he intended. They used to laugh a lot before he began working undercover. He was just beginning to realize how much that job had changed their dynamics. Now they had to find their way back to the easy comfort they had before.

She turned off the water and then rolled up the hose. "That felt good to do something normal."

Jack smiled as he watched her puttering about, then leaned back in the porch swing and set it to rocking. The simple joy of no longer living a lie was such a relief.

"Hey, baby, you do know you get the stitches out of your lips tomorrow?"

"Is that tomorrow? Yay! Finally I get to go somewhere."

He frowned. "There's no need for you to feel shut-in. We can go somewhere every day if you want to. I'll take you out anytime."

"I know. I just don't like being stared at."

"Oh, stop it and come here to me," Jack said, and held out a hand.

He was her magnet. She could never tell him no. She reached for his hand, then smiled when he gave it a tug.

"People have been staring at you for years because you're gorgeous. It's no different now," he said, then slipped an arm around her waist and pulled her down into his lap just so he could kiss the back of her neck.

She laughed because it tickled, but he already knew it, which was why he'd done it. When he had her in a better mood, he pushed off in the swing again and set it to rocking. Shelly leaned against his chest and pulled his arms around her.

Her curls were soft against his cheek. The weight of her breasts was warm against his arms. She was his love—so entrenched in his life there was no way to tell where one began and the other ended.

When he'd first seen her in the warehouse and

thought she was dead, his whole life had flashed before his eyes. Without her he was only half a man. She'd been so broken, and now all he could do was marvel at her resilience.

"So, I want to get your feedback on something."

"Okay, I'm listening," she said.

"Remember our trip to Hawaii?"

"Yes, on Oahu. It was wonderful," Shelly said. "We hiked Diamond Head. And we took the ferry out into the open water and boarded a little mini-sub to fish watch. It was like snorkeling but without getting wet. So touristy, and so much fun."

"Do I still have that floral shirt? The one I bought the day before we left?" Jack asked.

Shelly frowned. "No. You loaned it to Charlie one Halloween. He never gave it back."

Jack looked out across the backyard, watching sunlight glittering on the surface of their pool like diamonds.

"You're right. I did. I'd forgotten that."

Shelly rubbed the back of his hand in an absent motion.

"How do you feel about what happened?" she asked.

"You mean Charlie?"

She nodded. "You two were such good friends."

He shrugged. "He was my friend, but I wasn't his. If I had been, he wouldn't have done what he did. He just wasn't who I thought he was, and that was on me, not seeing past the lie he was living."

"I guess, but I didn't see it, either," Shelly said.

Jack shrugged. "His own wife didn't know what was going on. He got in debt and took the easy way out to solve that. I never once heard him mention owing money, or paying off a debt. I never saw that weakness in him to take shortcuts to what he wanted. He was a damn good actor and in a position within the Bureau to do some serious damage. What happened to him was his own doing. Hell, he even took the shortcut to resolving the problems he caused by killing himself."

Then Jack began rubbing her back in a slow, circular motion.

"Enough about him and back to Hawaii. What would you think about living there?"

Shelly gasped and then slipped off his lap onto the swing beside him and grabbed his hand.

"Seriously? What would we do?"

"I have a pilot's license. I wouldn't mind piloting a chopper from island to island for sightseeing tours. Tourists are a year-round business."

Shelly jumped right into the fantasy. "I can do my job anywhere. Every business needs an accountant."

They looked at each other and grinned.

"Are we being serious now?" she asked.

He nodded.

"Oh, I would so love to do this," she said.

Jack knew she had a lifetime of PTSD ahead of her and she didn't realize it. But not living in the house from which she'd been abducted would be a huge plus, and getting away from the city in which it happened, even better.

"Then let's keep this in the back of our minds," he said.

Shelly threw her arms around his neck. "We can do anything when we do it together."

He grinned. "I think I told you that our junior year in high school."

She rolled her eyes. "That's because you wanted me

to go with you and your family to your dad's hunting cabin up in the mountains above Denver."

He laughed. "Well? Was I wrong?"

Shelly sighed. "No. You were right, but that was also the weekend I decided I would marry you one day."

The grin spread across his face. "Really? Why?"

"You fell asleep with your head in my lap one afternoon and you were talking in your sleep."

His eyes widened. "You never mentioned this before. What was I saying?"

"You just kept saying my name over and over," Shelly said.

Jack frowned. "I don't get it. Why would saying Shelly make you want to marry me."

"Because you weren't just saying Shelly. You kept saying Shelly McCann. Shelly McCann. Not Shelly Hartman, which was my name at the time. It was like you were trying out the way the name felt on your tongue. I liked the way it sounded, too."

Jack leaned across the gap between them and kissed her forehead, then the tip of her nose. "I still like the way it sounds."

"Ditto," Shelly said.

"Speaking of doing things together, how do you feel about meeting the men who saved me?" Jack asked.

"Now?"

"Whenever," he said.

"I say let's get my stitches out and I'm ready. Do you want them to come here for dinner? I think I'm up for that."

"If they come here, we're having it catered."

"That sounds like fun. All the good food and none of the mess. Yes, please. What do they like?"

"Probably everything. They are the least pretentious people you will ever meet. I think the best way to describe them is unique."

"This is fun. We're planning a party. We haven't done anything like this since you began undercover work. I can't wait! Definitely, invite them."

"Will do," Jack said.

After that, they sat awhile in mutual silence, still swinging, but each lost in their own thoughts.

He was thinking about going inside to get them something cold to drink when Shelly's feet suddenly hit the patio, stopping the motion of the swing.

"What's wrong?" he asked, but she didn't answer.

It was as if she had gone on alert, her head cocked to one side, intently listening. Then every emotion on her face just disappeared—like she'd turned to stone and he didn't know what triggered it.

He was afraid to touch her for fear of setting off a full flashback, but he couldn't just sit and do nothing. He leaned a little closer.

"Shelly…baby, what's wrong?"

She grabbed his hand and moaned.

Then he heard the sound of an airplane flying overhead. Although they weren't in a flight path, it happened now and then.

"Shelly?"

She was shaking now, her gaze fixed on something only she could see.

"Baby, what's wrong?" Jack asked, as her voice slipped into a whisper.

"Planes. Taking off. Landing. Taking off. Landing."

Now he knew. She was back in that warehouse, still tied to the bed.

"Can't get loose. Can't see. People so close. Planes too loud. No one hears. Help me."

Jack got up, then stood directly in front of her.

"I'm here, Shelly! Look at me! I'm here!"

She took a slow, shaky breath and looked up.

"Jack."

He took her hands. "Yes, it's me. Let's go inside now. We've been out a long time. We'll get some sweet tea."

She was trying to wrap her head around what had just happened as she followed him into the kitchen.

One airplane flying overhead had triggered that. She was weary of waking up screaming—afraid to go to sleep. Just when she thought she was getting a grip on flashbacks, something like this would happen.

"I don't think I want anything to drink right now," Shelly said. "I'd rather go lie down for a bit. Later this evening we could go out for dinner if you want."

Jack slipped his hand beneath her hair and pulled her close. Her whole body was trembling.

"We'll see how you feel at dinnertime. I think resting is a good idea."

She looked at him. "Will you lie down with me for a while?"

"I would love to," he said, and walked her to their room. "On top of the covers or under them?" he asked.

"On top and maybe one of those lightweight blankets."

Shelly crawled into bed and rolled over on her side, facing the wall. She felt Jack climbing into bed beside her, then pulling a blanket up over the both of them.

When he curled up behind her and tucked his arm around her waist, she felt safe enough to close her eyes.

"Love you," she whispered.

"Love you, too," Jack said.

Jack felt her body beginning to relax. A few minutes more and he could tell by the sound of her breathing when she finally fell asleep. When he closed his eyes, his thoughts went to finding Shelly at the warehouse. He would never know the whole story of what she'd gone through, and in hindsight, it didn't matter. She was alive and they were home.

Adam Ito was trying to call out to a nurse to tell her something was wrong when he felt his bowels give way. The next thought in his head was that he hoped he was dying, because he couldn't move. Inside, he was screaming for help, but no one could hear.

My mother did this. Because I killed my brother, she killed me. She didn't have to touch me to make me die, because she cursed me.

Even in this state of being, Adam wasn't taking responsibility for any of it. The fact that he'd been tied to a chair, shot three times and left bleeding profusely didn't play into it. Or the extent of surgery he'd undergone afterward, or the continuous bouts of sudden rage that had been with him all his life. No. It was his mother who was to blame. So he lay in the feces, locked inside a body that wouldn't respond, cursing her for delivering him to this fate.

When he finally saw the nurse coming toward him with an irked expression, he knew she probably smelled the stink. She was pissed because she was going to have to clean him up. But then she suddenly gasped and ran to the bed.

"Mr. Ito! Mr. Ito! Can you answer me?"

He couldn't, which was obvious, and was relieved

when she immediately paged that doctor. He would come. There would be medicine to help this condition. Surely.

It occurred to him as he was waiting that he was as tied to the bed as Shelly McCann had been to that cot, and just as helpless. He'd intended for her to be afraid. But he didn't appreciate the shoe being on the other foot.

And then he saw that doctor come running into the ward and thought, *Finally.*

Grimley came through the door on the run, knowing that the first few minutes of a stroke were the most crucial. As he approached the bed, he could see the panic in the patient's eyes and sought to reassure him.

"Hey there, Adam. Looks like we have a situation. Let's see what's up, okay?"

Adam blinked, and Dr. Grimley gave him a thumbs-up, then began his examination. Prisoners often tried to fake an illness in an effort to escape, but there was no way to fake the facial droop and the deadweight of useless limbs. After a quick survey of the current symptoms, and his lack of reaction to any kind of stimuli, he looked up at the nurse.

"Is the X-ray tech here?" he asked.

"Yes, Doctor. Full staff."

"Then let's get him to X-ray. I want a CT scan on his head to check for brain bleed, but give him a quick cleanup first."

"Yes, Doctor," the nurse said, and went to get an orderly.

When the nurse returned with soap and water, towels and washcloths, and another followed with clean sheets, Adam was ecstatic. For a man who'd spent his life demanding nothing but the best, getting his butt washed and wiped just hit the top of the list of best things ever.

Ken and Kaho were resting. Kaho was asleep on the bed, but Ken had chosen to relax in their Jacuzzi. The hotter the water and the more forceful the jets, the better he liked it.

He'd been in the tub for almost an hour when he decided to get out. He was drying off when his cell phone signaled a call. He sat down on a padded bench to answer, surprised it was Grimley, the doctor from the hospital. He sat, listening to the doctor without speaking until he finally paused, waiting for an answer.

"Mr. Ito? Are you there?"

"Yes, I am here," Ken said.

"As I was saying, we will be moving your son to a different location for long-term care. Any recovery is iffy, and full recovery won't happen. The brain bleed was—"

"Excuse me, Doctor, but I do not have a son named Adam. I had two sons, but one is dead and one is forever banished from our home. I don't care what you do with your patient, but he is none of my concern."

Grimley was a little taken aback, considering they'd been here visiting earlier.

"I don't understand. You were just here and—"

"That was for my wife. She had something she needed to clear up with him, and now she is done. We're both done. Do what you want with him, and when he dies, he is a prisoner in the state of Texas. Do whatever it is you do with dead prisoners without family, but do not call us, because in our house, he is already dead."

Then Ken disconnected and set the phone aside,

feeling the weight of that burden leaving his shoulders. He got up and finished dressing, then glanced at the time as he went back into the sitting area. Still a few more hours until their dinner reservation, so he picked up the house phone, ordered a couple of appetizers, then sparkling water for Kaho and some sake for himself.

After checking to make sure she was still sleeping, he quietly closed their bedroom door, turned on the TV and waited for room service.

Fred Ray had been given the duty of cleaning out Charlie Morris's desk. Like everyone else on the floor, he was still struggling to come to terms with Charlie's fall from grace.

Charlie's partner, Nolan Warren, glanced up when Fred showed up at the desk with a box and sat down in Charlie's chair.

"What are you doing?" he asked.

"Deputy Director Wainwright ordered me to clean out the desk. I guess someone else will be sitting here soon."

Nolan frowned, then went back to work.

The drawers in the desk were all locked, but Fred had been given a passkey, so he began at the top on the right and worked his way down. Everything personal was put in the box, the things that were usable, like pens, staplers, etc., were set on top of the desk, and snacks or trash was thrown away.

He worked quietly and quickly, sorting through the contents. He paused once to look up and realized this was a view of the place he'd never seen. It was the difference between fieldwork and desk work—the difference between being seen as a sleuth or a secretary.

He glanced at the clock and went back to work.

* * *

When Shelly woke up from her nap, Jack was still beside her, reading messages on his phone. When she rolled over, he smiled.

"Hey, sleepyhead, do you feel a little better?"

She stifled a yawn and then stretched. "I do."

"Do you still want to go out for dinner, or would you rather order in? I'd be happy with Chinese delivery."

"Chinese sounds good," she said, and sat up and brushed her lips across his cheek.

"Let me finish answering this last text and I'll call it in."

Shelly nodded, then crawled off the end of the bed and went to the bathroom. When she came out, Jack was gone, but she could hear him talking. She went to get a pair of slip-on sandals, and when she got to the kitchen, he was digging out plates and flatware, getting ready to set the table.

"I'm just getting prepared. So, madam, what would be your choice of food for your dining pleasure?"

"Um, decisions. I think soba noodles with chicken and vegetables, and one spring roll."

"Comin' up," Jack said, then found the number on his phone for their favorite place and called in the order, then disconnected. "We're looking at an hour. You good with that or do you want a little something to tide you over?"

"I can wait," she said.

He heard her, but he went straight to the refrigerator and pulled out a little tub of flavored cream cheese and then got a sack of pita chips from the pantry. He put it all on the table and then went back to get their drinks. She was on her second pita chip when he returned. He grinned, took the lid off the cream cheese and shoved it toward her.

The next bite she took had a blob of cream cheese.

An hour and ten minutes later, the doorbell rang.

"I'll get it," Jack said, and grabbed his wallet on the way to the door. He came back laughing, with two sacks of takeout.

"What's so funny?" she asked.

"We had our same delivery guy. He told me my hair looked funny."

Shelly grinned. "Not a fan of the spike look, I guess."

"Evidently," Jack said, and set the sacks on the table.

"Good grief, honey! What all did you order?" Shelly asked.

"Good stuff. I'll share."

The meal began on laughter and ended with a groan. They were both stuffed, and there was still food left over.

"Breakfast!" Jack said, and started closing up the little boxes and putting them in the refrigerator.

"We still haven't opened the fortune cookies," Shelly said.

Jack got a quarter out of his pocket and sat back down. Their tradition was to flip a coin, and the winner got first choice of the cookies.

"Call it!" Jack said.

"Heads."

He flipped it, then watched it land.

"Ha! Tails. I win," he said, and then made a big deal of choosing, before pushing the other one to her.

"You have to read yours first because you won," Shelly said.

He tore into the wrapper, cracked open the cookie and pulled it out.

"Oh wow…listen to this. *New horizons await. They will change your fate.*"

Shelly tore into hers next, pulled out the cookie and broke it open. Her fortune fell out.

"What does it say?" Jack asked.

Shelly's eyes widened. "You're not going to believe this," she said.

"So enlighten me."

"Your future takes you to distant lands."

The smile slid off Jack's face. "You're kidding me."

"Read it for yourself," she said.

He read it, then looked up in disbelief. "Well, now. That kind of seals the deal, doesn't it?"

"It does for me," Shelly said.

"Together?" Jack asked.

Shelly got up and traded her chair for his lap.

"Always."

Eighteen

Jack came out of the bathroom with a towel wrapped around his waist. He was looking for the gym shorts he liked to sleep in when he thought he heard thunder. He went to the window to look out.

Shelly was sitting on the side of the bed with a pair of nail clippers in her hand, admiring his nearly bare body and happy their homes were together again.

"Is it raining?" Jack asked.

"Yes, right after you went in to shower. Such is the life of living in the subtropics. Will you help me? I broke a toenail and it's sharp on one end. I can't bend over far enough to do it myself."

"Absolutely," he said, then knelt in front of her. "Which foot? Which toe?"

She grinned. "Right foot, and the little one that cried all the way home."

He smiled. "Good one, honey. Okay, let's see what I can do about this."

When he bent over, without thinking, she combed her fingers through his hair.

He looked up, saw the want in her eyes, laid the nail clippers aside and dropped the towel.

Shelly reached for him, her heart quickening as he groaned.

She looked up. "It won't hurt me. I want you so much. I can do this."

She saw the flash in his eyes, and then he pulled the T-shirt over her head.

"You're on top," he said, and lay down.

He grasped her waist with both hands as she straddled him, and then held his breath as she slid down his erection. She was slick and warm and tight.

"Are you okay?" he asked.

Shelly's eyes were closed. "Not yet, but I will be."

She rocked against him.

He responded with a hard, upward thrust.

When they found their rhythm, it was easy to fall into the dance and even easier to lose track of time. Shelly was lost to everything but trying to catch the rolling heat coiling between her legs.

But Jack's control was gone. He grabbed her hips and pushed himself all the way up. One thrust, then two, and in the next, the climax slammed into her so hard she forgot to hold on and fell forward, letting that heated rush wash through her in wave after mind-numbing wave. Jack caught her just as he came. He lost his breath, and then his mind.

The rain passed before morning.

They woke just after sunrise and made love again because they could, then moved into the shower to get ready for her doctor's appointment. Between the soap and their hands, the last climax was both wet and wild.

Jack left her with a well-loved look on her face as he went to start the coffee, then came back to get dressed.

Shelly was ready except for shoes. She still needed that toenail clipped. When she handed him the clippers, he laughed.

"Oh yeah, the toenail." He quickly snipped off the sharp point. "We made love instead of making breakfast," Jack said. "But there's coffee to go."

"Works for me," Shelly said, and followed him to the kitchen, where he filled their to-go cups. She made sure that the lid was on firmly before carrying it to the car.

Jack leaned in and kissed her as she was buckling up. "For good measure," he said, and winked.

Shelly shivered. What a way to start a day!

They were back on the Loop, working their way to her doctor's office, when Jack's phone rang. He accessed the call via Bluetooth so he could keep both hands on the wheel.

"Hello."

"Jack, this is Nolan. We heard something through the grapevine you might like to know. Adam Ito had a stroke in the prison hospital. They're not sure what his chances are, but right now, he can't move or speak. At all."

"The irony of that does not escape me," Jack said. "That's how I found Shelly. Tied to that fucking bed, unable to move, speak or see."

"I'll be damned. I didn't think of it like that. Looks like karma bit him in the ass, big-time. They'll be moving him to a long-range care facility for prisoners, so I thought you'd want the update. In other news, how is Shelly? No hiccups in the healing department?"

"No physical issues at all," Jack said, and winked at

Shelly. "We're on our way to get the stitches out of her lips right now."

"Awesome," Nolan said. "Give her my best."

"I will. Thanks for the information. I'll pass it along."

Jack disconnected. "That was Nolan."

"Is anything wrong?" Shelly asked.

"Not for us. Can't say the same for Adam Ito. Nolan said he had a severe stroke in the prison hospital. He can't move or talk…at all."

Shelly's eyes widened. "So that's what you meant by irony!"

"Exactly. He's being transferred to some kind of hospital for prisoners."

"I hope the only way he leaves that place is in a coffin," Shelly said, and then shifted her focus to the passing scenery.

Jack gave her hand a quick squeeze.

When they reached the doctor's office, the visit was almost anticlimatic. Shelly's worry about it hurting to have the stitches out was unfounded. She was smiling as they left the office.

"It barely stung and I'm starving!" she said.

He grinned. "So am I. What sounds good?"

"It's almost eleven. Early lunch instead of late breakfast."

"Mexican?" Jack asked.

"Mmm, yes. Papacito's?"

"Absolutely," Jack said.

Ken Ito had been on the phone all morning, clearing the way to getting Yuki's body transported back to Japan. Many frustrating phone calls later, it became obvious that either they stayed here until the body was cleared, or they went home and waited for notification it was on the way.

It was Kaho who made the decision. "We go home. They ship. I do not wish to stay in this country any longer."

"Then we go," Ken said, gave her a quick hug and got back on the phone, this time to their airline to get a flight out tomorrow. Since money was never an object with them, the outrageous cost of twenty-four-hour-notice tickets was of no consequence.

Once the decision had been made, they packed before they went to bed and were in a car on the way to the airport by 7:00 a.m. the next morning.

It wasn't until the plane was taxiing down the runway that Kaho breathed a sigh of relief and reached for her husband's hand.

"It was painful to come with you, but I needed to make this trip to heal my heart, and I thank you," she said softly.

Ken lifted her fingers to his lips. "It was a hard trip for both of us. You are my heart. I needed you with me, as well."

And then the wheels left the runway as the jet flew up, up, up into the air.

Alicia Morris carried the last box of Charlie's belongings out onto the front porch. She wanted to burn them but couldn't start a fire in Houston without getting arrested, so she was donating them instead, and her dad was coming back to get them. They'd come earlier to get the baby and take him home with them so Alicia could tie up the business that came with death.

She was trying to wipe away every vestige of his

presence from her life, but it was harder than she could have believed. Finding their wedding pictures gutted her. Taking off her wedding rings and putting them away in her jewelry box made her feel naked. In a couple of weeks she'd be going home with her parents, and nothing that belonged to him was going with her—except Johnny. What little she did keep was for Johnny...for later, when he was older. He deserved to know what his father looked like. And maybe one day he'd give their wedding rings to his wife. She had yet to get to their safety deposit box, but that was on today's agenda. As soon as her dad took the clothes, she was going to the bank.

And now she was standing in the living room, listening to the silence. It already felt empty. The ties she'd had to this home died with Charlie. She'd get over the worst of this one day, but she would never get over his betrayal. She thought she'd known the man she married as well as she knew herself, but she was wrong—so wrong.

"What next?" she said aloud, and then remembered the office. They kept everything on the computer, but if there were personal mementos in the desk, she wanted them gone, too, so she grabbed another box and headed down the hall.

She groaned as she eased down into the office chair and swiveled toward the desk. Her body was still healing from childbirth. Life in one hand, and death in the other. She buried her face in her hands and started to weep. Life wasn't supposed to happen this way.

After a few indulgent minutes of more tears, Alicia pulled herself together—again—and began opening drawers. She had no idea what was in them, because Charlie always paid the bills.

The skinny drawer in the middle was neatly sorted into pencils, paper clips and notepads. Orderly, just like Charlie, she thought, and moved to the next drawer.

One by one, she emptied them of anything remotely attached to Charlie, then was down to the last drawer and glad of it. When she found a sonogram picture of Johnny in that drawer, she nearly lost it. She wondered what had happened to that, and laid it out on the desk to take with her.

She sorted and trashed, and sorted and trashed until that drawer was empty, too, then slammed it shut. She started to get up when she noticed the drawer was still ajar, and gave it a push, but it wouldn't go any farther. She frowned and tried again, and then again, before she decided something must have fallen in the track. So she pulled the drawer all the way out, then got down on her hands and knees to look. To her surprise there was a small book taped to the back of the desk, and part of the tape had come loose. It was the book that kept the drawer from going shut, so she reached inside and pulled it out, then she replaced the drawer.

Before, she would have been surprised to find out Charlie had secrets, but not anymore. She took the book and Johnny's sonogram picture and left the rest of it on the desk.

She got as far as the living room and then dropped into the recliner, kicked back, turned on the floor lamp by the chair. From the first page, she could see it was a simple notebook, one of the kinds that people who like to journal usually choose. The pages were lined, so the entries were neat—again a behavior pertaining to Charlie.

Every entry stated that the amount of money mentioned was a fee, then from that amount, a payment had been made to FR with a notation that said "one percent of fee."

There was no mention of where the money was, how he'd come by it, who FR was or why FR was being paid. There were about ten pages of notes pertaining to the three-year span, and nothing else. She guessed it might be part of what he'd been mixed up in, but it made no sense to her and then she saw her dad driving up and laid it on the coffee table.

She went outside to help load, but he waved her away, reassured her that grandmother and grandson were fine, and yes, she had enough breast milk, and if she didn't, she would let her know. They made plans to bring the baby home around 4:00 p.m. and he was gone.

Alicia walked back into the house with tears in her eyes and cried as she dressed to go to the bank. She almost forgot the safety deposit key and went back to get it, then left.

Their bank was a neighborhood branch of one of the larger banking institutions and she was grateful she didn't have to drive downtown to do this. The downside was, they knew her husband was dead, just not that he'd killed himself. She hoped she was long gone before all of the corruption he'd been involved in was revealed to the nation.

She arrived at the bank just before noon and grabbed the tote bag she had folded up inside her purse so she could empty the contents and close the account. She went straight to the safety deposit vault, signed in and then followed the attendant, who removed their box and took her to a private viewing room.

As soon as the attendant was gone, Alicia opened the box. To her surprise, there was another notebook, identical to the one she'd left at the house, and when she opened it, she saw dated monetary entries. It didn't take long for her to realize the dates of entries in this book coincided with the payment dates to FR in the other one, but she was still confused as to exactly what they were.

She laid that aside and began going through the rest. Besides a five-hundred-thousand-dollar life insurance policy, there was a pocket watch that once belonged to his grandfather, the deed to some land in Idaho that he'd inherited when his father died. There were keepsakes, and a picture of them that had been taken at the restaurant the night he'd proposed. She cried over that, then tore it in pieces, threw it in the trash and kept digging.

What she didn't expect was a sealed letter in his own handwriting, with the words *OPEN AFTER DEATH*. Her hands were shaking when she opened it, and within seconds of reading it, she thought she was going to faint.

> *Dear Alicia,*
> *If you're reading this I know I'm dead, and that was never something I could envision—us being apart.*
>
> *I'm sure you've already found the five-hundred-thousand-dollar life insurance policy on me, but in this economy, that won't last long. In my mind, the worst thing I could do as a husband was leave my family destitute. The second page of this let-*

*ter isn't really a letter. It is everything you need
to know to access the numbered Swiss bank account in your name.*

*There are millions of dollars in the account.
You will be wanting to know where that came
from, but all I will say is that I had a pipeline to
a gold mine, and leave it at that.*

*Don't think about where it came from. Just be
glad that it's there.*
I love you with all my heart,
Charlie

Alicia's hands were shaking. She felt like she was
going to be sick, and started putting everything from
the box into her tote bag, and then carried it out. She
stopped at the attendant's desk to turn in her key and
close the account.

"I'm moving," she said, and signed everything she
needed to sign to make it final, then had to make herself not run through the lobby.

The sun was directly overhead as she exited the
bank. After the chill of the air-conditioned bank, the
bitch-slap of heat was an immediate assault. As soon
as she got in her car and started it up, she turned on the
air-conditioning as high as it would go and then turned
all of the vents toward her face. She felt like she was
going to die. She now understood that those notebooks
had something to do with his illegal activities.

She was in a panic, wondering if there had been more
to his treason than being a part of black market military
weapons. Had he sold government secrets? Was he a
spy for a foreign country? How could he have accumu-

lated so much money in three short years? She needed to turn all of this in, but she was scared and ashamed to show her face at the Bureau. And the first person who came to mind was Jack. He might hate her, but she knew he was a fair man, and would help her make this right. Before she talked herself out of it, she sent Shelly a quick text.

I need help. Discovered notebooks Charlie had hidden. Payoffs…a numbered Swiss bank account. The possibility that he might not have been the only one involved. Either he had a helper, or was being blackmailed. Ask Jack who I should give all this to.

She hit Send, then started up the car and headed back to the house to finish packing.

Shelly was in the bathroom at Papacito's washing her hands when her cell signaled a text. She quickly dried them off and then paused to see who it was. When she saw Alicia's number, she sighed. At least it wasn't a phone call. It still made her sad to hear her friend's voice.

She pulled up the text, read it and then bolted.

Jack was eating chips and queso when he saw Shelly coming, and he knew by the look on her face that something had happened. He stood, seated her again and then sat back down.

"What's wrong?" he asked.

"Just read it," she said, and handed him her phone.

It didn't take long for Jack to react. "Oh my God. I wonder if this has anything to do with the snitch?" he muttered.

Shelly frowned. "A snitch? You mean Ritter?"

"Not until we're back in the car," Jack said.

She leaned forward, whispering, "Is this not over? What am I missing?"

"I've been thinking for a few days now that Charlie might not have acted alone. This information from Alicia might confirm that. I don't want to drag us back into this drama, but I can't walk away just yet. All I need is to see what she has, make sure she turns it in to Deputy Director Wainwright himself, and then we're all done. It's no longer my job to do anything there. The deal is, this is really Alicia's mess, and she's been screwed by all this, too. I can't imagine how she must be feeling. Text her back. Tell her to sit on everything and we'll stop by their house on the way home from lunch."

"Right," Shelly said, sending the text. "What a nightmare this continues to be."

A few minutes later they got a text back from Alicia. It was a red heart emoji.

And then their food arrived and the mood lightened once more.

It was close to 2:00 p.m. by the time they left the restaurant.

"Tell her we're on the way. We should be there in about thirty minutes," Jack said, and watched Shelly sending the message.

They got another emoji. This time it was a thumbs-up.

Alicia walked the floor until she saw them pulling up into her driveway and then met them at the door. She took one look at Shelly's healing face and started crying.

"I'm sorry. I'm so sorry," she said.

Shelly just shook her head and hugged her. "I told you before, I'm healing just fine. Look, the stitches are out of my mouth, too."

Alicia grabbed a tissue and began wiping her eyes. "I don't deserve this, but I am so grateful you guys are willing to help."

Jack gave her a quick hug. "None of this shit is your fault. Now, show me what you found."

"It's all laid out on the kitchen table. I have coffee. Do you want some?"

"Not for me," Shelly said. "We just finished lunch."

"Not right now," Jack said, and then they followed Alicia into the kitchen as they'd done so many times before. But this time Charlie was noticeably absent.

Jack started going over everything. Once in a while he would find something and ask Alicia a question, but not often. Most of this was explaining itself. Finally, he was through.

"I have to say, Charlie's penchant for keeping records and denoting details is going to blow shit wide-open somewhere. The main thing now is for the FBI to figure out who FR is."

"Will they let you work on the case?" Alicia asked.

Jack looked up. "Oh. I don't know why I thought you would already know this, but I've resigned from the Bureau. It's not official yet, but I'm not going back."

Alicia looked horrified. "Because of Charlie?"

"No, because of Shelly," Jack said, and touched her arm. "I had already intended the Ito case was going to be my last as an undercover operative. But having my job put her in danger was the final straw."

Alicia was trying not to feel envious. "What are you guys going to do?"

"You tell her," Jack said.

Shelly smiled. "We're planning on moving to Hawaii. Change of pace. Change of place. It feels like the right time to do it."

"That's wonderful," Alicia said, and realized she meant it. She had Johnny. He needed her more than ever and putting focus on what she had gained instead of what she'd lost was going to help tremendously in the months to come.

"Yeah, we're looking forward to exploring possibilities. But right now, let's talk about this. I want to call Wainwright. If he will come here to you, then you won't have to go to the Bureau at all," Jack said.

"That would be wonderful if he'll agree," she said.

"We'll soon find out," Jack said, and left the room to make the call.

Shelly felt sorry for Alicia. Her world was disintegrating before her eyes, and with a brand-new baby to raise. That was when it dawned on her that she hadn't heard the baby at all.

"Is the baby here?" she asked.

"Mom and Dad came and got him this morning so I could do some packing and tying up loose ends before we move. They'll be back with him soon."

"I'd like to see him before you leave," Shelly said.

"I want you guys to see him. He is perfect in every way."

Then the conversation shifted as Jack returned.

"I hope you didn't have plans. After Wainwright learned what you found, he didn't hesitate. He's on the way."

"Really? Oh, Jack, thank you. Just knowing this stuff will be out of my house by the time I go to bed will be a huge weight off my heart. I don't want anything to do with blood money. I want it gone."

Jack glanced at Shelly, who was looking a little weary. "Are you needing anything honey? Did you even think to bring pain pills?"

"Yes, I have them in my purse, but I'm good for now."

"Then I want to stay and make sure Alicia is cleared of culpability," he said.

Alicia started sobbing. "The relief of knowing this isn't all on my back is huge. Just when I thought things couldn't be worse, they were. Thank you, Jack. Just thank you."

At that moment, Jack was so pissed at Charlie all over again. "Well, dammit, honey. The truth is Charlie screwed us all over. But I still had a big question regarding the case anyway. This might point us in the right direction."

They were still talking about the case when the doorbell rang. Alicia glanced up at the clock.

"That will be Mom and Dad with the baby," she said, and went to go let them in.

The baby shifted the subject, and for the next thirty minutes, he was the topic of conversation.

The moment Shelly held him in her arms, every mother instinct she had activated. He was tiny, and warm, and smelled so good. And he was holding on to her little finger for dear life.

Jack saw the look on Shelly's face and smiled. Parenthood. One more topic they might have to take under consideration in Hawaii.

They were still playing with the baby when Deputy Director Wainwright arrived. Alicia's parents took the baby back to the nursery as Jack answered the door. It was Wainwright, with Nolan Warren and one of their federal prosecutors.

"Afternoon, sir. I really appreciate you doing this. We're in the kitchen. If you will all follow me, everything you need to see is laid out on the table."

Wainwright's expression was grim. The fact that this case kept getting deeper and more convoluted did not make him happy. Eventually, a statement would have to be made to the public and the press would have a field day with the news of a dirty Fed. The fact that there might be more than one just about sent him over the edge. He was hoping Jack McCann was wrong.

Alicia was even more concerned when she saw who the deputy director had brought with him. "Thank you all for coming. Have a seat."

"I think we should be thanking you for having the honesty to call it all to our attention," Wainwright said. "This could have made you very rich."

"It's blood money. I want no part of any of it," Alicia said.

Wainwright nodded, and then they all sat down. "Jack, explain to me what we have here. If I have a question, I'll stop you then to ask. Otherwise, start talking."

Jack began explaining the information as he saw it, while the prosecutor went through the paperwork. Jack told all of them about the disconnect he had between Ritter showing up on Dumas's crew and not being surprised to see him there.

"The bottom line, sir, is that my death that night would have served no purpose to Charlie. None of us had any idea he was connected, and Charlie knew he was in the clear. He was my contact. I told him everything. Someone else had a hand in planting my snitch, which means you haven't rounded up all the guilty parties. I don't know…maybe you can interview Ritter and see if he'll tell you who hired him. And maybe you can figure out who FR is, and why he was getting a cut of Charlie's take. I'll be in tomorrow morning to turn in my official letter of resignation, and my gun and my badge."

"I'll be there until eleven, and then I'm in court the rest of the day," Wainwright said, then eyed the prosecutor. "Start gathering all this up. Special Agent Warren will be lead on the case. Jack, you know when you turn in your resignation that you will be out of the loop of the investigation."

"Yes, sir. And that's fine with me."

"Understood," Wainwright said. "That being said, until we know for sure you two are no longer in danger, I will keep you informed of what's happening."

"Much obliged," Jack said.

Alicia watched the lawyer putting all of the paperwork and notebooks into his briefcase, and then they were gone.

"Okay, Alicia, you're good to go," Jack said. "Go be a momma now and know you're completely off the hook. Shelly and I are going home. Tell your parents it was nice seeing them again."

"I will," Alicia said, and walked them to the door.

She watched until they were gone, then locked the door and went to find her baby.

Nineteen

Paul Faber thought about Dude almost every day, wondering what had happened to him. He and Lou played cards at Muncy Peters's house last night, and before the night was over, they were all talking about the night they pulled him out of the water, and Muncy's emergency surgery on the island in the kitchen.

So when Paul got the mail the next morning and received a dinner invitation from Dude, he laughed out loud.

"Dang it, Dude is keeping his word, after all," he said, and went inside to get his phone. He called Lou first. He was waiting for a *hello*, when Lou picked up and just started talking.

"I just spent most of last night with you. Do you have something important to tell me, or did you just miss me?" Lou said.

Paul snorted. "Oh, shut up. Did you get your mail yet?"

"No, why?"

"Go look. I'll wait."

"Well, for the love of Pete, I'm not wearing any pants."

"Then put on some pants and go get the mail. I'm still waiting."

He could hear Lou grumbling, then heard him open the door. His mailbox was on the porch, so it wasn't like he had to walk anywhere to get it.

Within a couple of moments, Lou was back. "I got an invitation to dinner from Dude!" he said.

"So did I," Paul said. "It's for tomorrow night. Want me to pick you up and we can ride together?"

"Yeah, sure! What time will you come by?" Lou asked.

"Around six. An hour is more than enough time to get there. I'm gonna call Muncy and see if he got one, too," Paul said.

"Uh…what do we wear?" Lou asked.

"Something you'd wear to church," Paul said.

"I haven't been to church since high school," Lou grumbled.

"Then long pants and a clean shirt. Can you handle that?" Paul said.

"Yes. Are you curious?" Lou asked.

"You mean curious about who Dude really is? I know he's a Fed. I know he loves a woman named Shelly. I just don't know his real name," Paul said.

"His name is Dude, and I'll see you tomorrow," Lou said.

"Get a haircut," Paul added.

Lou yelped. "Crap on a stick! You're making a damn big deal out of going to eat a meal."

"You look like Bigfoot. Haircut," Paul said. He hung up, then found out when he called Muncy that he had an invitation, as well.

"I'll drive over to your house and we can all go together. And that way I'll get dibs on the front seat," Muncy added. "I don't suppose I should bring Dwayne?"

"Hell no, you do not bring that monster dog," Paul said. "But you could bring flowers."

"For Dude?"

Paul laughed. "No, dumbass. For his girl. Her name is Shelly, and I'll bet my dessert that she's there."

"Oh, well, then," Muncy said. "Yeah, I'll do that. See you tomorrow evening."

"Don't be late," Paul said. "It's rude to be late when someone's offering you a meal. Be at my place before five thirty. I have to pick Lou up by six."

"You are turning into a real Emily Post," Muncy muttered. "And if we're gettin' all picky about shit… If you're wearing sandals, get a pedicure. You don't have toenails anymore. You have hooves." Then he hung up.

Paul looked down at his bare feet and frowned, then he caught a glimpse of himself in the kitchen window and frowned again. Looked like he needed a dose of his own medicine. He went to find some sandals. He needed a haircut *and* a pedicure. And while he was at it, he was buying a new pair of pants. The only long pants he owned wouldn't button anymore.

Shelly woke up the next day excited and anxious. Tonight was their dinner party, but instead of having the meal catered, Jack found a barbecue joint that would deliver and had an order in for delivery tonight at six thirty. The guests weren't due until seven, so that gave them time to get everything out of to-go boxes and into bowls and on platters.

He'd ordered pork ribs and beef brisket, baked potatoes and baked beans, and a tub of coleslaw. They had two dozen buttermilk biscuits on the side.

Shelly ordered an Italian Cream Cake for dessert from a little pastry shop called La Baguette in a nearby strip mall, and for the first time in almost four years, she was going to get to use their good dishes.

She talked all the way through breakfast about what she should wear, and should she use a tablecloth or her pretty place mats. Jack finally stopped her.

"Honey. You're worrying about making everything look pretty, and I'm just hoping they're wearing shoes."

Shelly laughed. "Really?"

"Yes. Three single men, all in their midforties to early fifties, if I had to take a guess. But they are the nicest guys you will ever meet. Muncy is the one who dug the bullet out of my shoulder and sewed me up. He's rough around the edges, but as genuine as they come. Lou and Paul don't live together, but they're kind of like the Odd Couple. Paul is a less uptight version of Felix. Lou is the Texas version of Oscar. It's barbecue. If you put a tablecloth on the table, they'll be afraid to eat."

"Then I'll use the sisal place mats. They look like they're made out of straw, and give them a pile of paper napkins in the middle of the table instead of those made of cloth. We can also leave the beer in the bottles."

"Perfect," Jack said. "As for you, they're going to be enamored of you regardless of what you're wearing."

"I do have the Northern Lights going for me," Shelly reminded him.

Jack laughed. "Tonight is going to be awesome."

Deputy Director Wainwright wasted no time updating the director about what Charlie's widow had discovered, and was given the go-ahead to begin a full investigation. Wainwright had Fred running background checks on all the employees in the Bureau, civilian and special agents alike. Anyone with the initials FR was having their bank records checked for large deposits coinciding with the dates Charlie had posted in the notebooks. Even Ritter was on the short list because his first name was Farrell. Farrell Ritter. FR.

When Fred pointed out that his initials were also FR, Wainwright frowned.

"Well, is it you?" he asked.

"Uh...no, sir."

"Then alright," Wainwright said. "If you're lying to me, I'll personally lock you up and throw away the key."

"I swear, sir! Maybe you should have someone else run the background check on me just to be fair. I don't want to be the only one who didn't get cleared."

"Maybe I will," Wainwright said. "Now, go get busy."

At the same time, Wainwright sent Special Agent Nolan Warren to get a rundown on Jack's snitch. After coming up with nothing they could use, Nolan went to the jail where Ritter was being held awaiting trial, to see if he would talk.

Ritter was a scammer and a hustler, and the moment he walked into that interview room and saw the person who wanted to talk to him was a Fed, he began trying to figure out how he could work it to his advantage.

When the guard handcuffed him to the table, he frowned, but after the guard moved to the door, he eyed the Fed and then smirked.

Nolan had never worked with Ritter in any capacity, but he guessed from the look on the man's face that he was an asshole.

"Mr. Ritter, I'm Special Agent Nolan Warren. I need to ask you some questions, and it would be in your best interests to answer them truthfully."

"What's it worth to you?" Ritter asked.

Nolan just shook his head. "Wrong. I ask questions. You give answers."

Ritter shrugged. "Then ask away. But just so you know, I do not expect to have answers for any of the questions."

Nolan ignored him. "How did you come to be a part of Dumas's crew the night of the bust?"

"I needed a job. He had an opening?"

"Is that a question or an answer?" Nolan asked.

"Why, it's whatever you need it to be," Ritter said.

"Have you ever worked for Dumas before?" Nolan asked.

Ritter grinned. "I'm not sure. Sometimes I'm high when I take odd jobs and don't always remember where I was or who I was with."

"Jack McCann has stated that you were one of his snitches, and that you'd helped him with cases more than once," Nolan said.

Ritter nodded. "And that's the truth. If I know something, I'll gladly share it…for the almighty dollar. A man has to eat. I take my jobs where I can get them."

"Who planted you in Dumas's crew?" Nolan asked.

"Nobody planted me."

Nolan persisted. "Then why were you there?"

Ritter rolled his eyes. "You weren't paying attention, were you? I already told you… I needed a job. He had an opening."

Nolan leaned forward. "Have you ever been in a federal prison?"

A muscle jerked at the corner of Ritter's left eye. "You're the one with access to federal records. You tell me."

"I'd say you obviously haven't, or you wouldn't be trying so hard to get yourself put there…say for the next forty or more years. I'm not completely up to date on how much time you serve for crimes against the government because negotiations vary from case to case, but I do know it's a whole lot more than heisting a car, or getting busted for a dime bag of coke."

Ritter's smile was a little bit forced now. It was the first chink in the smart-ass's armor, and what Nolan had been waiting for.

"So, is your memory getting any better as to how you wound up in Dumas's crew?"

"I gotta have something for what I give you. That's how this works."

"No, that's how you worked it before you got involved in stealing from Uncle Sam."

Ritter shifted in his seat, and when he next spoke, Nolan heard a slight whine in his voice.

"If I tell you what you want to know, can we work a deal?"

"I am not a federal prosecutor. I have no power to give you anything except the promise that you will become someone's girlfriend when you get to prison."

Ritter stifled a moan. "I'm telling you the truth about no one planting me there. I did get the job on my own."

"Why?" Nolan asked.

"Will you at least put in a good word for me with that federal prosecutor?" Ritter asked.

"If your stuff is truthful, I will tell him you cooperated."

Ritter sighed. "Here's the deal. Morris has been paying me a little something for a while now."

Nolan sighed. He'd just found FR. "You're talking about Special Agent Charlie Morris?" Nolan asked.

"Yeah, Charlie."

"Why was he paying you?" Nolan asked.

Ritter shrugged. "I might have found out that he was playing both sides. And I might have told him it would be worth his while to give me a little something to keep me quiet."

Nolan's eyes narrowed. "That's called blackmail."

Ritter shrugged. "We just called it an arrangement."

Nolan sighed. "Okay, you were blackmailing Charlie. So how does Dumas enter into this?"

"He was just a means to an end," Ritter said.

Nolan slapped the table with the flat of his hand, making Ritter jump.

"Stop bullshitting me. How did you find out Jack McCann was working that job? Who wanted him dead?"

Ritter shrugged. "I found out through Charlie that Jack was there undercover. I didn't necessarily want Jack hurt. What I wanted was to mess up Charlie's thing with Adam Ito by having that deal go bad."

Nolan's heart skipped a beat. Jack was right. Once Ritter started talking, he didn't seem inclined to stop.

"I don't follow," Nolan said. "How would outing Jack screw up Charlie?"

"If the sale didn't go through, which it wouldn't when I raised hell about a Fed in the building, then Ito would lose his sale, and Dumas would lose faith in Ito, and Charlie would be cut off from both sides…buyer and seller. If this one went bad, the next time Charlie had a chance to broker another deal, he wouldn't have any takers, right?"

"But outing Jack doesn't make sense. Ito didn't know Charlie's name, and he didn't know he had a Fed on his team."

"But I did," Ritter said. "I knew both of them, and that's why he was paying me. To keep my mouth shut. Only, he stiffed me on the last deal and then refused to let me in on the one you busted. I showed him what could happen if a deal went sour."

"And you didn't think about what would happen to Jack?"

Ritter frowned. "No. He was just a means to an end. What you guys call collateral damage."

Nolan leaned back in his chair, stunned by Ritter's thinking process. The whole Bureau was in a fresh panic, wondering what the twist was to Ritter showing up on Dumas's payroll, and it was nothing more than a snitch's version of payback.

"I don't see the big deal here. I mean, what the hell? McCann survived, so no harm, no foul," Ritter said.

Nolan kept thinking of how close Jack had come to dying, and what Ito had done to Jack's wife to get to him.

Nolan shook his head. "Sorry, but you read that all wrong. There was harm—great harm. And that was a chickenshit way to treat a man like Jack, who always did right by you," Nolan said.

Ritter shrugged. "It ain't easy livin' on the street."

"It's way easier than life behind bars," Nolan said.

"But you'll soon find that out." Then Nolan stood and motioned to the guard. "I'm ready to leave now."

Ritter yelled, "Wait! What about the prosecutor?"

"What about him?" Nolan asked.

"So, are you going to tell him I cooperated?"

"I am going to tell him that you were running a blackmail scam, and when it went south, you targeted Jack to get back at Charlie."

Ritter's eyebrows knitted. "That doesn't make it sound good on me."

"That's because you didn't do good. You did bad—very bad."

"But you promised!" Ritter cried. "You're a Fed. You can't lie!"

Nolan looked at him in disbelief.

"Where did you come up with that? You were working dirty deals with a Fed whose whole life was a lie. And for the record, I didn't lie. You just tried to work a deal and then told on yourself. That's *collateral damage*, Ritter. You understand about all that, right?"

Ritter was still shouting when Nolan left the wing, thinking how happy the deputy director was going to be when he heard this.

The food arrived promptly at six thirty, which soothed Shelly's first concern. She and Jack put part of it in the oven for it to stay warm, and then put the coleslaw in the refrigerator.

They'd already picked up the cake before noon, and it was in the refrigerator, as well.

Every time Shelly went by the dining table, she had to stifle the urge to pretty it up. But the scent of barbecue was beginning to permeate the house, and the longneck bottles of beer were in a tin tub in the kitchen staying cold.

Shelly wanted to look nice for Jack's friends and was wearing her favorite summer dress. Pale pink with a high neckline and very little back. The loose fit, which kept it cool for summer, was saved from being ordinary by a hemline ending just above her knees. Her long curly hair was pulled back at the nape of her neck with her favorite silver clip, and the only jewelry she was wearing was her wedding ring and the sapphire ring Jack had given her for their anniversary. It still put a lump in her throat, remembering she'd received it the same day the Bureau came to tell her he was dead.

Jack was wearing black jeans and a red knit polo shirt. He'd spiked his hair just enough to make Shelly happy and was putting out some tortilla chips to go with the spicy salsa on the table when the doorbell rang.

Shelly looked at Jack. "They're here!"

Jack gave her a quick kiss and then grabbed her hand and took her with him as he went to let them in.

"Really?" Shelly said, as she hurried to keep up with his long stride.

"Yes, really," Jack said. "I have to show off the trophy wife first."

Shelly grinned and then stood beside him as he opened the door. Three very uncomfortable men were on the threshold. Two had flowers and one had a big box of candy. When they saw Jack, they grinned.

"Dude! Is that really you? Damn boy, you clean up real good," Paul said.

"Yes, it's me, Jack McCann, otherwise known as Dude, and welcome to our home. This is my wife, Shelly." And then as the men filed through the open doorway, Jack named them off. "Paul Faber and Lou Parsons are the two who fished me out of the bay, and Muncy Peters is the best medic the army ever shipped home."

The men were taken with Shelly.

"Nice to meet you, ma'am," Paul said. "The candy is for you."

"A pleasure to meet you," Lou said. "These carnations are for you, too."

"I don't know what all these flowers are in my bouquet, but I thought they were pretty. Only, they're not as pretty as you," Muncy said, as he handed her a mixed bouquet of flowers.

"They are all beautiful! Thank you so much, and thank you even more for saving Jack's life. I thought I'd lost him. The biggest miracle in my life was finding out he was still alive, and I have all of you to thank for it."

"That night and the ensuing week was the most excitement any of us had seen since the early days in Afghanistan," Paul said, and then wrapped Jack up in a bear hug.

Jack hugged them all, thanking them again for what they'd done, and saying how glad he was to see them again.

Shelly kept looking at them, at the dear expressions on their faces, and the way they kept looking at Jack. They liked him. They really, really liked him, and he liked them, too.

"Honey, why don't you show the guys where the beer and snacks are while I put these in water."

She led the way into the kitchen and got down her biggest vase. While she was arranging the flowers, the men had already popped the top on their first beers and were digging in to the chips and salsa.

This was turning into a real party.

Life couldn't be better.

When food finally reached the table, everyone was ready to eat. Jack seated her at the table beside him and let the other three sort themselves out.

"Don't brag on this food thinking I cooked any of it," Shelly said, which made them all laugh.

Jack grinned as he reached for her hand. "She's still not a hundred percent from her ordeal, and I didn't want her stressed out by trying to do too much, too soon. She is a damn good cook."

Paul glanced up and then pointed to her eyes. "Can't help but notice you're in the process of wearing out two black eyes. Were you in a wreck?"

"No. I was kidnapped," Shelly said, and picked up the bowl of coleslaw. "Help yourself and pass it around."

Paul felt horrible that he'd even asked. "I'm sorry. I shouldn't have—"

"Oh no! It's okay. I am alive today because Jack found me."

Jack nodded. "That's most of the reason why I wouldn't tell you guys anything personal about myself. I didn't want anyone knowing I even had a wife, but when my cover was blown, everything went downhill fast. They couldn't find my body, so on the off chance I was still alive, the bad guy snatched Shelly to get to me."

Shelly was determined to change the subject. "There are two kinds of barbecue sauce. Mild and hot as hell. Mild is in the container with a clear lid. The hot is in the one with a red lid."

They got the message and followed her lead. Muncy

was almost as excited about the biscuits as he was the pork ribs. He was slathering butter and reaching for the hot sauce when the meal began. By the time they were ready for cake, Muncy was calling her *sugar*, Paul was calling her *cutie pie* and Lou was trying not to stare.

Jack caught a look in Shelly's eyes and grinned. *Told you*, he mouthed.

She blushed. "Who wants Italian Cream Cake?"

All of the men, including Jack, held up their hands because their mouths were too full to talk. She hid a giggle and got up to get dessert plates, then cut the cake.

Just listening to all their chatter and laughter was the best medicine she could have asked for. It was wonderful—and so normal.

Paul quit on his third beer and was drinking coffee with dessert.

"Because I'm the driver," he said, and winked at Shelly as she refilled his coffee cup.

Jack had already spilled the beans about their move to Hawaii, and their reactions had been surprising.

Paul all but threw himself on the floor at the news. "No! Are you freakin' serious? That's my dream, to live on one of the islands, have myself a charter boat and take tourists fishing."

"Right, Captain Paul. And I'm going to be your first mate," Lou added.

Muncy frowned. "Well, hell, don't everybody go off and leave me behind. I think Dwayne would enjoy the islands."

"Who's Dwayne?" Shelly asked.

Muncy whipped out his phone and pulled up some pictures.

Shelly gasped. "Is that a dog or a horse?"

"Mastiff," Muncy said. "I raised him from a puppy."

"Is he friendly?" Shelly asked.

"He'll lick you to death," Jack said. "It's best to come bearing gifts…doggy gifts…big doggy gifts."

Shelly laughed out loud and, in that moment, sealed her forever in their hearts as one of the boys.

The next morning, Adam Ito was handcuffed to a gurney to take an ambulance ride through the city streets of Houston on his way to a long-term care facility for prisoners.

He was on oxygen now, with a future that wasn't looking too bright. He wondered after he'd had the stroke if they'd notified his parents, but people had quit talking to him. It was as if he no longer deserved information, since he couldn't respond. And then a day later, he overheard Dr. Grimley telling one of the nurses that his parents had been notified but refused to accept responsibility for him in any way, and left him to the state of Texas.

It was daunting to know that he, a natural citizen of Japan, would be buried in a land so far away. They had taken Yuki home and left him here to rot. Again, he had no concept of guilt for what had happened to Yuki, and being abandoned continued to fuel his anger, which was the only emotion he had left.

When they finally reached their destination and began pulling him out of the ambulance to wheel him into the facility, he caught a quick glimpse of blue sky, seagulls and the top of one tree, and then he was inside the building. Unless a miracle occurred and they put him by a window, he'd just gotten his last glimpse of the world.

Twenty

The next morning, Jack McCann made one last trip to the Bureau to officially resign, and he took Shelly with him because she asked.

When they walked in, they created their own level of chaos. Every agent on the floor came to say goodbye and wish them well. This was the one place Shelly didn't feel self-conscious. Everyone here knew what had happened and didn't judge her. She got more apologies than anything, and when they went on through to the deputy director's office, she was beginning to relax. She knew these men. She knew this world. But she had no words for how grateful she was that Jack was leaving it.

When they reached Wainwright's office, Jack took her hand and smiled.

"Let's do this, baby."

Shelly nodded.

Jack knocked, then heard Wainwright's voice.

"Come in!"

And so they did.

Adam Ito cheated justice by dying two days after his transfer. They buried him a couple of days later in a pauper's grave. Ironically on the same day Yuki's body was flown out of Houston.

In life their worlds could not have been farther apart, and in death, so were their final resting places.

When Jack was notified of Ito's passing, he breathed a sigh of relief, then went to find Shelly. Her response surprised him.

"It doesn't matter. I wrote his name on a sheet of paper the other day and then set it on fire. He's in hell now. Right where he belongs."

"I just love you," Jack said softly. "How about that flight to Oahu?"

She put her arms around his neck and kissed him.

No stitches between them. No ribs too sore to squeeze.

"Yes, yes, a thousand times yes."

"No more living in shadows, my love. We're moving to paradise."

Epilogue

The breeze off the ocean was particularly nice today, Shelly thought, as she shut down her computer. She worked for an accounting company on the Big Island of Hawaii, but she worked from their home on Oahu.

She walked out onto the lanai with a glass of pineapple juice, set it down on a little side table, then eased into the chair swing beside it and rubbed her tummy. Two more months and Miss Poppy would be here.

She loved the little mountain house they'd chosen on the island. It was far enough away from the city to escape the tourists, and just high enough that the daily showers that came with the afternoon weather had become one of her favorite things. They had a vegetable garden, flowering bushes and birds wearing feathers in colors more vibrant than any flowers on land, or any fish in the sea.

In the distance, she thought she could see an approaching helicopter, but it was so far away that right now it looked like a bug. Jack must be taking another group on an island tour. Every time he started out, he flew over their place just to let her know he was thinking of her.

From where she was sitting, the vastness of the blue water surrounding the island was drenched in sunshine, while the waves rolled in to shore, dumping the riders and their boards into the shallow surf.

There were fishing boats, and charter boats, and outrigger canoes dotting the water as far as she could see.

Paul and Lou were out there somewhere. She'd hear all about their day when they came over for dinner. Muncy was on ambulance duty until late, so he'd had to take a rain check on the meal. Driving the ambulance was a rush that never got old, and being a full-fledged paramedic made him proud.

He'd brought Dwayne with him, but they'd had quarantine to deal with before he was officially home, sleeping at the foot of his master's bed.

The massive size of the dog had been of concern to every neighbor Muncy had, until they got to know him. Now neighbors made excuses to stop by.

The breeze felt so good, and the shade was just perfect. Shelly was almost asleep when she realized that the chopper was finally close. She opened her eyes and then smiled when she recognized the colors.

It was Jack.

She got up from the swing and walked out from beneath the lanai to wave.

The quartet of men Jack was chauffeuring about the island saw Shelly wave.

"Hey, look. That lady is waving," one man said. "Wouldn't you love to live in a place like that?"

Jack's heartbeat jumped a lick as he saw her step out

into the grass. The breeze was lifting her hair and at the same time plastering her clothes against the bulge of her belly.

Jack grinned. "Uh…sorry, guys, but that's no lady. That's my wife."

* * * * *